Berit Ellingsen

NOW WE CAN SEE THE MOON

Berit Ellingsen is the author of two novels, *Not Dark Yet* (Two Dollar Radio), *Une ville vide* (PublieMonde), a Rococo-style fantasy novella (forthcoming), a collection of short stories, *Beneath the Liquid Skin* (Queen's Ferry Press), and a mini-collection of dark fairy-tales, *Vessel and Solsvart* (Snuggly Books). Her work has been published in W.W. Norton's *Flash Fiction International*, *SmokeLong Quarterly*, *Unstuck*, *Litro*, and other places, and been nominated for the Pushcart Prize, Best of the Net, and the British Science Fiction Association Award. Berit is a member of the Norwegian Authors' Union. Her web presence can be found at: http://beritellingsen.com.

SNUGGLY BOOKS

THIS IS A SNUGGLY BOOK

ISBN: 978-1-943813-61-2

Acknowledgements:

A big thank you to Valerie Polichar, without whom this book might not have been published. Many thanks also to Christopher Allen, Tobias Carroll, Don van Deventer, E.M. Edwards, Fabio Fernandes, Kathy Fish, Austin Gilkeson, David Gutowski, Andrew Hageman, Lorrie Hartshorn, Paul Jessup, , Judy Krueger, Michael Matheson, Adam Morgan, Kristine Ong Muslim, Steph Post, Richard E. Preston, Sam Rasnake, and Valerie Storey, for their kind support, and to Anna, Brendan, and Justin at Snuggly Books.

Cover photo by Jeff Kubina (Maryland Renaissance Festival) [CC BY-SA 2.0 (https://creativecommons.org/licenses/by-sa/2.0)], via Wikimedia Commons

BERIT ELLINGSEN

NOW WE CAN SEE THE MOON

NOW WE CAN SEE THE MOON

My storehouse has burned down
But now
We can see the moon.

—Mizuta Masahide (1657-1723)

1.

The Hurricane

At first, conditions were eerily still, with not a spring-barren branch moving in the trees, yet the gulls and sparrows and pigeons huddled on the roofs and lawns, as if they sensed what was coming. Then a dense fog rolled in, summoned by a stirring breeze that only seemed to thicken the mist. Waves began to form at sea, while on land the thinnest branches and the tallest blades of grass started to shiver, until the fog broke apart and revealed a sky black with storm clouds. The gulls shrieked and lifted and flew inland to calmer weather, while the sparrows huddled together inside hedges and bushes, and the pigeons squeezed into cracked walls and broken windows as quickly as they could.

Soon, the air began to shriek and lash the sea white. The meteorological services were following the hurricane closely, trying to predict its path and site of landfall, as well as its speed and strength. But owing to the chaotic nature of the atmosphere, the meteorologists were unable to determine where on the continent the hurricane would hit the hardest or with how much force. Some calculated that the wind speeds would be catastrophic, others were less confident and only recommended, rather than forced, evacuation of the coast. Thus, no comprehensive order of evacuation was given to the towns and cities along the continent, and the number of people who left varied greatly from place to place. No city or town council wished to pay for evacuating thousands or hundreds of thousands of people for what might be just a very strong late-winter storm. The coastal communities had enough challenges already: decreased revenues, high unemployment rates, frequent strikes, flagging social services, increased taxation, dwindling groundwater reserves, a failing fishing industry, an even-more-at-risk logging sector, and an infrastructure that hadn't been repaired or updated in years. Most towns and cities had already invested millions in floodgates, seawalls, levees, dikes, and canals to protect against the increased sea level and erosion of the coastline, as well as a violent winter storm like this. Thus the citizens closest to the coast were only advised to evacuate if they had the means to do this on their own and somewhere to stay inland. Instead, most communities asked people to cover the windows of their homes with planks or plywood, pull vessels up on land, secure loose objects from the wind, and store enough food, water, and medicines for three days in case the power went out.

By the time the unprecedented size of the hurricane and its extreme wind speeds were certain, it was too late to order a mass evacuation and risk that hundreds of thousands of people, perhaps millions, were caught in their vehicles on choked streets and roads. Then the sky blackened as if at dusk and the wind began to roar.

( )

Where the hurricane hit the coast directly, the wind speeds rivaled the strongest of those on the southern and western continents. All objects beneath a certain weight and size, such as cars and boats and trees, were lifted up and thrown around, including everyone and everything inside them. Heavier and larger items, such as trucks and boathouses and shipping containers, were pushed and rolled along the rain-filled ground, while they disintegrated into smaller parts as they were pummeled against the substrate. With bigger structures, such as wooden houses and barns and businesses,

8

the hurricane exploded the windows and peeled off the roofs. Once inside, the hurricane filled all spaces with its churning, pushing, pulling self, smashing the remaining walls and beams, as well as inhabitants and furniture, causing many of the structures to collapse. Sturdier buildings made from brick or stone or concrete had all their glass broken from the wind, flimsier parts such as external blinds or awnings or winter gardens ripped off, and their glass-walled foyers and lobbies cracked open from flying or rolling objects. Most such buildings, whether apartment complexes, officess, or hospitals, withstood the hurricane, unless they hid structural problems or had been severely weakened by age, in which case they fell or suffered severe damage, along with any living beings still inside them.

The combined force of the spring tide and the plummeted air pressure pulled the sea, already heightened by years of melting ice caps and now so raging it was more white than blue, far up on land. Thus, when the storm surge reached the coast, it hit like a massive flood wave, overflowing all but the highest floodgates, seawalls, levees, dikes, and canals, to engulf the towns and cities in its way. While the battery from the air continued, the water streamed up and around everything and everyone on the ground, spinning and smashing and cutting them like a blender. The storm flood and extreme amounts of precipitation completely overwhelmed the sewer system, causing untreated sewage to gush out in some places, or flood water to stream into the drinking reservoirs shutting down the flow of potable water in many towns and cities.

Power lines, transformers, rerouting stations, even large pylons fell, became submerged, or short-circuited into fire, blacking out power in several regions. The same happened with radio and phone towers, masts, and antennas, even some satellite ground stations along the coast. Data centers and server farms were flooded, went offline, or had to severely limit their functions, choking off even vital communication. Streets, roads, tunnels and underpasses, even small bridges, were flooded or filled with debris, rendering them impassable for the ambulances, fire trucks, police cars, and other emergency services that were still trying to reach all those in need during the disaster.

Inland, away from the flood, the pelting rain, sleet, and hail from the hurricane pulled avalanches of mud, soil, or rock across streets and roads, and in a few tragic cases, buildings and their inhabitants. The hurricane swelled rivers and streams and lakes, flooding some structures, undermining others, and blocking yet more. Trees toppled across power lines and railroads, roofs collapsed or grew holes, and thin windows bulged, shivered, and shattered in the high winds. Even outside of the direct path of the hurricane, and far inland, the destruction and chaos was profound.

2.

Early Spring

The team arrived on the continent in the middle of the night, in a wind and rain that seemed intent on smashing their helicopter to the ground. They shook and lurched and bounced with the aircraft and braced themselves for the landing.

It was their home continent, where most of them had been born and grown up and educated, and from which they had set out, hungry for adventure and eager to serve, certain of the necessity to do so. Time and circumstance had only proved them right, and with greater need in the world and increased responsibilities in the large and international humanitarian organizations they found work in, their competence increased to a level far beyond what they had possessed when they first set out in the world. Yet, they also knew that their capabilities were little without their support system, the organization and colleagues they had in the back, and its network of political supporters and financial benefactors, equipment and funds.

None of the team had envisioned returning like this, slinking in like thieves under the cover of darkness and inclement weather. Neither did they expected a hero's welcome, TV cameras and microphones at the airport; yet the times when their small crowds of parents and siblings and lovers and friends had waved and cheered at them in the arrivals hall, sometimes with flowers or gifts, that had felt like a hero's welcome, no matter how small and private. But tonight was different. Now their families and loved ones didn't even know they were coming, didn't know they had left their previous worksite, urged on by the president of their organization herself, and by the most recent and violent events. Their loved ones didn't know they were coming home, because only a few of the team had managed to get through the overloaded phone network and the non-responsive mail servers on the blacked-out continent for long enough to find out if their loved ones were even alive, much less tell them that they were on their way.

( )

Leah, the leader of the team, glanced over at Raymond, her second-in-command, who regarded the city they had been assigned to as his home, even if he hadn't lived there for years. This was the place where Raymond had met and married his ex-wife and where his son had grown up. But Raymond said nothing, just kept his gaze on the black oval of the helicopter window, where only the red emergency torches that filled their landing site with a feeble and smoking illumination managed to penetrate the darkness.

Over the last year, their assignments had brought them closer and closer to home. At first not geographically, but conceptually and socioeconomically. No longer did they land in rural villages and isolated towns parched by drought or flooded by rain on hard-packed soil. No longer was it predominantly farmers with crops that failed or livestock that died, or crowds of refugees, displaced by conflict or disaster, who needed their help. For years that was whom they helped, and that was who they, except for the very youngest in the team, primarily expected to help. But as the times changed more and more, the team was sent to larger and larger towns, then medium-sized cities, and finally, large cities, to aid not only farmers and refugees, but business owners, office workers, construction crews, service attendants, school teachers, travel agents, homemakers, medical doctors, university students, public servants, even low-level decision makers, in times of disaster. No longer only in tropical climes, but in subtropical, and even temperate regions of the world.

"It's globalization," Marten, the team's odontologist, would say every time one of his colleagues mistook one large city on one continent for another urban landscape on a landmass they had just left. And then it was no longer the familiar types of catastrophes they were called out to; drought, famine, flooding, or the natural disasters that happen on a planet where the surface moves and gives rise to earthquakes, landslides, flood waves, and avalanches. Instead, it seemed that ordinary weather and previously nominal seasonal phenomena had grown stronger and more intense, enough to damage cities and countries that previously never needed any outside help because their own emergency services were large, well-equipped, and well-trained enough to handle the freak occurrences. Now changes in season and weather happened with such force and on such a big scale that it overwhelmed the local capacity to cope. External help was called in; search-and-rescue teams, food and water supplies, medicines and health-care personnel, construction crews and engineers, and financial and political aid for long-term rebuilding and resettling. Forest fires scorched the cities on the oceanic continent, crop failures and dust storms starved the vast metropolises in the north of the eastern continent, drought and lack of water collapsed industry and agriculture in the south of the western continent. Those places were still far enough away and had violent weather often enough for the disasters there to be something the team could not imagine happening at home.

Yet, over the course of the year they found themselves in cities they had visited in the past as tourists, together with their parents or siblings or friends or lovers. Or in places they had dreamed of going to, that were on their list to see before they died, and which they now had the opportunity to visit and stay in for some time, but under completely different circumstances than they ever imagined for their trip.

( )

The helicopter deposited the team and their bags and crates and chests on a mound that peeked out of the brown and murky water, before the aircraft receded back into the sky.

"Can you hear that?" Gabriele, the team's disaster psychologist, asked.

"Hear what?" Jens, emergency physician, replied.

"How quiet it is." The city now was only capable of emitting natural sounds; the gust of the gale that swept through the darkness, the rustling of the bushes and grass on the mound, the splashing and gurgling of the water around them. The hurricane had muted the city to a hush. The team members could not help but wonder if the whole coastline, or even the entire continent, had fallen equally silent.

They couldn't linger in that notion. On the ground the inundation, destruction, and devastation was even more visible than it had been in the air. Everything that hadn't drowned had instead been smashed, snapped, broken, crushed, or collapsed by the wind, flying, or falling objects. Satellites and their human operators at ground stations and control rooms all over the world were working day and night to deliver quick and updated images of the affected areas. Now the fruits of that labor streamed over the satellite phone network to the team's only connected laptop to ease navigation, increase safety, and prepare all the emergency teams for the conditions on site.

All the buildings they could glimpse in the howling darkness were dark and damaged. Most were still standing, no longer gleaming and smooth from glass, but blind and gutted, with bones and innards exposed. A few had fallen over, both high-rise and low.

"One body over here," Marten said and held the beam of his flashlight out into the murky waves.

"I see one too," Edouard, one of the two forensic anthropologists in the team, said and swung his light further out across the water.

"Judging from the smell," Raymond said, "there must be many more than just those two around." Despite the temperate climate and the cool, windy weather, the smell of death was thick around them, mixed with the stench of sewage, rotting plants, and leaking hydrocarbons that always accompanied a flooding, no matter where in the world it took place.

❪ ❫

Leah recalled the first time she and the other senior members of the team arrived in a place of mass death, which had taken place to the south on the eastern continent after an earthquake devastated the coastline with a series of flood waves. Bloated bodies lay slung across heaps of debris and the roots of trees, over vehicles, tangled in seaweed or land vegetation, on the streets and on the beaches, with dazed survivors passing by. She recalled the terrible feeling, the darkening shadow from that first time, when she realized the situation wasn't as bad as she feared, but much, much worse. Now she wondered if that first raw shock of facing the repercussions of a major international disaster were resurfacing now, slow-burning like acid, because this was her home continent.

Leah glanced back, over her shoulder, to search for the border of destruction, the demarcation where disaster ended and normalcy began. During that first time of mass death, and at subsequent places, the line had been clearly visible, even painfully so. Because disaster, however devastating, however terrible, had a limit, was restricted to a certain area. Outside it, life went on as before, or as close to before as the inhabitants could muster. She didn't regard that as callous or selfish, it was life and it was reassuring. Even if the team remained inside the disaster area for weeks, they knew the rest of the world continued outside it, and they took comfort in that. Even when they were far away from that world, hours by truck on half-collapsed roads and paths, or on boat along flooded rivers or inundated bays, they could always retreat, go back for fresh food, clean water, to shower, sleep, relax, and reassure family and friends over the phone or mail.

So now, as Leah always did when she arrived at a new catastrophe, she turned slightly, turned back a little, to catch a glimpse of the rest of the world that lay behind them. Over the years the circle of devastation grew wider and wider and the time it took for anyone to move out of the disaster area seemed longer and longer, even with increased speed and accuracy of satellite imagery and navigation to help chart the safest and most direct route back. But now, as Leah turned for one last look at the rest of the world, she saw that it had shrunk so far behind them she could no longer see it. Now there was no line, no demarcation between before and after, past and present, disaster and normalcy.

3.

Leaving the Heather

Even in the mountains far from the coast and north of the direct path of the hurricane, the wind had made its mark. Now much of the moor was covered in water from the extreme amounts of precipitation that even the distant periphery of the violent low-pressure center brought, which the cold and wet soil had no chance to absorb. The hills and hillocks that scattered the heath had been gouged and scarred by landslides and run-off. Some of the trees that lined the ridges were broken or bent, leaning onto their surrounding trunks like walking wounded. The green stalks of winter wheat on the cleared flat of the moor were now rotting in the flood, and the farms that had plowed and sown those crops at the beginning of the mild fall now stood abandoned and dark.

Brandon Minamoto sat on the sandy floor of his broken cabin while he waited for the storms that followed in the wake of the hurricane to pass. Floodwater had rushed down from the low hillock behind the cabin, through the door of the structure's single large room, and out through the panorama window, along with most of the furniture inside. Now the wind from the broken window tinkled the glass shards on the mud-dusted floor, sounding like the leaves in a mythical forest, bringing cold gusts of rain. Yet, the cabin's remaining walls and roof held against the aftershock storms. He slept and sat through the chain of storms, inside the still, singular awareness he now recognized as himself. He had no appetite and felt no hunger. Only when he grew weak from lack of food did he rip open one of the sachets of freeze-dried camping dinners or oatmeal with salt and sugar stored in the now powerless and warm fridge, spooned the contents into his mouth with a little water from the cabin's own source, in globs he could barely taste. Constantly, there was a drop of sweet liquid at the back of his tongue, tasting like honey or nectar, but fresher, cleaner, like the light from a white star, nourishing him and turning his hunger into a shadow passing over water. This lasted for days, weeks.

When the weather finally cleared, it felt like he was pushed to his feet, into moving. Now he must pack his bag and lock what he could of the cabin and leave. He was needed elsewhere.

( )

He rose, a little light-headed but steady, not too hungry, wrung his thin sweater off, then the T-shirt, neither of them clean anymore, then undid his trainers, fatigues, and underpants, until he stood naked and shivering at the edge of the hearth. The sunlight glinted in the broken glass and the illumination that filled the cabin and the heath outside was bright and warm with spring. He bunched the T-shirt together, wet it in the water at the bottom of the cabin's floor hearth, and leaned over the square pit to scrub his hands, face, and neck. Then he rubbed the rest of his body with the moist T-shirt and stood to dry. There was a clean towel in the backpack, but he wanted to save that for possible emergencies or wounds. He tied his hair into a ponytail with an elastic band he had taken from Beanie in the apartment at Christmas, trimmed the nails on his fingers and toes with the nail clipper from the backpack, and shaved with the simple plastic razor in the tiny mirror from the top drawer in the kitchen. When he was done, he put the nail clipper inside the first aid kit, then placed it, along with the mirror and his headlamp, in the backpack lid.

He pulled out the clothes that remained after the flood and put on clean underwear, a dry T-shirt, mountain pants and jacket, clean socks, as well as his hiking boots. Then he rolled up the gray wool sweater, a few pairs of black cotton socks, a pair of thick wool socks, the remaining underpants and T-shirts, and stuffed them all into the backpack. The 30-liter container had no room for his well-used trainers, they couldn't take much water and were too bright and conspicuous, so he carried them to the kitchen corner of the cabin and placed them on the floor by the stove. The phone was at the bottom of the lake, so there was no need to worry about that. He removed the smallest note of cash left in the pocket of his mountain jacket, marked it with a blue ballpoint pen with a date more than two years in the past, retracing the letters again and again to thicken them so they were clearly visible over the printing on the bill. Then he folded the note together and placed it inside the right trainer. Michael, his boyfriend, would recognize the date and its associated place. If Michael or Katsuhiro or someone else from his family came to look for him, they must find something; he couldn't leave them with nothing, no trace of his whereabouts.

He rolled the sleeping bag up and tied its strings together. The now lumpy down made the bag thinner and colder than it had once been, but now in late spring that might only be an advantage. Since the moss-green cover had vanished with the water that rushed through the cabin at the height of the hurricane, he undid the straps of the backpack and squeezed the sleeping bag into them beneath the backpack itself. The items he couldn't carry or would no longer be useful he left next to the trainers; a knit sweater that was too thick to bring along, and the white shirt, black slacks, and thin leather shoes he had brought from home over Christmas.

At the back of the fridge he found a bottle of soda which he hadn't drunk because of the chemicals that might have leached from the plastic, but now he took the bottle out, closed the empty fridge, and stuffed the bottle into the backpack's vertical side pocket, meant for carrying a drinking container. His slim red steel canteen he rinsed, filled with water from the source in the hearth, drank deeply from it, then refilled it, and pushed it into the remaining side pocket of the backpack. Of the packets of energy gel and freeze-dried camping food he had bought at the beginning of spring, only a couple were left, and just one of the sachets of oatmeal with nuts and berries. He opened the little plastic bag, mixed the oatmeal with water from the hearth, stirred it with a spoon from the drawer in the kitchen, and ate the cereal slowly. It contained generous amounts of sugar as well as salt and he enjoyed the flavor, although he didn't feel particularly hungry. He nevertheless forced the oatmeal down, knowing he needed the energy. When he was done he felt more hungry than when he had started, a sign that his metabolism and digestion were increasing. He squeezed the packets of freeze-dried beef and turkey meals with longing, tempted to break up a few planks from the walls, make a fire to heat water for a more substantial meal, but doubted that he would be able to keep warm food down for very long. Instead, he balanced the dry, hard packets on top of the rolled up clothes in the backpack, and pulled the drawstrings together. The square plastic lighter, the scuffed compass he had had has since childhood, and the nearly new box cutter from the top drawer in the kitchen also went into the spacious pocket on the backpack's lid. The money that was left he rolled up and placed in the zip-locked inner breast pocket of the mountain jacket, along with the keys to his own apartment and to Michael's place, threaded onto the ring of a miniature steel flashlight.

When that was done, there was nothing left but to take in the cabin one last time. Even with the panorama window glassless, the sofa flowed outside, and the door askew, the cabin still resembled the structure he had arrived at in the fall to a surprising degree. He exited, pushed the half-broken door shut, pressed the key into the rust-spattered lock and turned it. With the added support from the bolt, the door now remained upright in the frame, partly able to resume its function as a barrier against the elements. For a moment he considered leaving the key there, but feeling still a distinct ownership of the cabin and realizing he wasn't ready to abandon it completely, he withdrew the key and took it with him.

The deck was dry but strewn with mud, sand, pebbles, plant debris, and even a couple of rocks larger than he would have been able to shift on his own. He gazed at the red buildings across the moor, where his neighbors had lived, but now nothing moved in the courtyard, the windows were unlit, and even the bright halogen lamp above the barn door, which used to glow orange day and night, was dark. He had no desire to walk over there only to find the farm empty. Instead, he turned away from the cabin and started on the familiar path that had nearly vanished in the underbrush.

（ ）

He hiked across the moor, not to the concrete platform with the rail lines extending in both directions, but to the nearest bus stop outside the town center. The bus stop was located by the parking lot of a long, low building that was styled like a log cabin, with grass and moss thick on the low gabled roof. The one-story structure housed a camping store with hiking and hunting gear, a small grocery shop that carried the same brands as the larger businesses in the town center, and a clockmaker's workshop that also offered postcards, maps, and other tourist items the three other stores didn't sell.

He had most of what he needed and not much cash left, but had spotted a few special drinking bottles the last time he had visited the camping store, and headed there first. As he opened the door, a bell above it chimed. He slipped quickly inside to stop the sound and continued past the rows of pitched camping tents, sleeping bags of various color and thickness, sitting pads, gas stoves, pots, plates, cutlery, cups, lighters, insecticide, lures, and tools on display. He picked up a cotton mesh scarf and an oblong plastic bottle with a filter visible through its clear surface. He had used similar devices before, the filter fine enough to keep most biological particles out, including bacteria and even viruses, but not chemical contaminants such as gasoline or diesel. That would be less of a problem, he hoped. On a rack at the back of the store hung fishing waders, long and thin like shed piscine skin. He picked a pair in artificial fiber, hoping they would breathe more than PVC, and tried them on in the store's single dressing room. The waders and filter bottle were expensive, but not as much as he feared. He spent most of the remaining money on packets of freeze-dried camping meals, which the store had a large selection of. Then he paid for the items, received a crinkly bag to keep them in, and left through the noisy door.

In the grocery store he found sachets of oatmeal with nuts and berries, complete vitamin and mineral supplements, and disinfectant hand wipes at a reasonable price. Then he only needed a hiking map of the whole region.

He had not been to the clockmaker's shop before, but saw faded and dusty maps among the clocks and watches and barometers and postcards in the display window. Inside that door yet another bell chimed, and he hurried in among the shelves, taking care not to bump or push anything over with his backpack. The white steel shelves were filled with table clocks in all imaginable sizes and materials, from wood to stone to glass, as well as hourglasses, drinking steins, and thimbles in an equally bewildering variety, many hand painted with local motifs. Further in were multiple stands with calendars and postcards with pictures the region, showing off its peaks, pines, lakes, and wildlife in all seasonal varieties. The selection of maps was nearly as great, ranging from detailed hiking maps of the surrounding area to extensive road maps of the whole continent. He chose a map of the region with the major roads drawn in red and blue, made his way past rotating stands of sunglasses and key rings and paid at the till.

But on the way out he spotted a doorway a single carpeted step, which led up to an adjacent section of the store, a windowless room with brown walls. There loomed a massive wooden cabinet with glass doors, its interior lit by horizontal lamps in burnished bronze. The solid shelves were filled with dolls, some wooden and looking like they were made for puppetry, others hand puppets of cloth. But the great majority were porcelain dolls, dressed in faux-antique clothing made from velvet, silk, and lace, their artificially gleaming hair ringlets of yellow, red, black, or brown, with eyes that shone in the gloom. He frowned, never having liked the staring orbs and pale hands of porcelain dolls, and turned away from them. The opposite wall was filled with other and finer constructions; cuckoo clocks, tiny chalets carved in great detail, some with proud finials on the gables, others with more rounded spears, some even equipped with miniature antlers and animal heads. They ranged from cream-hued to light-brown to nearly black, with hands in gold, silver, or bronze, weights of slender pine cones carved into preternaturally regular scales, pendulums in the shape of rowan, oak, or birch leaves, and the faintest outline of a tiny secret hatch above the clock faces.

Only then did he notice the ticking from the multitude of clocks, and as he became aware of the sound, it grew in strength and insistence. The clocks didn't show the exact same time, but the majority of them were close to midday. As he watched them, a couple of clocks intensified their ticking, the weights dropped a notch, and the door flaps above the clock faces vibrated with barely suppressed expectation. It was only a few seconds to twelve o'clock and then nearly all the crazy birdhouses would ring! The arms of the first clocks had already reached their apex and a deep resonance started up inside their intricate wooden bodies, preparing to call out the deep and hallowed tones of time, accompanied by the ridiculous artifice of clockwork cuckoos. Not once, or twice, or even three or four times, but twelve, in a horrible, torturous, time-delayed cacophony. He had been back from military service long enough that loud noises didn't bother him, so one or two clocks ringing would be fine, even five or six of them, but not twenty or thirty at once. The cramped room seemed to hold its breath in anticipation for the impending aural avalanche. He spun around, ran out of the room, and left the store as quickly as he could, not caring who saw him in his fear.

4.

Setting up Camp

When the team had arrived at the airport closest to the current disaster area they had been herded into the terminal, which was now only open for rescue workers and their equipment and served as a temporary coordination center for the emergency effort. Here, groups of emergency personnel from other aid organizations, local search-and-rescue, police, army, fire department, health workers, and representatives of regional authorities, were gathered in the executive lounge. They were given a short briefing and then assigned a part of the city to work in. Leah's team was one of only two identification groups, and the only international one. It was more than she had anticipated, but less than she had hoped for.

(( ))

With little information about the site and what it might require from them, Leah's team brought their own equipment, tents, tables, food, water, and communication systems to the mound.

"Tomorrow when it gets light, let's start looking for a building that still has four walls and a roof," Raymond said. They needed a place in the shade where they could unfold steel tables and place battery-operated LED-lamps on the floor, and filter-pump clean water for the makeshift post-mortem examination room. In order to store the dead they needed shipping containers or anything else that was solid and lockable, could hold dry ice, and function as a temporary morgue.

"Ice is on the way," Edouard said. "The other identification team has ordered a huge quantity from the nearest functioning population center. I just talked with them on the sat phone and they said they will reroute half the ice to us."

"Good," Raymond said. "Then we can start by setting up the small tents here tonight." These could easily be taken down and moved if one of the buildings nearby turned out to be safe enough for habitation in the morning. While the others pitched the two small tents, Edouard set up the water station, a fat, barrel-shaped filtering unit meant to provide families and small communities with clean water in developing countries. The team had several times had the pleasure of transporting similar filtering units to distant villages and communities to provide them with clean water. Now Edouard was glad he had brought one from the home organization's dwindling stores. Over the years, little by little, donations had shrunk and resources lessened, despite there being more disasters and more people needing help than ever before. Donor fatigue, the media and decision makers called it. There were simply too many disasters, too many little wars, too many people in distress, for the public to know who needed help the most.

Edouard took out a roll-bag of thick plastic from one of the crates that were stacked on the grass, shook it open, and brought it with him to the edge of the mound. There, he cast about with the strong beam of his large flashlight to see where the current of the floodwater might be the strongest and hence the cleanest. In the morning, he would inflate the small rubber rowboat he had brought with the pedal pump he had packed along with it, to be able to draw even faster-flowing and hopefully cleaner water from the flood. But for now he had to fill the roll-bag from the edge of the mound. He stepped slowly and carefully in case the drowned grass dropped sharply into the flooding, then squatted and pulled the roll-bag through the brown water. Then he rose and carried the dripping bag with him back to the top of the mound. There he opened the lid of the filtration unit and poured the liquid from the roll-bag into the plastic barrel. Gravity would now trickle the water through the filter, leaving the tank full of water free from virus, bacteria, protozoa, insect eggs, sand, mud, twigs, leaves, and other organic material. The process would even be able to remove some of the hydrocarbons and other chemicals that might have found its way into the floodwater here. The filter wouldn't be able to keep out all of the chemicals, but it would remove the worst, especially now when the filter was new and unclogged. The water wouldn't be entirely safe for drinking, but would be clean enough to wash in, rinse eating utensils, and most importantly, provide somewhat clean liquid for the identification work. While the first portion of water started dripping through the barrel, Edouard picked up the roll-bag again and went to fetch more water. The filtration unit would need two more rounds before it was full. After that it would be time to open the first crate of self-heating ready-to-eat meals to hand out to his colleagues, who by then would be finished setting up the tents and the primary equipment, and would begin to glance over at him for signs that it was time to eat.

❨☽❩

Edouard had grown up in a small but well-to-do family. Even now, his parents, his sisters, and he were still stuck in the conflicts and dependencies that had been established when Edouard and his sisters had been little and their parents still young. His sisters were still economically dependent on their parents, the youngest living at home despite having graduated from the most expensive and prestigious university in their country. This was a source of eternal conflict between Edouard's parents. His mother loved having her daughter close and didn't at all mind that she still occupied the same spacious and tall-windowed room as she did while growing up in their large, mahogany-furnished and marble-columned apartment in the capital. But Edouard's father resented this, as did his oldest sister, who lived, out of work, with friends in an apartment nearby, her rent, monthly expenses, and allowance supplied by her parents' high income. In that light, Edouard's choice of going into aid work after finishing his education at the same university as that of his sisters had been the least irksome life choice of the siblings, and could, with some good-will and a gray lie be called "international relations" to distant relatives and friends.

Having escaped the oppressive and repetitive stage play of mutual resentment and emotional dependency the members of his family had created for one other, Edouard was relieved to have made a loosely connected extended family with his colleagues instead. Thus, he was more than happy to do what he could to care for them and add to their wellbeing as best he could.

5.

To the Sand Castle

There was no bus connection from the small town to the coast, so he hiked for an hour back to the train platform nearest the cabin. As usual, the slab of rough concrete split by old rails extending north and south was empty of people. The platform was more than half a meter thick, yet nevertheless covered by thick underbrush that was green and fresh from the plentiful precipitation and the mounting warmth of spring. The overhead wires were almost ensnared in the young birches and rowans that stood along the line, but their leaves were pale and yellow, as if it were still autumn. He caught the first train to the coast, which took him to a town north of his home city. The car was almost empty, only a few heads visible above the rows of seats, so once he was sufficiently warm, he pulled the jacket off and dozed while the landscape rushed by outside.

At the train station in the coastal town he studied the rail connections to see if any of the local routes reached further south, but they were all canceled. The map and timetables were enclosed in displays where humidity was rising in the spring warmth and looked as if they were sweating inside. The yawning, hangar-like station was nearly empty in the midday sun, only seagulls, pigeons, and sparrows strutting about on the platforms. He checked the southbound bus routes and found two that were still in operation. They didn't go very far south, and one veered too far inland to be useful, but the other would take him almost thirty kilometers closer to his home. That would have to be enough. He waited quietly in the dust-filled rays that filtered in between the steel arches and beams and the air that echoed with announcements from the speaker-system.

When the bus, an old and rickety affair with ancient-looking stitched leather seats, roared into the station and stopped, he didn't board the bus immediately, but checked the departure time once more, then sidled over to the nearest ticket automat and stuffed one of his remaining bills into the slot. Ticket thus purchased and change received without having to interact with the bus driver, he wandered around for a bit, taking in the headlines of the newspapers in the station kiosk that sold flowers, magazines, snacks, and phone cards: Riots in the north protesting against the increased taxation due to the recent disasters. Drought and forest fires east on the continent, an oil spill in the polar sea after a maritime accident, more flooding in the south. But no mention of the devastation of the hurricane. That was more than a month in the past, and other disasters seemed to have followed since then and taken over the headlines.

(( ))

When he exited the bus at the route's southernmost stop, the first thing he saw was a gas station with the aluminum roof above its six pumps torn upwards and back, like the bared lips of the dog on the bus. The station's display windows looked like they had been shot out, glass shards glittering like rain puddles in a gaping steel frame. The asphalt was covered in clumps of concrete, deformed pieces of metal, pulped and dried cardboard and paper, rotten plant matter, an entire car wheel and several wheel caps, a plastic pallet, and a white hatchback rolled over on its side. Next to the ruined gas station ran the road, visibly littered with gravel and sand, but otherwise appearing to be in good condition. The bus doors hissed close behind him and the driver swung the vehicle back across the parking lot to return to the motorway and head back north. A few cars passed him, their chassis surfaces glinting in the sunshine, the roar of sound and push of air from them familiar, yet strangely unsettling after months of silence in the mountains.

He was still far from his destination, this was barely the suburb of the suburb of one of the many satellite towns that surrounded his home city, but it was a start. He was on his way home. He hitched the backpack up, clicked the clasps of the waist strap together, and began to follow the pavement south.

On both sides of the road were barren fields that were nearly flat, or had been bulldozed and leveled. They seemed to have been intended for future construction. A bright yellow excavator lay overturned by a ditch filled with brown water. Further out in the mud were the long, rectangular shapes of unfinished structures, palaces of glass and steel in various innovative shapes, with rounded corners, multi-colored windows, angled columns, or walls covered with steel latticework in bright, neon hues. He assumed these buildings had been corporate offices, warehouses, wholesale outlets, and business hotels. Associated with the unfinished shells were wide parking lots delineated in white or yellow paint. Once these spaces had been open and neat, but now they were littered with vehicles, most still upright, but bunched up along the edges of the lots, like runaway bumper cars, or remaining in rows, their windows turned to crunch, or blown end over end into heaps. One group of cars had tangled themselves into a rat king that had slammed its way through the entrance of the nearest building. Once inside they had lost momentum and settled in a cluster of broken steel and rubber inside the foyer, leaving rifts and cracks in the floor's dark and gleaming shale. Despair passed like a shadow over his mind. If this was how things looked outside of the hurricane's path, how much had been destroyed further south? And how many had been killed? What were the probabilities that his family and boyfriend had managed to survive the thousand little catastrophes that made up a natural disaster? He quickly pushed the speculations away, to not fall into dejection.

Most of the structures he could see had had their windows

blown out and their weaker points of architecture bent or crumpled by the hurricane or objects lifted up and hurled by it. Yet, some buildings seemed to have been passed over by the wind and were almost intact, revealing only a few missing windows, or wrecked, wrenched-up floors on the windward side only. But despite the destruction of the buildings along the road, the asphalt was free of cracks and debris, and cars passed by him at high speeds.

When dusk fell, draining the sky's blue to purple and pink, emergency housing started to appear alongside the road. The box-like wooden structures, construction site barracks, had been stacked three on top of each other, with unpainted plank-staircases reaching up to the flimsy doors. As he continued in the darkness, staying out of the headlights from the cars that occasionally passed him, more and more of the modest dwellings rose up on either side of the thoroughfare. But despite the great number of barracks, only a few of their tiny square windows emitted light and the tall street lamps that flanked the pavement were dim and dead, indicating that power had not returned to the area. He scanned the doors and walls of the barracks for white sheets of paper that could be lists of names of inhabitants or posters of missing people, but saw none.

A little after dark he left the road, crossed the shoulder and ditch, and slipped in among the rows of blue construction barracks. He chose one that faced the mud flat beyond the emergency housing and rolled in beneath the floor. There was only dirt there; no gravel had been deposited before the barracks were set up. He pulled the sleeping bag out of the backpack, wrapped it around himself, and curled up against the backpack. Above him the floor creaked and vibrated with the motion of its inhabitants as they crossed it, put something down, or sat on it. Breaths of warm air and the smell of people reached him through the floorboards, along with the sound of muted conversations, the cries of children, the barks of dogs, and, right before he fell asleep despite the cold ground and the chilling spring breeze, the sighs and groans of copulation somewhere in the space above.

6.

The First Weeks

The first morning in the drowned city revealed, after a thorough scanning with binoculars, that none the buildings near the mound seemed safe. The satellite images also showed that this part of the city had been thoroughly beaten by the hurricane and subsequent storms. Therefore, the team decided to set the rest of the tents up on the mound and unfolded the post-mortem tables inside two of the smallest tents to prepare for the arrival of the dead.

They set up the large tent, which could easily house forty people, at the top of the mound, and placed beneath its pointed canopy all the steel crates of equipment, and cardboard boxes with food and bottled water for the team and the survivors they might find during their work. These stores were certain to shrink as time went by, leaving more and more space for the team to sleep in. At the back of the large tent they unfolded two tables, and placed the small-sized and fine equipment and the medical supplies there, as well as the single map they had of the city, and the satellite-connected laptop. When the weather cleared, someone in the team would roll out the dark face of a foldable solar cell panel to recharge the laptop. But for now there was plenty of battery power left. The rear of the large, cone-shaped tent became storage space and nerve center for the team's work, while the front became sleeping, food preparation, and clothes-drying area. Finally, each team member placed one navy blue canvas cot where they most wanted to sleep inside the large tent and put the single bag of luggage they had been allowed to bring with them down on the cot.

The latrine they set up at the edge of the water, as far away from the large tent as it was possible to get on the mound of grass they lived on. Edouard placed the water filtration unit at the largest distance away from and upstream of the latrine, so that the team had a place to get water, do laundry, and clean themselves in private. The largest and heaviest supplies that had followed the team in the helicopter to the mound, such as two extra tables and an additional folded-up small tent and its poles, were stored on the meadow outside the large tent. The camp and the team's new home was ready for use.

❨ ❩

At first, rescue and evacuation of the living was the team's priority. It didn't take them long to locate the first survivors and help elderly couples, families with small children, or single individuals out of their apartments and houses, professionals and public servants from office buildings, toddlers and teachers from kindergartens, carpenters and electricians and plumbers from unfinished structures, road patrols and truck drivers from their tall vehicles, attendants and customers from shops and malls, chefs and waiters and patrons from restaurants and cafes, owners and artists from a gallery, researchers and curators from a museum, and healthcare workers and their patients, human as well as animal, from their hospitals. The team helped the survivors down from rooftops and stairwells and attics and trees where the citizens had sought shelter, not knowing what to run from first, the churning water that rose quickly around them or the shrieking hurricane that peeled the roofs off their houses.

These survivors had lived on what little food and water they had when the storm warning went out, or found sustenance in abandoned houses or stores that had been ripped open by the wind. Most of them were in good condition and could walk out of their shelters and into the rubber vessels on their own. The team evacuated the survivors to designated areas from which the survivors would be transported out of the city, first by boat or truck to other assembly spots, and from there in large buses to the emergency centers set up in the north.

Stadiums and concert halls and other large public venues that were still standing in the city housed many survivors who had made their way there from the neighboring streets and avenues. It felt good for the team to call these in, knowing that large groups of people had survived the disaster and would be out of the city soon. While the team waited for the evacuation transport to arrive they handed out bottled water, energy bars, and blankets to the survivors and treated those who needed medical attention for cuts from broken glass, bruises from falling objects, sprains from slipping on wet surfaces, concussions from flying debris, or fractures from being thrown around by the wind or the water.

But a small number of residents whose houses or apartments were above the water didn't want to come with the team. These survivors were missing a family member or a beloved pet and wanted to wait until they came back. Or they feared that their homes would be broken into, looted, and ruined if they left. Yet others said they had plenty of food and water and that the flood didn't reach to their floor, so they wanted to wait at home until the water went away. Most of these the team managed to persuade to come with them to the emergency centers and evacuation spots, but a few they couldn't convince and had to leave behind.

As the first week slid by and the water still stood high on the walls and the wind blew hard, seeming not to want to retreat or fall silent at all, the number of recalcitrants dwindled quickly and the survivors gladly followed the team in their rubber vessels to the assembly sites. More than a few of the inhabitants had hoisted flags and banners made by T-shirts or sheets to signal their surrender to circumstance and disaster for the rescue teams to come and save them.

( )

In the second week, the team found fewer survivors and more dead in the semi-collapsed buildings and hideaways and shelters that were left in the city. Few of the deceased had died from lack of food or water. Instead, they had perished of natural causes brought on or exacerbated by the natural disaster, or they were simply one of the number of people who die in every major population center every day. Some had passed over in their beds with boxes of multiple pills and bottles of water on bed tables next to them, others clearly ailing under blankets on their sofas, surrounded by tablets, tissue paper, oxygen tanks, or still hooked to their very own dialysis machine, such as a young woman Gabriele and Jens found inside a luxury apartment complex with golden surfaces and gleaming tiles. The blood in the thin, transparent tubes of the dialysis machine had gone dark and congealed from the lack of electricity to operate the device. Others, like an elderly man they found, seemed to have keeled over where he stood, perhaps from a heart attack, inside the beams of sunlight in the tile-floored, stained-glass-windowed hallway of a large suburban house. One elderly woman they found inside one of the tiny single-floor dwellings of a senior citizen housing complex slumped over a kitchen table that was set with a white rubber tablecloth and the plates and cutlery of a full Sunday breakfast. The fried eggs and bacon were hairy with mold, the slices of the toasted bread completely hard, the halved grapefruit hatching tiny red-eyed flies, and the pot of tea cold despite the knitted cozy that covered it. Yet the unopened, store-bought raspberry muffin that sat next to the pot of tea was still golden and sweating droplets of grease inside its plastic wrapping.

"Mary Celeste," Edouard commented as he started to search the dead woman's purse that stood next to the old-fashioned landline telephone on the kitchen counter for identification.

(( ))

Nevertheless, most of the remaining inhabitants the team found in the second week were still alive, but several were sick or poisoned, because in the lack of any other fluid and nutrition they had drunk from the floodwater or eaten stale or contaminated food. The team also registered more severe exhaustion, dehydration, malnourishment, hypothermia among the survivors than the previous week, as well as burns from trying to make fires to signal for help. More severe injuries also started to appear as the survivors had tried to navigate the floating debris of the city on their own and pick their way to the emergency shelters or evacuation spots where they knew they would get help.

Few, if any, survivors managed to leave the city on their own, and even fewer reached the shelters outside the city unaided. Some unlucky survivors had been injured in fights that erupted between family members, co-workers, neighbors, dorm mates, or strangers that were cooped up and unable to remove themselves from the situation while they waited for help or tried to reach it. These were latent conflicts that finally had been brought up and out in the open, like the debris that unmoored and floated to the surface in the flood.

7.

Into Emergency

He continued as soon as the faint light from the predawn roused him from his shivering and uneven sleep. Along the road the rows of construction barracks became longer and longer, until they seemed to constitute an entire town. In the late morning, he began to encounter people along the pavement, carrying cardboard boxes or plastic bags full of tins or bottles or cans of soda. He even passed a few people on bicycles, with plastic bags strapped to the luggage rack or dangling precariously from the handlebars.

He was glad for the increased traffic; clearly people were still living here. For a while there were multiple rows of barracks on both sides of the road, but during the day they became fewer and fewer and more vegetation and bushes appeared. Simultaneously, the amount of litter along the road increased: remnants of cardboard boxes, fast food wrapping, styrofoam cups, newspapers and magazines, shreds of toilet paper, lightweight refuse that could move far in the wind. The garbage rolled along on the asphalt, waved in the patchy, pale grass by the pavement or the staircase railings of the barracks, and cluttered the narrow lanes between the emergency housing. Past midday, clusters of bulging plastic bags began to crowd the pavement, obviously left there in the hope that they would be picked up by a passing garbage truck or other sanitary service. Many of the soft containers were torn and opened by the elements or scavengers, but whether they had been animal or human he couldn't tell. In a few places the garbage bags were so many and so large the stacks were the size of trucks, wafting a rank flatulence downwind.

Shortly thereafter he spotted the first tents on a slope across the road. They were bright orange, yet had none of the ostentatious complexity and variety of portable shelters meant for hiking or camping, with their scientific methods of resisting wind and rain with carefully selected materials and construction, indicating an individual daring and challenging of the elements, and of taking control of the situation and the environment into which the tents would be taken. In contrast, the tents he passed on the rise were simple, unsophisticated shelters, identical to one another, humble in their indication of the sudden and unplanned nature of the need they had been set up to fill, and of the ongoing necessity. A few tents were open, with people sitting outside them. They were cooking, eating, feeding children, or sitting passively, staring into the afternoon light. Between the tents inhabitants moved alone or in groups. As he watched, a small cluster of people left the grass, entered the pavement, and started following it in the direction he was coming from.

( )

Further ahead the knoll flattened to a park, with overgrown ponds, faded benches, and cracked walkways between the tents. The amount of litter on the asphalt and in the vegetation on both sides of the road had increased greatly. Now it wasn't just remnants of paper or cardboard or bags, but also heavier objects such as tin cans, wheel caps, and clothing. He even passed a large leather suitcase and a three-wheeled baby stroller turned over in the ditch.

In the park he spotted large tents made from a solid-looking, taupe-colored fabric, closed, but with crates stacked outside them and the tracks from many people muddying the ground. These tents reminded him of storage and supply tents in military camps he had been in on other continents.

Further down the road were stalls of portable toilets and a large pavilion-like structure, a tall orange tent that served more as roof than as a building. Here, personnel in dark coveralls and neon yellow vests moved back and forth among stacks of crates and water bottles. A long queue wound its way beneath the canopy, where the boxes and chests blocked his view, but the people he saw exiting carried flimsy plastic bags clearly weighed down by water bottles, cans, and other supplies. A sudden impulse to run across the road and up to the emergency center to see if they had lists of evacuees or identified dead flashed through him and he left the pavement, hurrying across the road towards the park.

He looked for a way to get inside the tent without having to join the long line or a way to get close enough to ask one of the staff if they had lists of survivors, but the stream of people who had received their supplies and were leaving the queue through the rear of the tent was so large and constant there was no way he would be able to push himself through the crowd in that direction. Instead, he followed the queue in front of the tent to its start and joined it. Even though the line moved constantly and fairly quickly towards the tent while more people entered the queue behind him, he felt impatient and restless. Every hour spent in line meant one less hour of daylight to travel in to reach the city. Yet, he needed to know whether they had any lists of survivors or dead here, or at least get close enough to see what kind of information they did have.

When he finally stood at the end of the line, one of the emergency workers handed him a transparent plastic bag filled with a few sachets of self-heating meals, a packet of whole-grain biscuits, some tin cans, a couple of bottles of water, and some chocolate bars. He asked the emergency worker if they had any lists of survivors and was told to look at the printouts at the back of the tent. He followed the flow of people who were leaving the queue with their food and joined a small cluster who were studying the sheets of paper taped to the rear wall. The paper was buckled with dried moisture and the black print faded by the sun. The letters were tiny and the surnames sorted alphabetically, but several sheets seemed to restart the sequence of names from the beginning to give room for more names. The lists were headlined "Registered Evacuees" and counted about a thousand individuals, which probably didn't include half of the number of people he had seen in the tent camp outside. It took him almost half an hour to skim through the lists, and in that time he found no familiar names. When he was done and could finally return to the pavement, he hurried on like the ground was on fire beneath him.

At nightfall he moved into the field on the lower and empty side of the road towards the silhouettes of the unfinished buildings that rose there. The muddy expanse was pockmarked with puddles that gleamed like coins in the golden light from the vanishing sun. The building he had seen from the road stood crumbled and dark. Its entrance looked like it had been rammed in, but whatever had caused the destruction was no longer present. The back of the long structure had been crushed flat and the side squashed into the ground. Strangely, the foyer area on the first floor was still standing, hollow like a small cave. He peeked inside the gloom. It seemed stable, did not creak or make any other noises in the evening breeze that indicated it was about to collapse. He swept the faint beam from his headlamp into the darkened space. The rear walls were hidden in debris—desks, office chairs, pieces of flooring from above, a tall potted plant, cracked computer monitors—and he couldn't see where the room ended. The floor was covered with a fine sand that had no tracks in it except for his own. Right inside the remaining wall a mottled gray sofa with thin steel feet had been pushed sideways against a concrete column. He shoved the sofa a little further inside, away from the shattered glass, put the backpack on the floor, and curled up on the sand-dusted furniture with the sleeping bag around him.

( )

The next morning he woke shivering in the breeze from the broken entrance. The sun wasn't yet fully up and the light was gray and flat. When he stood and stretched, sand crunched beneath his boots. Once the sofa must have looked sophisticated and expensive, but now it was rough, with threads in various hues of gray sticking out of it, like wayward hair. He sat down on it again and pulled out a sachet of oatmeal, nuts, and raisins from the backpack, along with a multivitamin pill, tilted his head back and ate right from the packet, then drank the water that was left in the soda bottle. If he found water he could refill it with the filter, so he hung on to the bottle for now. With breakfast done, he relieved himself in the inner corner of the semi-collapsed foyer, put the jacket and backpack on, and strode out of the cracked room.

He crossed the mud-field, returned to the pavement, and followed it south. For a few more hours orange emergency tents were visible on the higher ground across the road. There was a slow trickle of cars, mostly sturdy terrain vehicles, one or two vans, and even a construction truck and an in-transit cement mixer, but he didn't see where they were going, nor did he pass any construction work or repairs along the road.

A little after midday the camping site and its tents disappeared behind a curve and the road entered a stretch of woodland dominated by deciduous trees; beeches, oaks, elms, with the occasional cherry or maple standing among them. The road curved along a hill, which grew steeper and denser with underbrush. The tracks and beds from brooks and streams appeared in the vegetation above and below the road, which was entirely devoid of cars. He realized he hadn't seen a vehicle for hours, which he took to mean that the road ahead was blocked. He promptly left the asphalt and entered the shade beneath the canopies and the leaf-covered forest floor and followed the road from a distance so as not to be spotted by any car that might appear and try to stop him.

Along the hill, more and larger runoffs and interruptions appeared on the ground, indicating that large amounts of water had rushed down the slope, pulling with it the under-brush, sand and soil, even rocks and trees, and the occasional boulder. He passed trunks that had toppled over in the hurricane, some still healthy, others dead, as well as trees and branches that had been swept along by the water and now lay stranded in awkward or impossible positions on the hill; in the canopy of another tree, or entangled in the roots of another. Below him, he spotted a steel road gate with a sign that said "Road closed. No entry."

He followed the edge of the forest a little farther, past the gate, then continued near the shoulder of the road for faster progress, yet still in the shadow of the trees. As the thoroughfare wound southward, the asphalt grew more and more cracked, with water-filled potholes, and subduction-like crevices and overhangs in the ground, making the road impassable for vehicles.

8.

The Third Week

In the third week the dead became the majority, no longer the minority, even in the large improvised shelters the team found or the nearly undamaged and still solid-looking buildings where the remaining survivors had sought refuge. Some of the dead floated black and bloated in the still high and increasingly dirty water.

"It's time to start marking the corpses on the map, so we can could find them again later on," Leah told the team at the end of that week. She wasn't willing to give up the core of their work, the true reason why they were there, and not utilize their true expertise, no matter what the coordination center said.

Now, most of the living they found were sick or unconscious, and needed immediate help and evacuation directly to hospitals in the north instead of to the emergency shelters in the evacuation zone. A few the team found injured inside or near buildings that had collapsed, which the emergency teams only now had the capacity and time to search.

☾☽

"I'm spotting an arm over there," Jens said and pointed at a rubble of pale concrete and even paler dust.

"Are you certain?" Edouard said. "I can't see anything but rubble."

They moved closer to where Jens pointed, secured to the outside by a stretch of solid rope and protected by red climbing helmets and harnesses that curled around their waist and thighs.

"I see it now," Edouard said, and coughed in the dust that swirled in the air around them. They scooted closer to the exposed body part that was as gray and covered in dust as the blocks of collapsed floor and drywall around them. Jens removed his reinforced gloves and reached for the wrist of the swollen, gray limb.

"I have a pulse," he said after a short while. "Very faint, but definite."

Wasting no time with trying to dig the survivor out, they instead followed a medical protocol for earthquake victims and performed the medical tests and treatments possible via the arm. They measured the pulse more thoroughly, did a few blood tests for oxygen saturation, waste products that signified broken or severed limbs, and general infection to get some impression of the patient's vital signs. Then Jens located a vein to set a port for the intravenous introduction of fluid and salts while Edouard called the find in. The two nearest teams were from their group, and when they finally arrived, they carefully started to remove the debris around the patient to reveal more of their body. Jens continued to do various tests and give intravenous treatments through the port in the exposed arm, and after a while he saw the fingers start to move. Jens quickly took the hand.

"We're getting you out of there," he said. "Just lie still. Squeeze my hand if you can, but don't try to speak." Jens repeated the message in all the languages he knew, and Edouard added the ones he was familiar with. When they found a language the patient responded to, they proceeded to ask them questions about how they were feeling and whether they needed more fluid, painkiller, or any other kind of medication they depended on. While Jens and Edouard treated the patient, the rest of the team kept removing the rubble.

The work took hours and it was nearly dark when Edouard could finally tell the patient: "We're ready to bring you out now, so close your eyes and remain still." On beforehand they had given the patient as strong a painkiller as they could considering the patient's condition, which also provided a slight sedation to prevent sudden panic and more injury. Jens looked at his colleagues and the defibrillator equipment that one of them had brought. This was the critical moment where the sudden shock of being free of the rubble that pressed down on the patient, and thus increased the blood flow, could worsen the patient's medical status rather than improve it.

"Is everybody ready?" Jens asked. His colleagues nodded and together they started to lift the patient out of the crumbled wood and concrete. When they could see the patient's face, covered in dust and dried blood, Jens quickly put his dust mask over their eyes to shield them from the glare of the lamps the team had set up inside the crawlspace.

In similar rare and miraculous rescues, Jens had done the same surrounded by a crowd of emergency workers and volunteer locals in various avalanche and earthquake disasters. Often, the media had been present too, or someone with a tiny video camera or a phone, and filmed the miraculous, joyous, life-affirming event that a survivor rescue always was. Usually, afterwards, someone always tried to sell the recording to one news agency or another, local as well as international, and invariably they would succeed, for the clip to be shown worldwide after the devastating disaster. Jens had never thought it strange that anyone would film such an event, to celebrate it or later relive the moment, despite the shades of voyeurism and exploitation inherent in the act. To Jens, it was first and foremost a rebirth, the start of a rebuilding, a sign that hope should not be lost, that the odds could work in your favor, no matter how bad or impossible they seemed. Of course, such events were rare, and more often than not, those discovered and retrieved from beneath ruins were dead. In addition, it was not at all rare for victims to be alive, but fail to survive the rescue itself, or the demanding surgery and recuperation that followed, and which often required advanced medical equipment and procedures that were not available in the country struck by the disaster, or which no longer could be obtained.

It was all coincidences, luck, a lottery, Jens thought. Where any disaster happened, where the avalanche went or the earthquake struck, in what direction the buildings fell, where the walls collapsed, and which limbs they hit. It was random and merciless, yet more often than not it depended also on where you lived, who you were, and how much you earned. Everyone knew disasters struck the poor or the struggling, the unprepared or those whose governments ignored or downplayed risks in order to not have to deal with the issue, much harder. Then, no matter the extent of or type of catastrophe, followed the big question of whether the affected region or country had enough infrastructure and emergency personnel to aid the victims quickly, whether it was willing or able to accept aid from outside within a reasonable amount of time, and whether it had the economy and social coherency to help the fleeing masses then and there, not to mention whether it was capable of rebuilding cities and towns or resettling people and services following the catastrophe.

Death and disaster might be random, but the results of them were certainly not coincidental. At least not in the old world, the world as it had been, Jens thought as he held the cluster of plastic bags of intravenous fluid and medication of his current patient, and closed one palm gently around the tubes so they wouldn't fall out as the rest of the team carefully put the patient on a stretcher to carry the survivor out of the ruin. But who knew what the future would bring, even here on his own previously safe and wealthy continent.

( )

"Start taking pictures," Leah told the team at the end of the third week. "It's time we contributed to the walls." She had already brought the names and addresses of the dead the teams had been able to identify on the spot to the coordination centers outside the area of immediate disaster. Here, there was still Internet connectivity and electricity to run it, and rows and rows of monitors and computers had been set up to organize and direct the evacuation of survivors out of the stricken regions and into the emergency shelters and temporary housing beyond. At these monitors police, medical personnel, and aid organizations collected the names, former addresses, phone numbers of the survivors that were registered at the emergency shelters, as well as where they now could be contacted. Here, the names and addresses of the dead who had been identified were made available online, as well as listed on the walls and on large boards for the people who arrived in person searching for signs of their loved ones. The message boards also contained column upon column of hand-written posters and notes from survivors who stumbled from hospitals to health care clinics to emergency centers in search of the living and the dead: have you seen this woman, man, or child, please call this number.

A lucky few of the team had heard from their loved ones at home who were either staying where they were and had received help, or had reached an emergency shelter, or, the last and worst possibility, conveyed by shaking voices from other relatives or friends, were confirmed dead or still missing. Those team members, such as Jens and Gabriele, who had not yet heard anything from their loved ones, Leah took with her to the coordination center if they were available so they could help her update the databases with the team's lists, as well as search for the names of their loved ones and make calls to their home cities when the phone line was open.

Nevertheless, the team members didn't have much time or energy to worry about their loved ones, not here, not now. Instead, they made a conscious choice to trust the resourcefulness of their partners and family and friends, the efforts of the emergency workers in their home city, and the mercy of providence or luck or whatever higher power they believed in. Until it was confirmed otherwise they had to believe that no news was good news, and that there was not much the team members could do about the situation in their current location. This they did to be able to keep working and do what they could for the people at hand, without becoming paralyzed with fear and concern for their closest ones.

For as long as there was daylight the team worked outside, and when night and darkness fell and the few lanterns and torches they had seemed to be the only points of light in their sector of the city, they continued their job in the improvised examination rooms in the small tents. They tried to sleep through the silent nights, and gathered together when colleagues from other teams arrived with fresh food prepared in large containers for all the emergency personnel in the city, as well as for the few survivors who were still waiting at the evacuation points inside the disaster area.

The team took care of one another as best they could. When someone was more irritable or worried or quiet than usual, one of their colleagues asked them to take a break, sit down, have some water, get an energy bar or an apple, and talk. Those who were close friends, as many of them were, talked often and without reservations, without censoring themselves. In this way, they shared the ruinous images that surrounded them during the day and flitted across their mind at night, of the eyes and hands of those they lost during treatment and aid, of the lump of fear that sat in their bellies and grew worse when they thought of their loved ones at home, how the faces of the deceased and those of their family members and even they themselves seemed to merge and meld and become the one and the same until they could barely tell them apart. Then the team members cried together, or shouted, or even laughed to keep the fear of the future and the yearning for the past at bay. But most of the time the team members simply sat together, saying nothing, discussing naught, and remained in a silent, patient togetherness that did not seek to comfort or give or take or change anything, but simply stayed and breathed.

9.

Night at the Edge of the Abyss

Even here, far south of the cabin in the mountains, the canopies of spring foliage bore a strange autumnal hue, more yellow than green. Normally, at this time of year, the leaves would have been a green so bright they would gleam in the sun, and as the spring progressed to summer, they would slowly darken to a deep, moss-like hue. He didn't know what caused the yellowing of the foliage; a response to the increased levels of carbon dioxide in the atmosphere, or a change in the ultraviolet radiation that reached them from the sun due to alterations in the cloud cover?

In the mid-afternoon he arrived at a place where a broad swath of the road was missing, along with trees and underbrush and topsoil, reaching from the summit of the hill and stretching so far down the slope he couldn't see where the bare patch ended. The grassless, naked scar indicated that a river, not a tiny trickle or a small stream, had rushed down the incline, pulling with it the vegetation and the surface in a single, violent event. He closed his eyes and imagined the rumble and vibration of the landslide as it started on top of the hill, while the wind and the rain from the hurricane pummeled the ground, pushing and pulling on it with unceasing force until it gave way, liquefied to mud and chunky water, and tumbled down the hill. Engulfing the rest of the hillside in a wave, the landslide increased its influence and power as it went, peeling yet more of the surface away from the bedrock, and finally launching it over the edge at the bottom of the slope, like so much refuse, into a roaring, raging waterfall of mud and debris. But then the wind slowly decreased and the rain died down or turned into a gentle mist, the clouds cleared, and the sun crawled back, revealing the track of the landslide, raw like a wound. Boulders and rocks still clung there, as did a mud-dusted trunk or two, but mostly there was just sand and pebbles. Below him, past the edge of the slope which lead to who knew where, a stripe of blue rippled between the wall of vegetation that bracketed it: the ocean, now gray and overcast and distant, but gleaming nonetheless.

The last time he had been in the ocean, it had been bone-chilling and muscle-cramping, sapping the life out of him even as he struggled against it. That was only a few weeks ago, but it felt like years, decades. These waters looked milder, yet cloudy and dim. He nevertheless thought he could hear the sound of the surf beating against the unseen shore beyond and far below the slope, much gentler than the sea in the north. He sat down right inside the line of trees, by the edge of the steep, broad scar that was left after the mudslide, and watched the ocean for a long time.

《 》

As dusk fell a breeze started up, clearing away the clouds. The horizon lit up in deep pink and purple, so different from the sweltering, orange twilights that stank of gunpowder, dust, and sweat which he remembered from the southern continent. The colors at nightfall in both his mother's and his father's countries held the same bright pink hues as here, despite being situated on two different continents and latitudes. He thought of his parents and his brother, of Michael and Beanie, wondered where they were now and whether he would ever be able to find out in the fog of prevailing disaster. Then, curtailing his darkest speculations, he withdrew from the backpack a sachet of freeze-dried ground beef with tomato sauce and pasta. Better to feed his body than his concerns, and lack of nutrition always made worries worse. He shook the foil bag so all the powdered sauce and meat would collect at the bottom, tore the top away, and pushed it open. He mixed the dry contents with water from the canteen, stirring with the plastic spoon that had been attached to the bag with a dab of glue. There was just enough water in the steel canteen for him to rehydrate the meal, down a multivitamin pill, and still have a few mouthfuls to drink. At air temperature, the water was too cold to fully rehydrate the food, instead turning it into a thick, tomato-flavored mush with hard pieces of ground beef and even denser pieces of pasta. It was neither delicate nor appetizing, but it was rich, nourishing food, which he needed, so he chewed it well to crush the dry pasta and beef, and forced it down, despite the vomit-like texture and artificial flavor. He consumed all of the freeze-dried meal, even scooped out the powdery remains at the bottom of the bag and ate that too, then pulled the bag apart and licked the thick foil clean, because he knew how hungry he'd be the next day, how much he'd regret it if he wasted the food he had. He drained the canteen, shook the last drops free from it and onto his tongue, screwed the cap on, and returned the container to the backpack's side pocket. His stomach revolted slightly at the sudden influx of highly nutritious food, but he kept it down by breathing slowly in and out of his nose until his body settled and started to digest the meal.

◖◗

As the horizon dimmed to black and more clouds came seeping in, he became aware that he had been looking at something for a long time, but had been too busy eating and surveying the marks of the hurricane's violence to register it. Below him on the slope, almost, but not quite, hidden by the falling dusk, was an even darker shape on the ground. Its outline was almost completely circular, reminding him of pictures from the oceans of the southern continent, where in certain rare places deep cobalt pits were visible in the bright blue water. At first he thought that what he saw was some kind of shadow or optical illusion caused by the night filling the canopies and the underbrush. He stretched his neck and blinked like an owl while trying to get a better view of the odd object. He had heard that with the exception of the sun and the full moon, nothing in nature was perfectly round. The circle was the mark of civilization and humanity. Yet, here was something that seemed natural, but was nevertheless a perfect, even circle. It looked like a dark disc on the ground, and like the gravity well of a black hole, it drew his eyes towards itself again and again until he had no other choice but to rise, pull his backpack on, leave his precious shelter among the trees, and move down the slope towards it.

He approached the blackness gradually, cautiously. He had hoped for some lunar light, but no moon came out, so he had to put the headlamp on and spend some of its precious battery power. The bluish-white beam from the lamp was strong and steady, yet dimmed against the density of the forest and managed to penetrate the gloom only a few meters ahead of him. His instincts told him to lie down on the ground and crawl on his belly towards the black hole to distribute his body weight as much as possible, the same he would have done on thin ice, or in hostile territory. Here, the slope seemed to shake slightly, with tiny, near-imperceptible tremors, but that must be his imagination. Perhaps the soil was still unstable from the mudslide. He continued forward in the plodding yet familiar fashion, as he had done many times on the southern continent. Now the ground was nearly level with the disc and he had to stop occasionally and crane his neck to check how far he was from the edge of the blackness. A little more, and then there was something like a suction in the air, a sudden vacuum, and sand and pebbles clattered over the fall that yawned in front of him. He froze and held his breath. The tiny tremors started up again, and he couldn't tell if it was his own body quivering with tension and expectation, or the ground vibrating from unseen geological processes.

The black hole was nearly perfectly circular, its walls plunging almost completely perpendicular to the surface. It looked like someone had pulled a giant cork out of the earth. He recalled having heard of sinkholes tens of meters deep, but he had never seen one before now. He wished he had a camera to share the witnessing of the black hole, yet in another way the lack of methods with which to document the moment would preserve it forever in his memory. The air that rose from the deep smelled of earth, mud, and stagnant water. He also thought he heard distant dripping, as if from a deep, natural well. Perhaps there was water at the bottom of the sinkhole, or the collapse had ruptured a pipe. A draft rose up from the darkness, like a cold and sepulchral breath.

He remembered a story he had read as a boy about a nature spirit who embodied itself from the salt water, the driftwood that collected on the barren beaches, and the reeds from the tarns and ponds at a cold and remote northern coast. While traveling south, the embodied spirit met an elderly scientist who wanted to prove that the Earth orbited the sun and not the other way around, the scientist's young apprentice, and a gray cat the spirit turned into a horse. Together the group, which his younger brother Katsuhiro called "the traveling actors." meaning "freak show," journeyed to the capital. This city was built on the remnants of a giant spiral conch shell, where commoners and craftsmen occupied the bottom tier of the mother-of-pearl, and higher social classes, such as soldiers, lawmakers, and nobles, lived on the increasingly smaller and higher platforms of the shell. At the top was a meadow with an enormous castle, consisting of huge buildings that had collapsed into one another until they resembled a single, gigantic, multi-winged complex seemingly with no end. At the spire of the shell burned an eternal flame, which illumined and warmed the city and its region, like a miniature sun. Because of this flame the capital's scientists believed the sun to be orbiting the Earth instead of the other way around.

The scientist and his friends traveled up through the tiers of the conch to the royal palace to seek the source of the eternal flame. Instead, they found the corpse of the king sitting in a bed the size of a bedroom and the bedroom filling an entire cathedral. Tributes and tithes and taxes from the region surrounding the city as well as from the giant shell's many tiers flowed continuously to the upper royal level. But the travelers discovered that all the goods and money and food and jewelry, that cost the lower classes their lives to produce, were simply dumped into a wide hole in the floor. When the nature spirit saw that, it became so enraged it put a torch to the head of the dead king. In a moment of playfulness or malice, or perhaps a little bit of both, the spirit kicked the head off the corpse's neck, causing the skull to fly through the air and into the hole. But the skull caught fire on some candles on the way and the cavity it fell down into was filled with gas from the decomposing food and items that had been discarded into the hole, as well as the city's dead, who lay buried in endless, labyrinthine crypts beneath the castle, because only in death did the citizenry finally reach the level that sat closest to heaven. This was the true source of the eternal flame at the tip of the conch. Now the burning skull ignited the gas, setting off explosions that shook the cathedral-castle, forcing the group of travelers to flee outside and down the tiers of the conch-city while everything blew up and fell apart around them.

He recalled being shocked as well as delighted when the skull of the wasteful dead king blew up the castle at the end. His brother had found the story trite and unlikely, and had taunted him for liking it. Now, however, there was no one else around to criticize him for it and he let out a loud laugh.

The true diameter of the sinkhole was hidden from him by the night, even with the illumination from the lamp, but from what he could see of the edges that vanished into the gloom, the sinkhole was at least ten meters across. He swept up a handful of sand and pebbles, stretched his arm out into the darkness, and opened his palm. The falling material whispered as it left his skin and fell silently into the void. He held his breath and waited, but there was no plop or click or clatter of debris reaching the bottom of the hole, even after a good while. He peered into the gaping space as sharply he would approaching an event horizon, but there was only silence and darkness. The pit was neither evil nor a bad sign, but a result of the geological characteristics in the area. It simply was, no matter what he or anyone else thought about it. He rested his chin on the hard, abrupt edge and simply breathed, now at peace with the presence of the sinkhole, feeling the blood flow through his body in regular, warm waves, aligning itself with the surf that whispered against the shore far beneath the hill.

10.

The Fourth Week

In the fourth week, the number of living the team now found in the city had become so small they began to focus fully on what they were specialized to do: bring the names of the dead back. That was what they had dedicated most of their professional and adult lives to, what they had worked at on all continents of the world; whether together with local authorities and organizations, or independently, openly or attached to covert operations in regions ruled by regimes that would prefer that certain truths were not known, but which the international community or invested parties sent the team and similar groups to unearth in the name of justice or prosecution.

The labor varied with the location and conditions of the place the team found themselves in. Thus they had different routines for whether they arrived early or late to a disaster zone, whether they worked with the recently dead or with remains that had been buried for years, whether they assisted the locals or worked on their own, whether the climate was cold or hot, dry or wet, whether there were many dead or just a few who needed to be identified. But no matter the circumstances or the place, the team's work was rarely quick and never easy.

Now they followed a protocol for mass disaster in flooding and inclement weather, with minimal outside assistance, resupply of resources, or transport of the dead. The protocol worked sufficiently, although this time, differently from most other instances, there was no Internet because the hurricane had flooded power plants, transmission stations, and transformers, and blown down countless electricity pylons and masts. In addition, campuses and buildings that had housed Internet routers had been flooded or collapsed, making it impossible to say when connectivity would be restored. The same was the case with the mobile phone system; countless towers and antennas had been ruined or lost power, making phone coverage extremely random and spotty.

"Let's bring the corpses out of storage and start working on them," Leah said when they were all sitting with their bags of self-heating breakfasts in their laps and preparing for another day of searching the remains of the city for survivors and dead.

❪ ❫

Leah made hand-drawn copies of the records and diagrams they used for the identification work and usually filled out in their online system. During the examination of the first corpses, which the team had retrieved from the water surrounding the mound and stored on ice in the few large steel crates they possessed, Raymond and Edouard and Marten noted their findings in notebooks and on paper pads and filled out Leah's hand hand-made diagrams in pencil. They stored the paper records in one of the small steel crates they had brought bags of intravenous fluid in, which was now empty. There were no possibilities for doing more extensive identification tests or postmortem examinations because the hospitals were still filled with injured from the hurricane, and the local coroners were busy identifying the dead retrieved at the periphery of the disaster area.

Now, when Leah hitchhiked out on the motorized vessels of the neighboring rescue teams, she brought the caskets of the dead that had been provisionally examined by the team with her out of the city for burial, as well as their meticulously written and archived records. The large rubber boats or rigid-hulled inflatables wound their way through the flooded city streets slowly and carefully, until they escaped the harbor, where they gunned their powerful outboard engines to all but fly across the sea northward. At the coordination center, Leah logged onto the identification databases that were available on the still unstable Internet connection and decimated servers, and made a final check for the corpses' identification in dental records, fingerprint databases, and archives of medical and genetic information. This way she managed to identify a few individuals and add them to the list of confirmed dead, while the rest she registered in the database as unknowns, with as many of the identification characteristics as the team had managed to examine and describe on paper. From these trips Leah brought back what little of food and water supplies, as well as medical equipment and paper journals, she could obtain from the coordination center.

11.

The Haunting

He woke behind the fallen tree trunk he had curled up against inside the line of trees, removed his gloves and jacket to air out some perspiration, and stretched and yawned to loosen the cold muscles. Then he rolled the sleeping bag up, ate a portion of oatmeal, nuts, and raisins, and drank the last of the water in the old soda bottle. Now he had to find a clean stream, but with the filtering device, it could be any kind of water, as long as it wasn't polluted by chemicals. It could even be the water from his own body, although he hoped not to have to do that for a long time yet, and he would only be able to twice in a row without drinking anything else in between before it would start to damage his organs. He put the gloves and jacket on again, as well as the backpack, and continued into the forest.

Away from the road, with only the compass for navigation, the vegetation seemed endless. The distance to civilization — roads, buildings, people — was not far, judging from the map, but inside the yellow-green brightness of the foliage, the overpowering scent of soil, moss, and leaves, and with no sounds other the hush of the wind, the occasional bird song, and the creaking of trunks and branches around him, the rest of the world seemed far away.

At noon the sun broke through the clouds and rays of light filtered through the pale canopies. He was out of sight, yet still progressing towards his goal, and he was certain there were no others in the forest. Any evacuees would have passed through weeks ago. He found no tracks, broken branches, fire pits, or other signs of recent human activity, which made his body relax and the walking easier. After a while he heard the sound of running water up ahead and picked up his pace to reach it. Between the broad trunks and the translucent foliage, the liquid face of a brook appeared, blazing in the midday light. He followed the water a short distance to check whether it was runoff from a field or a meadow further up, but saw no clearing ahead, so he knelt by the edge of a small pool where water rushed above the pebbles at the bottom and swirled and danced on the surface until it tumbled over the lip to the next pocket downstream on its tireless journey towards the sea. He leaned forward and sniffed the water for the scent of any chemical or out of place smell, but there was nothing, only the fragrance of running water and fresh vegetation. Reassured, he lowered the filter bottle gently into the liquid to stir up as little debris as possible, then scooped the plastic container back up with a slow, steady motion. He pulled the pump handle out from the bottom of the container, pushed it a few times, and thumbed the lid open. A burst of clear water squirted from the head of the bottle, overflowing after having been pushed through the complex filters inside it. He shook the drops off the mouthpiece and drank. He had to trust the bottle; the similar ones he had used in the past had been reliable and safe even for hundreds of liters. He drank what he needed, then moved upstream a little, past the mud he had already stirred up, pulled the container through another pool, and filled the steel canteen and the soda bottle with clear, clean water from the filters.

According to the map, the patch of forest was only a few kilometers wide, but either through faulty navigation, or a subconscious reluctance to leave the trees in apprehension of what he suspected lay before him, it took him a full day to cross.

❨❩

The next morning a thick fog settled on the landscape, its tiny drops cooling his face and breath. Soon after he left the hill, he came to a long field where young pine trees stood in dense rows, like vines in a vineyard. He followed the lanes to the end, where the field opened up to rows of other plants, some kind of saplings, apple or cherry or plum, blossoming white flowers on their nude branches. At the end of the field was an expansive greenhouse and a cluster of other buildings, which he assumed to be indoor plant nurseries, storage, and perhaps an outlet plant store. Bounding the field was a tall yew hedge, and on the other side of it a road. He crouched down behind the hedge and checked the compass. The road went in the north-south direction, so he traced the hedge south until the field ended, then crossed the nursery's wide and nearly empty parking lot. Only a few vehicles, bowled over by the hurricane, lay rusting on the asphalt. Beyond was an empty intersection where the traffic lights blinked a fearful, restless yellow. He hurried past them and across the road.

For a long stretch there were only fields, meadows, and pastures, interspersed with farms, the occasional private home, some with a small business on the first floor and a driveway for customers to park in at the front. The area consisted of gentle hills, and grass had already started to grow on the southern slopes, but the sprouts looked thin and nearly yellow, like the foliage in the forest, and the dips and troughs in the landscape cradled pools of brown water that reminded him of the flood on the heath.

As he turned south along the road the area changed from semi-rural to residential, with more and more hedges and medium-sized houses. Some of the private homes showed signs of damage; missing roof tiles, gables crushed by trees, broken windows, sections of verandas and terraces broken up and strewn across the lawns. He thought he saw movement behind some windows, but all the houses were dark, and he met no one on his way through the neighborhood.

Yet further south the houses thinned and a few low apartment complexes and tenement buildings appeared along the pavement, then more and more businesses: a shoe store, dry cleaner, bakery, hairdresser, bridal gowns, toy store, lamp shop, locksmith, and more. Here, in the center of the town, the destruction was more overt. Many windows were broken, the tops of some structures looked like they had been swatted sideways, and cars and trucks lay haphazardly in the street, full of soil and mud. A clearly visible line of dirt on walls and trees and posts marked the height of the flooding and showed that the water must have reached almost to his waist. That meant most homes and businesses had been waterlogged and damaged. Perhaps even the sewer system had broken down and was still not functioning. He saw no other humans, no moving vehicles, or living animals, except for a crow sitting in a still, naked tree, and a circle of seagulls high in the sky. The sun almost managed to burn through the clouds, but not quite, giving the daylight a sickly, jaundiced hue. The wind was chilly and constant, hurrying him along the city streets at a fast pace.

☾☽

As he progressed south, the area he was crossing turned residential: two-story wooden houses with gabled roofs, horizontal siding, bay windows, decorative shutters. Several homes showed damage—broken windows, a hole in the roof here, a torn-off veranda there—but most of them remained structurally sound and were still able to effect a barrier against the elements, were still shelters against the world. Tiny raindrops slashed through the air. He spotted a house up ahead with a For Sale sign on the roofed porch, the siding painted a dove gray with white window frames, shutters, and front door. In front there was a small garden with a low boxwood hedge to show off the dense, healthy grass beyond and slender cherry and apple saplings that had been planted in perfectly circular beds on the lawn, the branches weighed down by strings with white stones that swung in the wind. The saplings must have been too flexible to be broken by the hurricane, but it was strange that the stones were still hanging in their loops of twine.

He pulled open the white picket gate that led from the pavement to the front door of the house. Daylight had almost fallen and its windows were gleaming black planes. He turned and scanned the houses across the street. Their glass panes were dead and flat as well, with one house missing half its roof, which had crashed into the second floor of the neighboring home. Those houses looked far from habitable and showed no signs of repair.

The white door of the property he was in had an oval window where red and green glass had been framed by lead to form an image of a bouquet of tulips. He tried the handle; it had once been gold, but had now oxidized to a burnished surface where rust sat like gnats on the ruined smoothness. He half turned and smashed his elbow through the stained-glass. As he had expected it cracked easily and cleanly along the lead joints of the flower pattern. With the miniature flashlight on his key ring he pushed the remaining shards away from the window frame, snaked his hand inside the door, and snapped the lock open.

The entrance beyond was dark. As he entered and closed and locked the door behind him, despite the broken window, fallen shards crunched beneath his boots. Right inside the door hung the plastic rectangle of a home alarm system, but its diodes were dark, no power pulsed through the wires, and the once-white cover was gray with dust. Next to the security electronics hung a rack with a couple of keys left in it. He unhooked them quickly and stuffed them in his pocket, in case they might be needed.

As he had guessed, the kitchen was through the first door in the hardwood-floored hall. It looked out on the porch and the garden and the street beyond. The lilac counters and white kitchen table had a fine sprinkling of dust, telling him that the house was indeed abandoned. He pulled the satin steel door of the refrigerator open so the bottles and cans on its shelves clanked and trembled. The interior was warm and dark, and whatever had been edible was no longer recognizable as such. A pool of sluggish, slimy water trickled down from the icemaker in the door and down onto the cans of soda, beer, and orange juice beneath it. He reached for them, but then a wall of stench hit him so hard it made him gag, his mouth filling with saliva. He kicked the door shut so its contents rattled again and retreated to the hallway, covering his mouth and nose with one hand. From there he peered into the kitchen. A smelly pool from the fridge was collecting on the dusty hardwood floor.

The stench of rotten meat reminded him of a time in middle school when the teacher had displayed the lungs and trachea of a pig in science class. It was almost summer and although the dead organs had been frozen when they were presented for the gasping class, they rotted quickly in the spring heat. The aging, stern teacher, rumored to be a former army major, pushed a piece of rubber hose down the ringed trachea and asked for a volunteer to come and breathe air into it. He slid down on his chair to be less visible to the teacher, knowing he might throw up if he had to push his own breath into the rotting flesh and taste the air that no doubt would be expelled back. The poor student who ended up by the desk at the bottom of the circular classroom, grew white and trembled as they put the orange rubber tube to their lips, inflated the pig lungs, and quickly let the hose go just as the lungs exhaled, to the jeer of the rest of the class.

The smell also reminded him of corpses rotting uncovered and uncared for beneath a violent sun because they were suspected, and correctly so, to be bait for more locals to be shot. He quickly clamped down on that memory before it could rise fully in his mind.

(☽

The first cabinet in the white and dove gray and recently refurbished kitchen contained a full set of expensive-looking china. The plates, saucers, bowls, cups, and mugs were painted with highly detailed, naturalist-style illustrations of flowers and plants common on the continent, with a broad filigree pattern of genuine gold along the rim. The sight stung him with unexpected force. Was this what the planet's natural resources, environments and climate, the whole habitable world, had been ruined for? Gold-painted simulacra of what had once been abundant, yet not valuable enough to protect, other than as decoration and whatever use it had for humanity? He took out every single piece of the porcelain set and frisbeed it through the air into a tinkling, broken heap behind the kitchen table.

The other cabinets contained tins of soup (oxtail, tomato, cauliflower, mushroom), vegetables (artichokes, palm hearts, green asparagus, white asparagus, red beans, white beans, sliced mushrooms), and meat (turkey, ham, cocktail sausages), sachets of powdered sauce (white, brown, butter, red wine), spices (black pepper, white pepper, red chili, green chili, garlic, cloves, rosemary, thyme, nutmeg, ginger, vanilla), packets of pasta in various shapes and sizes, some even dyed black with squid ink, and pouches of pre-made bread and cake mixes (fine bread, whole wheat, pancakes, waffles, apple pie, chocolate muffins, strawberry tart) and various types of biscuits, sweet as well as savory. He took the bag of squid-ink pasta, a tin of mushroom slices and one of ham, and two packets of sweet digestive biscuits.

Beyond the kitchen was the living room, facing the garden in back and a steep slope covered by slender deciduous trees that in the absence of people had grown tall and wild, threatening to engulf the roof and the balcony with their canopies. In the living room was a long and comfortable-looking sofa, above which hung two large reproduction prints of a man and a woman walking along a beach and of one of the most famous bridges on the western continent. The coffee table and TV bench were as dusty as the surfaces in the kitchen, and toy cars, dolls, children's books, and wooden puzzles were strewn on the floor. In the corner by the sofa was a red plastic crate filled with yet more toys, its soft sides bending under their weight. He nearly stepped on a plastic tugboat and kicked it beneath the table. If for some reason the bedrooms were occupied or otherwise unfit to sleep in, he could spend the night on the sofa in the living room.

Cradling the cans and packets of food in his arms, he moved noiselessly up the cream-colored carpet on the stairs, and quickly surveyed the upstairs floor. Three bedrooms; one nursery with crib, dresser, and mobiles, one room belonging to a little girl, and one to a pre-teen boy, both rooms complete with bed, shelves, closet, TV screen, toys, musical instruments, clothing, and shoes, in various stages of mess.

The master bedroom was surprisingly small and had a narrow floor-to-ceiling window that had either not been covered with curtains because the bedroom was on the second floor and facing the mass of trees that was about to swallow the house, or the draperies had been removed in an attempt at making the house look brighter and more modern in preparation for the sale. To have such a large window in the bedroom and not cover it up seemed almost exhibitionistic. Between the entrance to the room and the bed, a two-door cabinet made of teak, a material it was prohibited to import and sell, had been squeezed in. Its doors were open, spilling clothes from the shelves on the left side, some down to the floor. The door on the right side was open as well, revealing a vertical space so full of clothes that some of them didn't fit inside it, but hung askew from the rod. A bundle of dresses and suits, several layers thick, had been slung over the door. Propping it open was a chair of the same red-listed wood as the cabinet, on which yet more strata of clothes were piled, while another heap had slid down from the smooth back of the chair. Whatever clothes the inhabitants had taken with them when they left had not made a visible impact on their stores. He suddenly felt a great resistance to sleeping in the broad and perfectly made up double bed, which was shaped vaguely like a sled and carved from the same restricted-trade wood as the cabinet and its chair.

The bathroom had been recently refurbished as well, even though the house was probably less than five years old. It displayed a long counter with two sinks in white polyester resin that looked so shallow they'd immediately overflow if anyone tried to wash their hands in them, a shower cabinet twice the size of a regular shower, floor covered in slabs of

66

gray sandstone, LED spots crowning the ceiling. He opened the medicine cabinet first. It was full of pill packets, all empty of the blister-wrapped tablets that had once been there. According to the labels they were to be taken against depression, anxiety, insomnia, migraine, heartburn, hyperactivity, high blood pressure, elevated cholesterol, fever, and diffuse muscle pain. There was a name he recognized as antibiotics and could have taken with him, but that box was empty as well. Even more plentiful than the pharmaceuticals were the cosmetics; the other cabinets were crammed to the edges with makeup and nail polish in a palette of colors, anti-wrinkle creams, moisturizers (his and hers), body scrubs, dental bleaches, whitening tooth pastes, mouth washes, fragrances, after-shaves, hair dyes, gels, waxes, sprays, treatments, conditioners, fragrances, and deodorants, with several bottles missing, judging from the voids left in cabinet. On the floor under the drawers beneath the sink lay the plastic wrapping of a twenty-roll package of toilet paper, with a few more rolls inside one of the drawers, which he helped himself to. On the white resin between the two sinks were more voids from items that had been removed when the owners had left. Remaining was a miniature steel tree full of jewelry; necklaces, bracelets, rings, chains, and watches, all silver-plated, brass, nickel, rhinestone, leather, or plastic.

Between the master bedroom and the smaller rooms was a panorama window overlooking the garden and the road. A tan wool sofa stood with its back to the glass, instead facing the black surface of a 50-inch television screen on the opposite wall. The sofa had a chaise-lounge module at the end and was full of pillows in matching colors, with an umber blanket slung over the back. He put the food and the backpack down by the sofa, but continued to check the house. A small door next to the nursery revealed a cramped closet with stacks of plastic boxes, some translucent, others opaque. In the pale chests he could make out yet more clothing, shoes, toys, and stacks of documents. On the unpainted floor stood a vacuum cleaner, a toolbox, a child's bike, a printer, a small TV, and a skateboard. The bottom shelf held several packs of beer, three large bottles of carbonated water, and a few flasks of brown liquor. He sniffed the air; it smelled of dust and plastic, with a hint of alcohol, probably from the bottles. He took out the beer and the water, placed the water on the sofa, but carried the alcohol into the bathroom and put the bottles by the toilet. The toilet didn't flush as there was no water in it, but it didn't seem obstructed or overflowing. As long as he had liquid to flush with he could use the toilet. The beer and liquor would serve him better that way.

Downstairs in the kitchen he found more porcelain plates, this time with swirling blue flowers, some unadorned water glasses, and designer steel cutlery. He brought a plate and a glass, along with a knife and fork, back upstairs. There he turned the sofa so it faced the window instead of the blind surface of the television screen. Then he removed his jacket, opened the tin of ham and of mushroom slices with the tabs provided on the cans, cut half the ham into slices, and ate the thick pieces with the mushrooms. The ham was salty; the mushrooms could only dampen it a little, so he added some digestive biscuits and chased it down with carbonated water. He ate at a leisurely pace at the short end of the sofa while he watched the garden and street below. After he had eaten just a little more he felt full, and drank only water from then on. Shortly after nightfall his eyes grew heavy. He moved to the chaise-lounge part of the sofa, spread the sleeping bag over himself, and leaned back into the pillows. Almost immediately a brightness engulfed him and he fell asleep in the dark and quiet house.

◖◗

From his sleep he heard himself sigh and moan and call out garbled words and vocalizations. Not certain what dreams or recollections precipitated the sounds, he let them pass through his mind and body as they wished. There was, after all, no one around to hear him, and no one to feel ashamed in front of.

But further into the night he dreamed that his parents,

Katsuhiro, Michael, and Beanie had hidden in the attic of the house, behind a trapdoor in the ceiling he had missed and which was only visible from the couch. Quietly, his loved ones left their cramped and dust-filled hiding place, descended the collapsible ladder to his place on the sofa, to stand in silent accusation of his abandonment of them while they watched him flop about and cry out in his sleep. He wanted to rush up and apologize for leaving them so many months ago, but when he finally managed, through deep concentration and long-time practice, to wrest himself from the grip of the dream, push motion back into his body and will his eyes open, there was only the weak illumination of a dimly overcast morning in the room. His mind was so heavy with sleep that he immediately fell back into dreams and didn't stir for hours.

When he finally woke again, it was long past midday, and the room was nearly dark. The sky was filled with rushing clouds the color of lead, and large, round drops trickled down the white-framed view. Feeling groggy and lethargic, he forced himself up. The room was chilly and despite the down sleeping bag and his mountain pants, boots, and sweater, he was cold and shivering. Using the last of the water in the plastic bottles from the house, he prepared a sachet of oatmeal and a multivitamin pill, and ate it to the sound of the cascade of rain that hit the glass.

After he had cleaned himself in the bathroom, he put on his jacket and backpack again, rolled up the sleeping bag and tied it to the bottom of the backpack, then trotted down to the living room. There, he pushed the sliding glass door open as far as it would go. The wind took hold of the diaphanous white curtains and pulled them out in the diagonal rain, and a fashion and a sports magazine lifted from the coffee table in front of the sofa and flapped like released birds out on the dusty floor. He stepped out onto the yellow leaves on the veranda and bowed with a flourish to the rustling canopies that hunched over the windowed gables like vampires over their victims.

"It's all yours now," he said.

12.

Past the First Month

As the weeks grew beyond the first month, even the dead the team found had clearly been survivors, subsisting on canned food and bottled water in mildewed apartments or humid house floors that sat above the water. But then the survivors had perished either for lack of food and drink, or from injury from accidents, or even self-inflicted damage: Someone swinging from a belt in the rafters in one of the old storage buildings near the docks that had been divided and refurbished into modern apartments. Another one looking as if they were asleep on the bed in a small house, pill bottle still in their hand. One who had aimed at and successfully hit a cluster of car wrecks dead in the water three floors beneath their window. There were no letters or notes that could explain the apparent suicides. All the emergency workers could do was search the bodies and living spaces for identification, make a note of "suspected suicide", along with the name and address, and bring the information back to the mound.

◖◗

Whenever they discovered suicides, Gabriele was always quiet and careful, partly out of respect for the deceased and the tragic circumstances of their deaths, but also because it wasn't always apparent whether the person was dead by suicide or someone else's hand. Perhaps in the chaotic circumstances following a large-scale disaster, people with murderous intent or proclivities would find the opportunity they needed, and making it look like an accident or a suicide in the aftermath of disaster might be easy. Then, there was also the irrational but nonetheless definite fear that the killer might still be around, lingering in the house or apartment or office building or commercial space that Gabriele and Jens searched, and would attack if the emergency workers ever voiced a suspicion of foul play at the site. Thus, Gabriele consciously refrained from searching the adjoining rooms, closets, and storage spaces near a suicide, and never voiced aloud speculations of criminal activity in the field. Only if she had specific evidence from the site of the suicide, or found indications of crime during the post-mortem examinations she helped out in or observed, did she mention them at camp.

(( ))

Equally tragic and maybe more unsettling, the teams also found small tent camps and evacuation spots where the survivors had received food, water, and medicine, but then had not left for the larger assembly centers to the north and the more substantial emergency housing there. Those survivors had died because they had not received further help and been unable to reach nearby shelters, many of which were now empty and cleared out because by now the emergency coordination considered the city to be evacuated and had shifted the majority of the personnel to the emergency shelters, tent camps, and evacuation housing outside the disaster zone.

"Why didn't these survivors leave, when they had the chance and knew they had to?" Jens asked Gabriele, since she was the specialist in disaster psychology.

"The answer is as simple as it is difficult," Gabriele replied, in the accent typical of the southern countries of the continent. "These people stayed behind while everyone else evacuated because they hoped that their loved one were still in the city and that they would find their way home, perhaps even returning from the emergency centers outside."

"People do not behave rationally in disasters," Jens quoted. He and Gabriele had heard that maxim often from Raymond and Leah. Now they repeated it to themselves and the few colleagues in the team that were younger than them.

( )

Weeks had passed since the hurricane, but subsequent storms and gales and heavy precipitation still pelted the coast, washed over it in long slow waves, bringing unseasonably low temperatures and much more rain than usual. The water remained in the city; the moist horizontal line of algae and mud that grew on all structures and drowned vehicles, and which displayed the height of the inundation, sank only a few centimeters, leaving the streets and buildings rotting in the water, like the black and bloated corpses that floated in it.

Now the city was quieter than when the team first arrived. Back then helicopters shuttling emergency workers in and survivors out of the city, as well as military aircraft on the way south where the devastation was said to be even more profound, roared through the sky. At the coordination center at the periphery of the city there was the occasional bus or column of vehicles taking the living, wounded, and dead out to the hospitals and evacuation housing in the region beyond. In the team's camp, vessels with outboard motors hurried back and forth in the flooded streets, ferrying survivors, emergency personnel, and supplies, the sound of their engines echoing against the drowned concrete. But as the weeks progressed, fewer and fewer vessels, airborne or plowing the floodwater, passed the grass-covered mound.

Now, when the members of Leah's team spoke to one another or to emergency workers from other teams who paddled or rowed past them in small rubber vessels, their voices sounded loud and sharp in the lidless air. This made

them dampen their voices to a whisper, and keep their conversations, about the number of survivors and dead that they had found and the weather and the conditions in the city and at home, short. At night the lights in the team's camp were the only illumination visible against the black silhouettes of the empty buildings and the flooded streets. Only on the rare occasions when the cloud cover broke for long enough for the team to catch a glimpse of the moon and the stars did they see any other light.

((

Finally, the team found no more survivors, and the city seemed to have been fully abandoned to the dead. The team had worked at many different types of emergencies, caused by natural disasters or armed conflicts or both. But none of the team members had been to a place that seemed completely emptied of living people. This was a new and frightening experience.

The quiet reminded Marten of the silence that rings in the air right after a landmine or a bomb has gone off: a deep hush in which everything for a moment has stopped and is holding its breath, until the ears start piping and the survivors screaming. Only this time, the hush didn't let up, but remained.

As the team lay in their cots in the big tent, inside a night that was so dark they couldn't see their own hands when they held them up in front of their eyes, Marten wanted to ask Edouard if he had heard anything from his parents or friends. But knowing that the standard phone and Internet communication was still silent even at the coordination center outside the city, there wasn't much to ask about. He knew that if his own mother had been with his sister and her family as was the plan when the hurricane hit, instead of in the dementia village where she lived, they would have taken her with them. If she had remained in the village, the nurses and assistants would care for the elderly inhabitants as well as they could. He had no way of reaching his family or anyone else. Marken knew that Edouard hoped that his parents and two younger sisters had left for their house in the ski resorts in the mountains when they heard the hurricane was approaching the coast.

Skiing and mountains. Last winter Marten had taken a week off with childhood friends and gone snowboarding as high up as they could afford to spend the holiday, where there was still snow and the entire world was silent and white. Not muted and slamming-in-the-wind quiet because it was broken, like here, but hushed by the snow and the winter, with ice crystals whispering against his legs and the board as he carved his way down the off-piste slope. He had filmed himself in high-definition on the new waterproof sports camera he had bought for the trip, done spins and flips so lumps of snow slapped the lens and trickled down its glass. He had even done a front flip while holding the camera at the end of a stick, for extra show-worthy footage, and when he landed that had sprayed up enough powder to cover the entire front of his body.

Marten had uploaded the video then and there from the mountainside, without editing or filter, while the others jumped and played around him, because he had been so eager to put it up on the video site and show it to the world. It was by far his best snowboarding video, doing his most impressive trick in the most beautiful place he had ever been, where the peaks were sharp and jagged as knives and the white gleaming in the sun. The video looked like it could have been shot among the world's tallest peaks on the eastern continent, or even on Mount Vinson on the Antarctic continent, which Jens always went on about, but the video had only gotten twenty or so likes.

That had annoyed him a little, although Edouard had looked appropriately impressed when he returned to the team and showed his colleagues the video, and had laughed when the snow rushed up in Marten's face. Yet after that,

Marten had realized that the reason why he had been so eager to film the trick and put it online wasn't just because he had wanted to impress the others. Mostly, he had wanted to freeze that moment in time, to keep the memory for the entire rest of the future, to always be the person he had been when he had been young and unafraid enough to flow down that mountain in the deep snow. A moment held in time, unchanging and unforgettable, like his mother's few remaining memories. But now that moment was gone forever, and all he was left with was a canvas cot on a raised field of grass inside a dead city.

13.

Flood Country

The rain fell hard and the gale pushed him in the back and nipped at his clothing, but he remained dry and warm inside his windproof, water-resistant garments. He pulled the mesh scarf up over his nose, and with the jacket's billed hood and the leather gloves, he felt cocooned against the elements. The early afternoon was almost dark, like the winter days he recalled from an exercise in the far north. From time to time a ray of sunlight pierced the clouds, sending a shimmer of illumination across the rain-wet ground, reminding him of the northern light that had spilled and billowed across the endless night sky in the Arctic.

He encountered several long cracks and tears in the asphalt, perhaps from a burst pipe or subterranean gas leak, but crossed them without needing to slow down much. As the rain kept on, ridge-backed streams of water appeared in the street, braiding and twisting and rushing towards the drains along the pavement. As the afternoon subsumed into evening, the water became more and more visible, increasingly affecting the thoroughfare, until the asphalt was covered with water and he had to keep to the pavement to remain dry.

The further south he pressed, the deeper the water grew, until even the pavement was submerged. He retreated to a lawn whose lowest lying parts were barely moist. There he took the waders out of the backpack, removed his mountain

boots, put on the pair of thick wool socks at the bottom of the backpack, and pulled the waders up on top of his trousers. The wetlands garment was so wide it accommodated the inner layer of clothing well, and when he pulled the adjustable suspenders out, they were more than long enough for him.

Shortly after that, the water rose to well above the boots of his waders and he felt like a child walking through puddles on the way home from school. But the flooding couldn't have been caused by the current rainfall, which while plentiful seemed normal, but must be remains from the hurricane and subsequent inclement weather.

( )

The suburban houses and lawns gave way to a stretch of grassland, with a line of dense thuja trees shielding the road. He suspected that behind the trees ran one of the multi-lane motorways which connected the city to other urban areas of the region, and that he was currently following the older and narrower road which stretched from the city's limits to its center. Since the motorway and its raised sections, turnpikes, and bridges, might have collapsed or been damaged by the flood, not to mention the vehicles that might still block the thoroughfare if people had tried to evacuate the city in a hurry, he decided to avoid the motorway and enter the old road instead. If it was possible to follow it, he would sooner or later reach the honeycomb towers north in the city.

After nightfall deep, prolonged vibrations began to rumble across the sky, the audible sounds like an iceberg, only hinting at the mass of infrasonic noises below the threshold of his hearing. Distant, bluish-white fractures flashed across the sky in quick sequences, lighting the path for him a few seconds at a time. Yet, it was the increasing rainfall and building gale that forced him closer to the line of thuja trees for shelter. The lightning seemed sufficiently distant and the coniferous trees young and healthy enough not to make it too risky. In the brief moments of glaring light-and-shadow, he saw the roofs of several vehicles to the side of the road. He rushed towards them, at first thinking that even if their windows had been broken, a chassis might provide some shelter against the raging rain. But as he drew closer he saw that the cars and vans and trucks had either been pushed or rolled into the ditch, where they lay half submerged, like beached whales. Most of the cars were on their sides, with only a wheel and a front corner peeking out of the rain-pocked water. Only a few vehicles were still level, with the roof above the surface. He nevertheless approached the convoy, slowly, carefully, so as not to get swept off his feet in the knee-high and increasingly churning water. There he spotted one car that was standing more or less upright in the ditch, and whose windows gleamed with glass in the strobe-light. He hurried over to it and took hold of the broad handle of the door, but then he saw the shapes hunched over the steering wheel and the dashboard on the passenger side. Another blink of lightning revealed, even through the rain-streaked windows and the rumbling darkness, that the bodies inside were so bloated and swollen they barely looked human any longer, and had been dead for weeks. He pulled his hand away as if from fire, yet the next moment he had to rub the water away from the glass to be entirely certain. The next ripple of lightning confirmed the distended outlines of watery decomposition. He moved quickly away from the car and the column of drowned vehicles, back to the slightly higher ground on the other side of the road to avoid the water from the cars. Then a piercing, icy fear that also his parents, brother, boyfriend, and friend might have been caught in their vehicle while trying to evacuate the city descended on him and drove him hard into the night.

He had hoped to get close enough to the honeycomb towers to see them from a distance that night, but with the flooding that still remained, advancing became more difficult and much slower. As he continued in the southeastern direction along the road to the industrial region east of the city, the water became increasingly deeper. He feared he would have to seek shelter in the industrial district, something he didn't particularly want to do because of the heaps of toxic slag and waste that had been deposited by the factories there and which the hurricane and flooding might have spread throughout the area, so he decided to head in a southern direction, even if that meant leaving the old road and its relatively flat surface beneath the water.

Finally, forced by exhaustion and lack of illumination in the slowly fading thunderstorm, he found a slab of concrete that stuck out of the water like a lopsided table. After checking that the slab was steady and not standing directly beneath anything that might fall down and crush him, he crawled up on the rough concrete, and despite the rain and cold fell into a quiet blankness.

( )

In his dreams he felt a gentle weight on his arm of something small tucking itself near his chest to sleep there. He thought it was one of his two Eastern-bred cats, which used to curl up next to him in bed and purr and snore loudly, but which he had left with Beanie when he moved from the apartment to the mountains.

As he realized he was awake and rising towards the surface of sleep, he expected the weight to dissolve with the dream, but it didn't. He opened his eyes yet refrained from moving. A mosquito buzzed past, so large and limp-legged he could hear the whine from its flight. The morning had hoisted a bright and warm sun high in the sky, the air fresh and clean after the thunderstorm the previous night, and the concrete around him so warm it was nearly painful. Lying on his arm, half rolled up like a fat hose, was a snake. He froze and peered down at the sleeping reptile. Judging from the dark band that zigzagged down its back, it was some sort of adder. He wasn't certain if all adders were poisonous, but didn't want to find out. Tears started to fill his eyes and blur his vision, but he swallowed them back and forced himself to lie still, as he had done, unseen and in nearly as close proximity, to other and more dangerous human opponents. The wait was long and terrible, and knowing what might happen if the snake struck only made it worse, yet he had to consider it. There wasn't much he could do if the serpent bit him, other than hope to tolerate the poison. If his body didn't, the only possibility was to try and reach help inside the city, which might be farther away than he could handle. He might die before he saw his parents and brother and Michael and Beanie again, all because he had stupidly forgotten that snakes and other wildlife would, like he did, seek the few spots of dry land that remained in a flood. He wanted to ball his hands into fists, but daren't disturb the creature, so he bit his lips instead. He could almost feel the adder breathe, slowly and placidly, like a cat sleeping in the sun. For a long while he was terribly tense and tears rolled from his eyes down to his temples and into his hair. But after a while he couldn't hang onto his fear any longer, the mental and physical strain too much, and he accepted that he was not the master of the situation. He started to relax, thought of a time he had concealed himself in the shadow of a burrow which belonged to a family of meerkats and the curious animals had clambered all over him, sniffed his nose and ears and gun, and finally used him and the spotter as platforms for their watchful survey of the landscape. He had nearly fallen asleep again when a cloud passed in front of the sun's disc, for a moment graying the sky and cooling the air. The adder stirred, woken by the vanished warmth, and flicked its tongue into the air. He held his breath in terror, but the reptile only slithered across his chest, down the side of his concrete billet, and vanished out of sight.

He drew a long sigh and shivered for a while, growing sleepy again, but didn't dare risk the adder returning. He sat up and stretched, his muscles sore after the wait and his clothes damp, but still much warmer and drier than when he had gone to sleep in the predawn darkness.

《 》

In daylight the world revealed itself as an ocean. The rippling, glittering water covered everything. Only objects above a certain height stuck out of the surface, like the bows and masts of sunken ships. He recognized most of the objects that protruded from the flooding: trees, bushes, the shovel of a front-loader; the screaming yellow of a fallen tower crane, the shards of its broken cabin sparkling in the sun; the concrete skeleton of a building in progress. Other structures had been crushed or bent or drowned to unrecognizable and reduced to tangles of steel beams, slabs of concrete, or piles of broken bricks.

He stared at the new world, horrified and fascinated at the same time, reminded of a dream he'd had of a polar sea littered with drowned cruise ships and passenger planes, squeaking and groaning when moved to make room for new wrecks. The ocean that now surrounded him was warm and alive, yet it was as much at the mercy of the elements as the oneiric graveyard ocean had been. As in the suburbs and satellite towns he had crossed, there seemed to have been no attempt at diverting the water or pumping it away, to restore electricity or sewer function, or to clean up the rubble, even now, weeks after the hurricane. Instead, the area seemed to have been abandoned, left to the wind and the rain. That knowledge hit him like a punch in the gut, and he wondered what scale of disaster would cause such inaction, how much of the coast had been hit, and how far inland it reached.

He wouldn't find those answers now. Since emergency shelters and housing had been set up further north, at least some of the evacuees from the affected areas had received help. Perhaps all resources had gone into the relief effort, with little for the cleaning up and reconstruction, at least for now. He crouched on the slab, sniffed the air, and scanned the water for the telltale signs of foam and iridescence from gasoline or other chemicals. But there was only a vague scent of pine trees and sun-baked concrete. The floodwater was brown and opaque, but held no froth or oily colors. He scooped up a little water in his palm. It didn't smell of any apparent chemicals. He took the chance and filled the filter bottle, pumped, wiped the cap, and drank. It tasted stagnant and muddy, with an undertone of sand, probably from the concrete. It wasn't exactly good, but as long as the filter kept the harmful biological agents out and the water wasn't full of chemicals, it didn't matter that it was turbid or unappetizing.

He used a little of the filtered water for a multivitamin pill and the last sachet of oatmeal left in the backpack. There should be more in the apartment, unless Beanie had taken all the non-perishable food with her when she left. When he was done he pulled the filter bottle up from the side pocket of the backpack, rolled it up in the towel and stuffed it in the backpack. He undressed, rolled the mountain pants up into a tight cylinder, and pushed it down into the side pocket where the filter bottle had been. It was warm enough to wear only the waders and even that might, if the temperature rose much further, become uncomfortably hot. Then he folded the mountain jacket together and fastened it beneath the lid of the backpack, hoisted everything on, and slowly stepped into the flood, like a bather at the beach testing the temperature of the sea.

( )

As the sun climbed towards its zenith it grew hotter, but also more humid. Clouds started to gather in the sky, first as small condensations of fleecy white which the sun's rays had no problems burning through, then heavier and denser clouds, which eclipsed the solar disc for longer and longer periods. He was grateful for the graying weather, because he had suddenly realized he had no sunscreen, and was glad he had the mesh scarf to cover his head and neck.

The water, which reached well above his thighs and seemed to grow a little deeper for every kilometer he advanced towards the bay, nevertheless cooled the waders and his skin. At times it felt like the water was leaking into the waders, perhaps through a seam or the soles, and he stopped, climbed a staircase or up into broad window sill to check the fabric. But it was all the cooling effect from the surrounding water. He found no leak and the only moisture inside the waders was perspiration from his own body.

(( ))

In the afternoon he entered a neighborhood which he had lived in as a student at the university in the city. Both sides of the road sprouted short streets that ran perpendicular to the main thoroughfare. From these bristled four short driveways, two on each side, each leading up to a garage and a brick house with a sharply angled shed roof. The entrances to these houses were floor-to-ceiling glass in sturdy pine frames, with a solid door set into the transparent wall. On the other side of the houses the slanting roof afforded two stories, with a sliding door displaying the living room on the first floor and the narrow mezzanine on the second, facing a modest garden.

Parallel with the main road was a narrow strip of park that cradled the houses at the end of each street. The parkland was shielded from the busy road beyond by a wall of dense deciduous trees, flanked by an unlit gravel footpath. He knew that because the room he had rented was at the end of the neighborhood, in a white wooden house three stories tall, with squinting, wooden-shuttered windows beneath a hipped roof, standing out from the identical, sharp-angled, glass-walled structures that lined the short streets. He had lived in the third of the four tiny bedrooms on the second floor, each room rented to a student. The first time he walked back to the house through the neighborhood he had forgotten which street the building was on, couldn't even remember what side of the main road he had exited from when he left. He had followed the footpath up and down the park until nightfall and he finally found the right side street and the white wooden house, giving him ample time to study the architecture of and the lives led inside the mostly curtainless and brightly lit interiors of the angled brick houses along the park.

Now he recalled that the main road through the neighborhood had had a small drain in its middle which the side streets had slanted gently towards, so that it probably would be further below the water than the footpath in the park. Accordingly, at the first intersection, he took off into one of the perpendicular streets, followed it to the end, and waded into the water-covered garden of the house there. The wall of trees between the park and the once busy road behind it was as dense and tall as he remembered it, but had the same autumnal tint as all the other vegetation.

The once-so-modern houses were mute witnesses to the destruction that had taken place around them. Most of them were still standing, although a few displayed holes and cracks in the roof. In others the large glass wall in the back or the smaller one in the front had splintered or collapsed, with a few unlucky ones having the entire side caved in or large parts of the ceiling ripped off by the wind. On the lawns outside the houses, furniture and belongings floated. He spotted a sofa and two chairs in a screaming orange color bobbing halfway inside and halfway outside a living room, while jackets, dresses, trousers, shoes, boots, and other garments floated shredded and bled of color everywhere in the murk, along with remnants of paper, photos, a basketball, a TV with the screen cracked, parts of a kitchen, a washing machine, a faded pet carrier with a wire door.

One house near the end of the park had been lucky enough to keep all its walls and even its roof, yet this home too was inhabited only by water. As he moved through the garden he thought for a brief moment that the glass spheres suspended from long black wires inside were still glowing with electric light, but it was just the sun refracted off the front wall. Behind it, brown water filled the living room like an aquarium, its motion decoupled from and independent of the flooding that surrounded him on the deck outside. The dark glass displayed his mirror image, dwarfed by the dense, rain-heavy clouds in the sky behind him.

14.

Soon They Would Be Home

The deliveries of food, water, and ice from outside became more and more rare. The food they now received was no longer bags of expensive and nutrition-dense self-heating or freeze-dried food, but tins of canned meals and even individual ingredients that needed to be cooked together. When Leah had a clear sense that the supplies were arriving less and less frequently, she started marking the dates of their arrival in her notebook, and began to ration the food. Finally, she realized that more than a week had passed since a rowboat or a rubber vessel from one of the other teams had stopped by, and she could not say with certainty when she last saw a plane or a helicopter pass overhead. Thus, slowly but surely, without any message from the coordination center or the home office, via the laptop, the supply of food and water to their camp, and the transportation of the dead out of it, ceased. The few times Leah managed to get through the static on the phone to the central coordination and the organization's main office, the line just kept ringing and ringing or she heard only the annoying beeping of a busy line.

When a rubber vessel or a canoe did pass the camp on the mound, Leah lifted her head from the corpse she was working on or the water she was filtering or the food she was preparing, and waved with outstretched arms at the emergency teams onboard. Generously, kindly, they always approached the mound or slowed down for long enough to exchange a few words. They too must know that in situations like these, information was almost as valuable as water and food.

《 》

"Next time let's go somewhere far away from here," Gabriele whispered to everyone and no one in particular as they lay in the tent one night. "Somewhere less wet and dark."

"Like where we were before this?" Jens said, recalling the dust and heat of that place, and the fear and distress of their departure.

"Perhaps not, then," Gabriele concluded, while she quietly wondered if they would ever manage to leave the place they were currently in.

But then the number of teams who passed the mound on vessels that sat deep in the water and were filled to capacity with emergency workers and crates of equipment seemed to increase sharply in number. And now when Leah asked these colleagues where they were going and why they were leaving, they answered:

"We've been ordered to pull out because we're needed on the western continent," or "We're going home to help those we can there."

"What's happened on the western continent?" Leah wanted to ask, but when she tried to get more out of the emergency workers who roared or paddled past, they only shouted that they didn't have time to explain or simply shook their heads and held up their hands in apology, and hurried on their way while the smelly floodwater sprayed up in their wake.

《 》

Despite hearing that other groups had been asked to go to the emergency shelters to work there, and that some had left on their own decision to return home, Leah's team continued as before. Up at dawn to wash as best as the muddy and toxic circumstances allowed for, eat the food that was left, which still seemed plentiful, do the work they had come to do, body after body after body. Since they could no longer check records directly, they could only examine the bodies and register what they found as thoroughly as possible. It was more record-keeping and archiving than anything else. That was all right, they had been trained not only to gather information but to organize and store it as well. There was still much to do, and it was satisfying work. With the lack of ice, they improvised, found other solutions that were appropriate for the time frame and circumstances they were in. They were used to doing that too.

But finally came the message Leah had feared, yet expected. It came from the coordination center outside the city and not from their home organization itself.

"All teams are to leave the city, with immediate effect. Efforts will now focus solely on the emergency centers and temporary housing communities outside of the disaster zone. We can no longer support anyone's work or presence in the city. If you have no means of transportation, we will provide it for you and for any equipment and tools that can be disassembled and packed quickly. Please confirm to the nearest communication center your coordinates and the amount of personnel needing to be withdrawn, as well as the number of kilograms of equipment and supplies. We aim to have everyone out of the city within the next 48 hours. Once you report in at the communication centers you will be given new assignments. There is no need to confirm this with your home organizations, as it has already been cleared through the right channels."

The members of the team looked at one another, some in sadness and some in joy, but all in relief. They were going back. Soon they would be home.

15.

The Honeycomb Towers

He didn't stop at any of the other houses, nor at the home across the street which he had rented as a student and whose top floor now lacked an outer wall and parts of a ceiling, resembling a cut-away diagram or a scale model of a structure. Instead, he went south and pushed his way carefully through the water to avoid stumbling or cutting himself on submerged debris. The flooding grew increasingly deeper and he realized he should avoid the low-lying motorway and the train station below his apartment.

Somewhere along the drowned streets and houses and bus stops and lamp posts and hedges and gardens, he spotted, in a flash of lightning that split the evening gloom, the wrought-iron fence and finialed gate that delineated the old cemetery near his home. He waded across the road and into a parallel street to get further away from the corpse-touched waters, then progressed slowly down that road. As it started to slope towards the hillock where the honeycomb towers had been built, the easternmost of the nineteen-story structures came into view. The high-rise looked like it probably had during construction, a six-sided pillar of concrete, the stairwell and elevator shaft nearly hidden by the floors and walls of the surrounding apartments. On the side that was visible to him, only a few balconies still clung to the wall faces. The other apartments looked like a giant hand had tried to rip them from the structure. Some of them had parts of the floor-to-ceiling glass front still intact, others were just a gaping hole in the wall, with no floor left. With a sinking heart he saw that the top floors of that tower were gone, looking as though it had been snapped in two a little above the middle.

His pulse shot up and a sudden desire to start running towards the hillock and the other honeycomb towers rushed through him, the impulse to throw himself forward into the dirty, rain-ringed water and swim the rest of the way, debris or no debris. But he reined his mind in and instead forced himself to continue as slowly and carefully as he had until then. He couldn't risk having an accident or getting injured now, not when he was this close to his goal. Warm and moist inside the waders and the water-resistant jacket, he vaulted past a mud-spattered guardrail and up the cracked asphalt of the driveway to the parking lot in front of the towers. The broad, wan beam from his headlamp could only reach a few meters into the drenching darkness, but he nevertheless craned his neck and stared up into the night where he knew the other high-rises were, trying to catch a glimpse of them. Finally, more lightning tore through the sky and he spotted the mangled balconies and exposed apartments of the next two towers in the row. They were no longer the regular, symmetrical structures they had once been, but nearly fleshless skeletons, with remnants of walls and balconies hanging from them like rags.

He reached the top of the slope where the parking lot began. A row of cars had been blown over the edge and into the bushes below, and there reduced to a pile of twisted, rusting metal. In the gloom and rain he ran across the rain-drenched asphalt to reach the front of the honeycomb towers and assess the damage from there. Being out of water and moving on dry land was a strange sensation after days of wading in deep water. His pulse and the noise of the gale were blasts in his ears, drowning the world in sound.

He was distantly aware that he could no longer feel his body, not even the feet that splashed through the rain on the glistening, gravel-strewn asphalt. Finally, he rounded the westernmost tower, the one that had been built first—it was at least standing—and went on to the second building. The rain streamed down his hood and face and collar, even moistened the scarf around his neck. He tilted his head back, covered his eyes with his hands, and squinted up into the sky, like a child lost in a rainy evening and looking for the light from the windows at home. Another lightning bolt cracked the night and rolled its vibrations across the sky. The second high-rise was still standing, even some of its balconies were left, and the top floors didn't seem to have broken off. He waited anxiously, shifted his weight from one foot to the other while he sneezed from the precipitation that streamed into his eyes and nose. Finally, another dagger of lightning blinked, confirming what he had just seen. The top floors were still there.

He sighed and breathed and something settled in him, and he could simply watch the broken, wall-fluttering structure that had been his home for years. He watched it for as long as he needed to, then shook the hood of his jacket free of raindrops, and found a way down from the parking lot. On the side of the slope a large plastic pipe had been exposed by rain and sliding soil. The pipe looked large enough to stand in, so he entered it, sweeping his beam back and forth to look for dangerous debris. The pipe was almost dry, with a thin layer of sand covering the plastic on the bottom. Suddenly exhausted and unable to go on, yet more worn out mentally than physically, he sat down, shrugged out of the backpack, and leaned into its comforting thickness.

( )

He woke from cold, hadn't had the energy to unclasp the sleeping bag from the backpack before he'd been overtaken by sleep. The wind was still high and had changed direction; now it breathed a cold drizzle into the pipe. The jacket and waders and backpack were covered with bulging raindrops, which captured the gray daylight inside their tiny, perfect domes, coalesced into one another and ran down the fabric when he stood and lifted the backpack. He stepped out on the scarred slope. Despite the wind the clouds were thick and low, almost like fog, and the air smelled of decay, organic as well as inorganic, of sewage, and of standing water. He had only been to a flooded area once before, as part of relief work during his service, but the stay had been long enough to impart the memory of the smells of inundation, giving him a hint of what the city would look like in full daylight.

He strolled up the incline and along the parking lot at the edge of the bushes, then walked quickly past the crushed entrance to the first tower. The glass doors to the foyer of the second high-rise were completely gone, leaving only a kinked steel frame from which a few large shards dangled, clinking in the gale. In the shredded doorway a dark hyperbola in the dense, short-pile carpet showed how far inside the rain had come. Here, the carpet was soaked, while in the lighter-colored areas it was merely moist. The fabric squished beneath his boots as he crossed it, leaving dark imprints that slowly faded as they refilled with water. There were no other footprints in the foyer, or other signs of recent passage. One of the elevators was open, but the lights on the call buttons and inside the car were lifeless and dim. The foyer creaked, dust and fine fragments of drywall sprinkled from the ceiling further in. He froze and listened for mounting squeaks and crunches, the telltale signs of increasing slippage and collapse, but the noises abated as the wind gusts passed.

The high-rise with his apartment had survived the hurricane, perhaps because the surrounding honeycomb towers had shielded it from or broken up the most violent winds. Judging from the previous two nights, the structure had also tackled several bouts of subsequent poor weather. He was nevertheless acutely aware that the fifth and easternmost building had broken during one of those storms and that the top floors were missing from two of the other towers. The higher up, the more exposed would the apartments would be. The building didn't seem to be on the brink of imminent collapse, but he'd have to be as quick as possible.

◖◗

He entered the black maw of the stairwell that wound itself up through the structure and started climbing. Eighteen floors. When he had bought an apartment on the next but uppermost floor, it had seemed a very good idea. Now he was less certain.

The stairwell was dark; even the emergency exit signs above the doors to the hallways were dead. He lit the head-lamp, hoping it had still power left. The beam woke to life, a little more yellow than before, indicating decreasing power, yet still unwavering and clear. Knowing it was better to climb slowly than to hurry and then have to stop for breaks, he kept a low but steady pace, keeping one hand on the steel banister. At first he tensed for every squeak and groan from the tower and wanted to stop to listen for the steel-and-wood crescendo that signaled impending doom. But as he ascended higher into the stairwell, he knew that he was too far up, too far away from the entrance, to even have a chance of making it out if the building was about to fall down, so there was no point in listening for it. All he could do was continue up into the darkness.

Clouds of dust danced in the beam from the headlamp and what he took to be drywall chalk fell from unseen sources in the gloom, adding to the contamination. He wet the scarf with water from the soda bottle and pulled the fabric up over his nose and mouth. It wouldn't keep out much of the dust, but it was better than nothing. After a while he became aware not only of the snapping and creaking of his surroundings, but of a steady, regular noise that followed him up the steps. It took him a few seconds of tense listening before he realized it was the sound of his own breath, amplified by the concrete walls and the long drop beyond the banister.

◖◗

The first time he heard his own breath like that had been during an exercise in the Arctic. A course in polar survival and combat had taken the unit to an island a little more than a thousand kilometers from the North Pole. When he stepped out onto the runway, the wind was unlike anything he had experienced before, so freezing and dry it felt like he had landed on Mars. As they left the airfield, the brightly painted buildings and the network of snow-plowed roads and above-ground pipes of the settlement, and drove out into the white, it dawned on him that the conditions were so severe that even small mistakes that would have been negligible at home could kill him. It was fully possible to get lost in a whiteout and freeze to death minutes away from the tent. Even falling into the ice-floed water at sea could be deadly, draining the life out of him before he could be pulled back on board. Up until then, death, even in harsh and barren territory, had been most likely to arrive from opponents in combat, or through carelessness or bad planning. Dying from lack of water, overheating, or general exposure to the elements had been a possibility, but shade and water had never been impossible to find, and the human threat had always been the greatest.

But here, it was clear that nature itself was more formidable and stronger than anyone or anything else. Seeing it was like being afforded a glimpse of the world as it might have been without a human presence. He had always trusted his resourcefulness, training, and comrades to slip out of dangerous situations alive, but in the Arctic, that might not be enough. As a result, he felt terribly exposed, vulnerable, like he had been flayed of skin. The sensation was disquieting enough to hamper him during training and interfere with his sleep. But one afternoon when they were moving down a wide, snow-covered valley, the pale Arctic sun set behind the mountains in the distance, painting the landscape pink and the shadows blue. The low breeze fell to a whisper and the world became completely quiet. With no birdsong or hush from trees or hiss from sand, his own breath and heartbeat seemed to be the only sounds in existence. It was as if the entire silent, frozen landscape breathed along with him on his tiny spot at the floor of the valley all the way up to the slowly darkening dome of the sky and the large, white stars. The polar landscape had accepted him, taken him in as part of itself, would accept him and all his actions, whether they were selfish or compassionate, legitimate or unjust. That moment made the sensation of skinlessness vanish, and he started to appreciate the polar conditions, no matter how dangerous or uncomfortable they were. When the course was over, he didn't want to leave, and boarded the waiting plane with reluctance, knowing that he must someday go back.

《 》

The recollection made him smile. He felt almost as skinless as he had back then, but the sensation of deeply being a part of the world around him, of belonging to it and of being in the right place at the right time, was as present now as it had been then, comforting him greatly.

He kept ascending, around and around the long drop of the stairwell, past landing after landing after landing. A cold draft whispered through the structure, probably from open doors and cracked walls above and below, yet the climbing made him sweat inside the waders, which forced him to stop a second time, to pull off his jacket and outer sweater, and attach them to the backpack. But finally he could climb the last landing, the top floor just a single turn of stairs above him, and pull the door to the corridor open.

Bits of paper, fabric and wood rolled along the carpet. From the left side of the hallway the gray sky was visible through cracks and missing doors. Somewhere, loose wood clapped in the gale, making the floor shiver. He advanced slowly into the corridor, keeping to its right side where the damage seemed less. Through the torn doors and split walls across the hallway, he saw that some apartments were missing the balcony or the entire front wall, while the interiors looked like they had gone through the spin cycle of a washing machine. Other rooms were missing sections of the roof or the floor where rain had leaked in. Yet other places fires had started, perhaps from failures in the electrical system or even lightning, charred shadows rising from curtains or tables, but then the flames had burned out by themselves or been stamped out by falling debris, or extinguished by the power-independent sprinkler system that may have functioned even after the hurricane, like the moving limbs of a freshly killed octopus. But no matter what had happened to the individual apartments, the destruction was total and unlike anything he had seen before in his home city, even on that continent, ruined and transformed by multiple elements several times over.

At one spot in the corridor the floor trembled so much he had to step sideways along it as if he were moving on a narrow ledge. There, two apartments were missing not only their balconies and outer walls, but their entire floors had fallen into the abyss beyond the building itself, or down into homes below, leaving the hallway fully exposed to the sky. Beams and struts jutted from the missing floor like broken bone. He balled his hands together and continued along the wall, trying to time it with the rhythm and the sway of the building. But when he was a little over halfway across the gap a sudden gush of rain hit him. He started to flail, the beginning of a long fall, but managed to shift his weight enough to press himself against the wall. He remained there for a small eternity with his eyes squeezed shut. Only by breathing along with the wind and the rain, and telling himself he was only meters away from where he must be, did he manage to open his eyes, unclench his body, and inch past the last missing apartment.

But finally he was at his own door, which stood slanting from the upper hinges in a strange mimicry of the entrance to the cabin after the flooding in the mountains. The smooth, cobalt blue surface had splintered, revealing its unpainted interior. There was no sign that anyone had been there after the hurricane. He clambered over the remnants of the door and took in his home, which vibrated much less than the open part of the hallway had.

〈 〉

The glass banister of the balcony was gone, but the concrete structure itself was still there, even one of the plastic chairs, pushed against the wall that separated his jut into the air from that of the neighbor's. The living room window had cracked, yet only the section where the sliding door had been was gone. The vertical blinds, previously white, now gray from the wind and the rain, whipped in the freedom of the elements. Several of the narrow vanes had been ripped from the rail and slung over the drenched sofa. By that piece of furniture his sky-colored glass lamp had crash-landed on the floor and the small table it used to occupy lay overturned, yet the sofa was still standing by the wall where it had always been. Now he was glad he had mounted nothing on the walls, but kept them blank, preferring the changing hues of the day as it progressed from morning to evening to anything a static work of art could provide. The tall chairs at the kitchen table had been flung around, several of them against the front door, causing it to crack, and the kitchen table itself had sailed into the chest of drawers in the entrance. Every surface and fabric in his home was wet from rain and wind.

Yet, the bathroom was almost like he had left it, save for a puddle of muddy water right inside the door, a few scattered splinters of wood, and some towels that had taken momentary flight and lit on the tiny, bluish-brown iridescent tiles on the floor. He wanted to check if there was any water left in the pipes, but didn't dare turn the faucet in case the pipes would begin to vibrate and disturb the precarious equilibrium of the building. In the bedroom the same smooth gray sheets he had left on the bed were still there, only lightly sprinkled with dust and drywall chalk, the corners of the duvets neatly tucked in at the ends in a way he never did. When he saw that he smiled. Poor Beanie, she had cleaned and tidied before she evacuated, tried to leave the apartment as it was when she moved in. The doors to the closet were shut and the rack Beanie had set up next to it to hang her own garments was still there, but nearly empty. Only some thin blouses and skirts had been left behind, some having fallen to the hardwood floor in the breaths from the living room, others still on their broad lacquered hangers.

He moved back to the living room and the kitchen. The cats' steel bowls and the pet cage that usually sat on top of the clothes rack by the front door were gone. He scanned the apartment debris for the carrier, but couldn't see it anywhere. It seemed that both his housesitter and the cats had managed to leave the apartment before the hurricane. That might mean that Michael and Katsuhiro had evacuated as well, perhaps together with Beanie.

On the steel surface of the fridge door a neon-green post-it note with letters in large, black marker caught his eyes. The note had been fastened with all ten round, white magnets that hung on the door, and displayed his name in capital letters in Michael's large and solid hand. "You can reach us here", the note said, followed by a phone number he thought he recognized as belonging to Michael and Beanie's aunt in the north. He pulled the note gently out from under the magnets so as not to tear it, folded it in two, and put it in the inner zipper-closed pocket of his jacket. Then he had to lean into the fridge and cry for a while.

16.

The Gateless Gate

The empty, broken apartment no longer felt like a home and he took only a few things from it; the sachets of freeze-dried camping food and oatmeal he had stored in the cabinet, a packet of batteries for the headlamp from the top drawer in the kitchen, plus the small first aid kit in the bathroom to back up the one already in his backpack. Then he left the apartment as he found it, teetering on the edge of its own abyss. The door still hung askew in its frame. He slid over the broken barrier and left it open.

◖◗

The long climb up through the apartment tower and the search of his hurricane-damaged home had made him thirsty. Despite the real danger and possibility of the building collapsing, there was no way he could leave without checking the state of the great amount of fresh water that rested above him, not the least because he had no idea how clean or polluted the flood further inside the city was. He made his way slowly and carefully through the partly flayed corridor back to the steel door at the stairwell. The tower trembled in the wind, rustled and clattered its debris in rhythm with the gusts, and howled and whistled as the air pushed its way through cracks and crevices. He told himself that it'd be quick, that the water up there was vital if the flooded city was contaminated with chemicals and dead bodies, and forced himself to continue. The top floor was just one more landing up, yet it shivered more insistently and with much larger amplitude than the eighteenth floor had. He pushed the heavy door open, slipped through, and closed it slowly behind him to prevent it from slamming and causing hazardous cross-vibrations.

The hallway was unlit, yet he could see that the door to the showers was missing, as was much of that room itself. Where a window had stood—in the wall between the benches provided for the apartment tower's residents' clothing and shoes— and in the shower stalls themselves, the narrow white tiles ended in a cloud-filled drop. No access through that room. He advanced down the shuddering corridor to the thin glass door that led directly to the pool room. Strangely, that fragile barrier was fully intact, unbroken, and he opened it and entered.

The fashionably large and once white satin-finished tiles in the pool room were now gray and filmed over by muddy rainwater that had spattered the walls. The white plastic deck chairs and garden recliners that occupied the long wall by the pool had been deposited in tangles of bristling legs and armrests in the corners in the back. The panorama glass wall had been pushed in and the shards then swept out by the hurricane, along with most of the arched glass roof. Two chairs had been knotted together and pushed all the way to the edge, but had snagged in a horizontal beam of steel frame, and stood upended and shivering there, with two legs over the precipice and two holding onto a sliver of remaining window.

However, the wall of the pool itself had held, the concrete reinforced with clusters of iron rods since it was built to hold back millions of liters. The wind had nevertheless churned up and pushed out much of the water across the edge of the pool, which was still drooling into the sky. When he saw that he couldn't help but smirk. He slowly approached the water's edge. The fluid made familiar lapping noises as it pushed against its constraints. That sound alone had once been enough to slow his breath and heart in preparation for diving down into the blue depths to glide along the tiles on the floor. Now he restrained himself from pulling his clothes off and diving into the water the way he had loved to do. But that motion and force in the pool would almost certainly break the remnants of the outer wall, and cause all the water to rush over the edge and into the sky along with him. That sudden redistribution of weight might also be the final strain the quivering tower could take, making the rest of the building collapse. Had he not found the note from Michael on the fridge, but instead, the starved and dehydrated corpses of his boyfriend and Michael's sister, who had been housesitting in his apartment, he would have been tempted to dive into the pool, to commit one final act of violence. But now he only wanted a little of the water.

He crouched by the edge and gazed into the undulating depths. A bit of sand and some glass shards and metal debris glittered on the bottom, yet the surface of the water looked clean. The acrid smell of chlorine still rose from it, but by far not as strongly as it had when the room was whole and less harshly ventilated. A little chlorine was probably just good, neutralizing the contamination from the debris and the water that had rained in. The filters in his bottle would take care of the rest. He took the plastic bottle out and passed it slowly through the still transparent, still blue water, while he wondered how much time would pass until he could dive into a pool of clean, bright water again. He drank what he needed of the purified water, filled his red steel canteen and soda bottle, then retreated slowly back to the hallway and the uppermost landing, knowing that the rain and the wind would soon wash away the muddy boot-prints he had left on the tiles.

☾☽

The trip down was harder than going up. Now he was more wary of the groans and creaks in the stairwell, the trembling and shivering of the walls, and the darkness that rose up from the unseen drop and pressed against him. The urge to run, to flee down the stairs two steps at a time to get out of the building before it collapsed was almost overpowering. But he had to take it slowly; one misstep and he'd find himself descending in a much faster and more injurious way than he wished. He had to take the time he needed, despite flinching at every snap and startling at every pop from the walls. His descent seemed to take eons. When he finally slipped out from the shadow of the last landing, across the wet carpet in the foyer, and out into the gray and rushing daylight, he was trembling.

☽☾

He took in the tower one last time—the missing balconies, the dead aircraft-warning lights at the top, the curtains and blinds that flapped like trapped birds from the broken windows—before he turned and crossed the parking lot. Now he had to reach his brother's apartment in the city center. If Katsuhiro had managed to leave before the hurricane arrived, their parents might have gone with him, maybe together with Michael and Beanie. But continuing south to lower ground meant even deeper water and less dry land, and would require something more substantial than just his waders.

He looked about and recognized a line of trees in the distance, the edge of the bog whose black surface, reflecting the golden light from the city center, he had admired so often from his living room window and the pool on the top floor. The pedestrian overpass that crossed the motorway below the apartment towers had now become a true bridge, leading from one spot of land separated by the flood to another. He carefully descended the rain-gouged slope below the parking lot to where the bridge began. Its concrete foundations and the multi-lane motorway that passed below it were completely hidden in dark water, but the span of the overpass rose well above the surface and didn't look too badly damaged by objects that had come floating in the flood or flying in the hurricane.

He continued out on the concrete construction, ready to leap off the railing and into the water should the bridge start to crumble beneath him. Yet it hardly shook with his steps as he reached its shallow apex and progressed down its distal end. On the other side he saw a child's sneaker and a black suitcase slung into the vegetation, but saw no signs of their owners, neither footprints nor clothing nor bodies.

((   ))

Closer to the marsh, islets covered in deciduous trees, bushes, and perennial weeds bulged out of the flood. He crossed them by wading out from each mound and then jumping towards the next as far as he could, hoping to land on the slope of the receiving islet instead of in the water-filled dip between them. He splashed and windmilled, but avoided getting too wet and wiped his face with the sleeves of his sweater, which was still dry beneath his waterproof mountain jacket.

However, inside the fen proper he had no choice but to wade into the murky water, and did so while aiming for the flooded knolls and clusters of trees that were visible in the new lake. He had read somewhere that humans had developed the ability to walk upright because they lived on grassland that flooded regularly. In order to cross the water, the early humans had to get up on their hind legs to wade, the way some species of ape do when they forage in marshes. This could also explain the diving reflex and other adaptations to water that humans seemed to have evolved independently from the other great apes. As he pushed through the flood, its surface well above his waist, holding his arms raised to keep them dry, that theory seemed more than plausible.

In the summer the marsh usually dried up into a muddy meadow, and in the winter it became a plane of thin ice with reeds and cattails protruding from it. Only in the spring and autumn was the marsh a true wetland, with half-submerged lumps of grass and bushes. But now the bog looked more like a tarn or a pond. The water had drowned and thus removed many of the familiar features, and the gray sky was dimming. He lit the headlamp and swept the pale beam across the insect-dappled, leaf-adorned water. The wind was increasing and he felt the needle of a raindrop on his cheek. It seemed like the storm was picking up again at dusk, as it had the previous nights. He waded and splorched along the edge of the flood lake, circling a cluster of slim beeches he was certain he recognized. He had always used those trees as a navigational marker in the fen, yet now he could see nothing at the bottom of the water near them, not even when he used a thin branch to churn up the substrate, making the smell of mud and decaying plant matter rise up, and, to his relief, no other and meatier stink. Was his memory that poor? But then he spotted a cluster of gaunt, leafless birches that were surrounded by floating leaves and tree limbs, out in the water. He pulled his boots up from the mud and moved to the snarl of vegetation and debris. From there, he could just about make out something that was darker than the water itself, both harboring and resisting the inundation, just a few meters out into the flood lake. The outline was so familiar he let out a laugh when he saw it. This was the birch he had carved; he just hadn't seen it flooded before. Only one of the submerged punts was there, he couldn't see the other, but one was much better than none.

How many times had he stood at the edge of that pond and gazed down into the water that was trapped inside the old vessel? When the weather was warm and the marsh dry, the fluid inside the narrow line of wood turned shallow and translucent, almost revealing what lay at the bottom of the craft. In the winter the liquid trapped in the vessel's narrow embrace froze to a blank surface, while the marsh water around it remained black and still, with frost-covered straws that quivered in the wind. He had once broken the icy surface inside the punt with the heel of his boot, stepped through it into the dry bowl below, just to see what was there, but the old wood had hidden only sand and pebbles.

Now the vessel was there, its image rippling like a dream beneath the surface, the flat bow still holding water both inside and outside itself. He passed the beam of his headlamp over the birches briefly to see if the declaration of love he had carved there was still present in the wood, but it was too dark to see much and growing darker still, so he had no time to look thoroughly. He didn't particularly want to go swimming alone in this dark, dank flood lake, but knew he couldn't go on without the craft to find the answers he needed. And he'd rather swim here, where the water seemed untainted by chemicals, than in the city center where it most certainly would be polluted.

He stood on the bank, stripped off the waders and the rest of his clothes, then waded into the flood. Even though the punt was close to the bank, the water reached to his neck and he could feel the tangles of twigs and branches that covered the bottom, mixed with leaves and mud. He inhaled, then crouched down, took hold of the edge of the punt and pushed, trying to overturn the craft beneath the water. The old wood shifted, yet didn't roll or let go of the bottom. He went up for air before he needed it, inhaled, and dove again. This time he placed one foot on each side of the hull and started to shift his weight from side to side, rocking the vessel slowly. The water dimmed with silt and sediment, and he closed his eyes to protect them from the particles that swirled up around him. He rocked back and forth for a short while, then went up for air. When he next went down, he pushed at the vessel again, and this time he could feel it give way, tip more and more, the sand and mud collected in the hull falling out in thick, dark clouds. It was a long time since he had done any breath hold and the exertion made his heart beat hard and his lungs burn. With the last oxygen he had, he gave the punt a good push, before he broke the surface again. It was almost dark, only the faintest glow was left in the sky, and the trees across the pond were black shapes against the tawny dusk behind them. He treaded water for a short while, then inhaled, closed his eyes, and went down again. This time the punt shed the last of its contents, let go of the bottom of the marsh with a groaning crunch, and finally floated to the surface.

17.

A New Vessel

He splashed some water into the old hull to rinse off more of the sand and mud that remained there, but then noticed he was shivering and immediately waded back to the bank, pulling the punt with him. He pushed the vessel up on the rain-slick grass, just far enough so it wouldn't slide back into the flood lake. Then he took the filter bottle out of the backpack and used the liquid from the pool to rinse his face and hands of marsh water. With teeth chattering from the chill he lit the headlamp and inspected himself for ticks from the grass, in particular his armpits, behind his knees, the crook of his elbows, his genitals, and around his ears, throat, neck, and scalp. He couldn't feel anything, but took out the little mirror from the lid of the backpack and scanned as much of his shoulders, back, and buttocks as he could see in its small surface.

There was something in his left eye, a grain of sand or an eyelash, stinging and creating a small blur in the corner of his vision. He blinked and peered into the mirror, could barely see both eyes in the narrow space. In the white of his left eye something small and black protruded from the surface, weaving slowly, as if tasting the air, stretching and begging. When he realized what it was, he froze in shock. Without thinking, he grabbed the filter bottle, pumped it hard twice, and pointed the ensuing jet into his eye while straining it open with one hand. Sight was his strongest and most precious sense, all his life depended on it, even more so in the flood.

When he lifted the mirror to his eyes again and squinted down into it, his hands shook so hard he could barely see anything. He inhaled, held his breath for a few second, and slowly exhaled, as he had been taught long ago to calm fear and steady his hands for aiming. Then he lifted the mirror again. The tiny leech was gone from his eye. There was no shadow on the surface of the sclera, no oblong form biting into the eyeball and nourishing itself on his blood and fluids. The spray must have gotten rid of the parasite since it hadn't yet attached itself with both ends. He lifted the upper eyelid, then the lower, worried that the leech might have slid beneath them, but saw or felt nothing there. The mucosal lining of his eye was red and irritated, yet it felt different than when the leech had been there, and nothing clouded his sight anymore. He drew a deep breath and poured some more water into the eye for good measure. He would have to check it in the days ahead to make certain that he hadn't simply sprayed the body of the leech off and that its head and mouthparts were still there, inflaming the eye. He drew a long and shivering breath, then stood and dried himself with the hand towel from the backpack. Back inside his clothes he grew a little warmer and fell asleep on the grass behind the old, salvaged craft.

( )

Morning came, foggy and raw. He mixed the last of the filtered water from the pool with half a bag of freeze-dried stew from the apartment, plus a multivitamin pill, and ate that for breakfast. The meal was cold and sloppy and the dice of hard beef hurt his gums, but it was filling and nourishing and not too salty. Tiny drops swirled in the air, beading the branches of the half-drowned trees and the bowed necks of the reeds. Every sound seemed to come from far away, thick and muted, like in a soundproof room.

The water from the swimming pool was gone, but with the relatively clean state of the marsh, he took the chance of filtering its water to fill the canteen and the soda bottle. He had no oar or paddle, but spotted a thin, nearly branchless sapling trunk that floated in a tangle of broken canopies and rotting leaves that had collected further down the bank. Wading in, he pulled at the slim wood, and wrenched it free from the skein of dead twigs with a snap. The bark of the ash sapling was liver-spotted, yet smooth and free of offshoots, and would make a decent staff to push the old vessel through the water with until he could find something better.

He had never punted before, but assumed he would be able to pick it up by necessity, and pushed the old craft out into the flood lake. No water bubbled up at the bottom of the moist wood or squirted through unseen holes in the hull. That was a good sign. Smiling, he placed his backpack in the bottom of the punt and stepped in. The craft shifted and lurched, forcing him to crouch to stabilize the vessel and become used to its motion. When the punt grew still, he lowered the makeshift rod into the dark surface of the water and pushed off from the grass.

The dark flood lake hid reeds and leaves and decomposing plant matter, whose remnants and scent he whirled up with the stake. The far shore was obscured by the morning mist, and there was only the sound of water dripping from the pole and distant, weak bird calls. He was grateful for the fog. Even just sitting in the punt made him feel exposed, too visible. He would have preferred to stay in the vegetation, but he had to continue. He breathed the moist air in, out, in, out, and its tiny droplets collected on his face and gloves and hood.

He steered the punt towards the opposite side of the flood lake, where the water grew even deeper. Here he wouldn't have been able to wade. Near the bank he detected a current, a small motion in the water, swirls and whorls that pointed to where the marsh now flowed in the new avenues and paths afforded it by the flood. He let the gentle movement catch the punt, push it over the soft, grassy bank, and into a network of slim channels that led deeper into the marsh. The silhouette of a heron appeared out of the fog and lifted, and he heard the warbling of ducks and geese, but saw none. He even thought he detected the rhythmic, sharp calls of frogs inside the whiteness, despite the cool weather. Feeling more in balance with himself and his surroundings than he had done since he started the journey home, he pushed the vessel ahead with unhurried calm. When he felt more certain of his balance and the punting motion, he got up on one knee and used the pole from that position, which allowed more powerful strokes through the still, grass-bristling water.

The depth of the flood varied constantly. A few places reeds or bushes scraped against the flat of the punt, and he had to wade in to push the vessel free. Other places he had to drag it past obstacles such as fallen trees and the occasional boulder that rose out of the surface. Once, he had to pull the punt over what looked like the top of a concrete block, but from there on the water turned so deep he had no problems crossing it in the small craft.

The water from the marsh flowed out into a motorway with multiple lanes, flooded high with black, gasoline-glistening water. The mist concealed the vegetation at both sides of the road, giving the impression that he was in the middle of a broad, slow-flowing river. He thought of the long, warm river in the south of the western continent that snaked through half the landmass of tropical rainforest. He had heard that those rivers were now often in drought from lack of rain and would dry up to wide, serpentine mudflats, while the lush, humid rainforest turned to grassland. Then, when rain finally did fall, the ground was too dry and hard for the enormous masses of water that arrived, and the forest would flood, letting the great river and its countless tributaries rise far above their banks. He wondered how life was now for the many towns and villages, even cities, along those waterways, and in what condition the complex network of living beings and food chains which the enormous forest supported were now. Before he started on his journey home it had seemed that the whole world was changing, its temperature, weather patterns, ocean circulation, animal migrations, all the environmental systems, leaving millions of humans displaced, on the move, or homeless, all over the planet.

He hadn't thought it would happen on this continent, or to him, but that assumption had been wrong. Yet, it had happened and must be accepted. He breathed and punted and let the water take the vessel where it wanted.

( )

Through the still, iridescent surface he could see the roofs and outlines of cars he passed above. Here and there a van or a truck broke the surface, most of them upright, a few on their side, which were easy to avoid. The water smelled of diesel and gasoline, and he pulled the scarf up over his nose and mouth, hoping it would block some of the stench. He was glad he had filtered water from the marsh and filled the canteen and soda bottle, which he sipped from occasionally.

Soon, the motorway narrowed to a city street and the buildings on both sides of the water grew taller and closer. He had reached the center of the city. Now its streets resembled the canals and waterways he had traversed with his family in an old town that was situated in a shallow lagoon south on the continent, yet his current location had glass and steel towers instead of wood and brick mansions. He spotted something that looked like clumps of rags floating in the water, but as he came closer it turned out to be dead bodies, so waterlogged and half-eaten by birds and other animals that only their remnants of clothing indicated that they were human. Once he had seen the first bobbing corpses, he recognized more of them and kept his distance.

One cadaver had been trapped in a surge that rushed in from a sloping side street and over the edge of a concrete flower bed. The height difference between the concrete and the asphalt below created a small waterfall, where water churned constantly, pulling the corpse down beneath the surface and back up to the froth again and again. He remembered from the emergency training before departing to a flooded town during his service that such eddies of swirling water were especially dangerous, even when they were small, because other objects would also be trapped there, potentially causing injuries, and adding to the difficulty of getting out of the current. Right below the little waterfall, he saw at least two different heads pop up and disappear again, and didn't stay to see if more bodies had been caught there.

The blank facades of high-rises loomed out of the mist. He scanned them for signs of life, light, or motion. A few times movement caught his eyes or he thought he saw a brightness in the distance, but it was only a bird lifting from the railing of a balcony, or light-colored blinds wafting from a broken window.

As the day waned, he drained the canteen and the soda bottle, but could not refill them because the water smelled distinctly of gasoline, diesel, and other chemicals, with an undertone of decomposition he neither liked nor intended to sample. He suddenly yearned to see the ocean again, a true sea, not the dank intrusion of the flood, but clean, moving, living water. Inside the hush of the mist he steered the punt out of the core of the city center and into the streets that pointed towards the shore. When it had grown nearly dark and a cold, humid wind started up, which nevertheless did nothing to tear the fog apart, he pulled the staff up and let the punt float in the torpid water. He was near enough to the bay that he might be able to see the ocean tomorrow. The fog would keep him hidden until then. He went to sleep on the now-dry wood at the bottom of his vessel, with the sleeping bag and backpack sheltering him.

18.

The Corpse Counters

By the time he sensed them through the paralysis of dreamless sleep, they were already too close, coming up at the side of the punt. Instinctively, he held his breath and remained still. One of them bent over him, a shadow blocking the daylight, and lifted the mesh scarf he had pulled over his face as camouflage and protection against insects.

"Is he alive?" someone, a woman, said close by.

He opened his eyes, clasped the nearest wrist and struck the face above it as hard as he could from his supine position. The man that was bending over him swayed with the punch. He put both feet on the man's belly and gave him a good kick.

"Ooff!" the stranger said as he fell backwards—disappointingly, not into the flood, but into the vessel he had come from. The whole world rocked with that motion and water splashed up between the punt and the inflatable three-bench rowboat. He pushed forward after the man, but a fan of liquid hit him in the face. It was sudden and cool enough to slow his momentum for a second.

"Stop! Stop!" the woman in the rowboat shouted. "We're medics, we just want to help!"

He spat and wiped the fluid away from his eyes. It tasted faintly of sewer and rust, but didn't sting more than clean freshwater did. Now he saw their bright red coveralls with reflective yellow trim on the sleeves and chest, and the surgical gloves on their hands. If they were medical personnel, he couldn't hurt them.

"Take it easy," the man breathed, a welt already blooming on his cheek.

He sat down, but kept the man and the woman in view. They looked unarmed.

The two exchanged glances. Their hair was as greasy and ruffled as he felt and their coveralls were smeared with stains.

"Are you hurt?" the woman said while looking at his face and body, not just him, but his physical and mental status, in a way he recognized from other medics. "Are you in need of assistance?"

"I am," the man said behind her, but she ignored him.

"Are there more people further in?" he asked.

"No," the woman replied.

"Yes," the man said. The two looked at each another again. The man had a scruff of dark blond hair with paler streaks in it and looked to be in his early thirties. The woman seemed to be a few years younger than the man and had straight light-brown hair tied into a long ponytail at the nape of her neck.

"We're the last ones here," the woman said.

"Excluding the dead, of course," the man said.

"Just the two of you?"

"No," the woman said. "We're a team, a small one."

The man grimaced like she was betraying a secret, but didn't say anything. He still couldn't see any bulges of weapons or ammunition clips under their clothes, not even protective vests. Next to them sat a steel case with a handle on the lid. Their craft was so glaringly yellow it would be impossible to hide. It reminded him of the vessels his family sometimes rented at the beach he was headed towards, tiny rubber rowboats that were easy to paddle, but hardly more solid than a beach mattress and just a fraction safer to use.

"Who are you working for?" he asked.

The woman mentioned the name of one of the largest aid organizations, not only on the continent, but in the world. Were things so bad they needed help from other countries?

"What about you, then?" the man said. "Why are you here?"

"I live here," he said. "Or I used to."

"We'd better talk at the camp," the woman said. "All right?"

"All right," he said.

"Good." She leaned forward and pushed a neon-yellow rope through the rusted ring at the stern of the punt, tying it in a clumsy but tight knot. Then the strangers brought two white plastic paddles up from the bottom of their rowboat and pushed the blades deep into the water.

( )

At a grass-covered mound that rose like a thatched dome out of the floodwater, they disembarked and tied the rowboat to a lamp post. He climbed out of the punt and pulled it up the muddy bank as far as it would go. On top of the low hillock stood a large open tent, its pointed roof and octagonal shape resembling the structures he had seen in the park on the way to the city. The breeze wafted through the space, lifting the ends of the open flaps. He had expected other stragglers, people who were injured or waiting to be evacuated, like in the town he had passed. But inside the lawn-scented shade of the tent, there were only stacks of plastic crates and cardboard boxes of various shapes and sizes. In the back, a large collapsible table held an array of smaller containers and caches, paper maps, toolboxes, and an orange plastic case that looked like it might protect a laptop computer for field use or a satellite phone.

Someone in a red coverall and neon yellow vest pushed a foldable canvas cot over to him and he sat down on the navy blue fabric. As soon as he did, he was overcome by such a sudden, overwhelming tiredness that he took the chance of not resisting. No one seemed to be in a hurry to talk to him, and he was soon lying on the cot, gazing up into the puckered zenith of the tent. A little later someone approached and handed him a white plastic cup with transparent, clean-looking water, which he sat up and drank before he lay down again.

A broad-shouldered, middle-aged woman with dark hair and skin leaned over him and touched his clothes. When he swatted at her, she put a hand on his chest and said: "I just need to check that you're not a danger to my colleagues." He let her search him since he had nothing to hide. She took something out of the inner chest pocket of his jacket, leaving a scent of disinfectant and sweat behind.

"Wallet but no identification, a few notes and coins," the woman said to a tall, solid-framed man in his fifties with thinning, silver-gray hair, slightly watery, but gentle-looking eyes, and a generous gut hanging over the belt. They were both dressed in light-colored slacks and jackets, with solid boots that had seen much use. He wanted to eavesdrop on them further, but a brightness flared up in him and engulfed the world.

( )

When he woke it was dark outside, while a wide-brimmed steel lamp glowed in the interior of the tent. The woman who had searched him and the man she had addressed were sitting further inside, together with the man and the woman in the rubber vessel, as well as two young men he hadn't seen before. Ceramic bowls were perched in their laps and they had cups or cutlery in their hands. He watched them and listened to their voices.

"Found a few more to the east."

"Where?"

"Out by the roundabout."

"Are you checking them tomorrow?"

"Yes, as early as possible."

"Found data on the female, added her to the list."

"We're down to the dental records on most now."

"Sometimes that's all we need."

"But most of the time it isn't. Not by far."

"Yes, I know."

"I'm so damn sick of this place. Heard from anyone yet?"

"No. We have wait till the end of the month."

"Come on!"

"First survivor in two and a half weeks, congratulations."

"Three weeks."

"Not a survivor, a traveler."

"How did he get in?"

"Ignored the roadblocks, probably."

"Any records?"

"Not yet."

"By the way, don't expect to get more supplies. Sorry that I haven't told you before."

"What?"

"No?"

"No."

"Can you at least ask them about it?"

"I knew you'd say that, so I did."

"And?"

"The answer was no."

"Jesus."

"There are other sites, with people who need help."

"What do they think we're doing here?"

"You know how it is."

"We're the ones sitting here, you're out and about."

"Yes, but . . . "

"We've got some bags left, it'll be fine." Silence, but not too tense, still relatively relaxed.

"Well, I'm going further west tomorrow, have a feeling there will be more there."

"Be careful."

"We'll be ready for it."

"Could be difficult if there's more than ten."

"One by one, as always."

"I'll see what I can do with the ice."

"Yes, thank you." More silence, the sound of cutlery against bowls, and running water.

"Good night then."

"Good night."

They stood and dispersed into the unlit parts of the tent where he could still hear their voices, but not see them.

☾☽

A little later the tall, solid-looking man with the light-colored clothing and silver hair stepped over the crates and approached him. He sat up, trying to clear his mind, chase the sleepiness away. The man took a bottle from the table behind them, squeaked the cork open, poured water into a cup, and held it out to him.

"Thank you," he said. He drank and the man disappeared for a moment. When he returned he held a bowl of food in front of him. Canned meat and vegetables, soft and warm, not just reconstituted freeze-dried powder. He took the bowl. "Thanks," he said again.

"You're free to leave when you wish," the man said, "but we'd be very happy if you gave us a name first so we can delete you from our lists of missing persons."

He considered giving the man Michael or Katsuhiro's name to check if they were missing, but what if his own name was on those lists and wasn't crossed off so his family could know he was still alive? He gave the man his real name.

"Thank you," the man said, writing on a small pad he took out from one of the front pockets of his jacket. Other notes had been scribbled in blue ballpoint ink there, with a spindly, curling hand. The stranger rose and turned towards the table, but did not open the orange plastic case there, or anything else.

He ate the moist, canned meal and drank the clean, mild water. The dish tasted of beef, potato, carrot, onion, and turnip. The water was gently flavored from minerals, probably calcium, potassium, and sodium. It was so good he felt a little faint. He could almost sense how the dissolved nutrients rushed to the parts of his body that needed them the most. The tension which the moderate but near-constant hunger and thirst, as well as the journey itself, had created in him eased, making him shiver, despite the relative warmth in the tent.

The solid-framed man took a bottle of water, broke the sealed cap, then leaned back against the table.

"I'm sorry that my colleagues startled you."

He glanced up at the stranger. "My apologies for attacking them," he said. "I wasn't expecting anyone."

"Neither did we," the man said. "Not after all this time. I'm Raymond, by the way. I'm a pathologist, and like the others, I'm working to collect and identify the dead that may still be here."

He took the man's hand. "Are there a lot of dead around?"

Raymond looked at him. "There are still some left, yes."

"They were killed by the hurricane and the flood?"

Raymond's face contracted and he felt the tip of an unease that wasn't directed at him. "Most of them," Raymond said. "Others had been unable to evacuate and starved to death before the emergency teams could reach them. Some drank water that was contaminated with chemicals, because there was nothing else to drink. Some had illnesses that were exacerbated or precipitated by the stress of the disaster, such as heart disease, asthma, or depression."

Hearing that, he felt heavy, listless.

"Did you perhaps see any bodies on your way in?"

"A few, maybe four or five, close by," he said. "Some in the vehicles on the motorway to the north. Then a whole column right outside the town limits." He saw no point in not telling the stranger.

"Do you recall approximately where?"

He nodded.

"Can show me on a map tomorrow?"

He nodded again and spooned up the last of the food in the bowl.

"Why are you here, then?" Raymond met his eyes directly.

"I'm looking for my family," he said. "We live here." He braced for the "No, where are you really from? The Eastern continent?"

"Are you local?" Raymond perked up.

He nodded.

"I am too!" Raymond said. "At least I was, a long time ago. My son grew up here, we had a lovely apartment near the city center. Always good to come home to. When he moved out we rented it to two students. But I . . . I don't know what happened to them in the flood."

His pulse quickened, but he realized the source of the sudden emotion was not himself, but Raymond. Something sat like a barb in the man's flesh as well as his mind, kept away with just the thickness of a paper sheet. The pathologist seemed sturdy enough, but there was something brittle in him, not his body or his external persona, but further in. He recognized the sensation from officers he had served with during his time of service, and in friends there, and shrank from it. But that didn't work; he couldn't get away. He could only sit and feel the emotions that churned inside the other man, and pity him.

"I'm sorry to hear that," he said, not knowing how else to address the troubles in the other man.

Raymond swallowed. "I'm certain they evacuated with the others."

He nodded.

The pathologist seemed to pull himself free from whatever was bothering him, and stood. "Let's not keep the others awake any longer. We can talk more in the morning. I hope you can get some rest."

"Thank you," he said quietly. "You too." He sat on the cot for a while, digesting the food and the water. When someone turned the lamp in the tent off, he lay back on the curving canvas and listened to the people around him fall asleep and start dreaming. It was a long time since he had shared sleeping space with so many people, yet it remained strangely familiar, as if he had never left that life.

Beyond the tent's sheltering fabric the evening breeze rustled in the vegetation. He felt his body's weight against the fabric and the heft of the cot against the grass and the soil. It was as if the night and the sky and the grass wrapped themselves around him and cradled him to sleep.

19.

Comfort and Closure

The next morning he woke when the others rose, and got up too. While they undressed and cleaned their bodies with washcloths and water from a filter system and tap behind the tent, they turned away from one another or hunched down behind the stacks of crates and boxes for what little privacy there was.

In the close presence of other people he felt anchored, defined in a way he never did when he was on his own, yet it wasn't a wholly uncomfortable sensation. He took the tooth-brush from the backpack lid and the remains of the water in the bottle Raymond had given him the night before and shuffled to the bank where the small inflatable and the punt bobbed on the floodwater's gentle motion. The eyes of the others were at his back, but since he had left his clothes and belongings on the cot, he assumed they understood he wasn't leaving, just off to brush his teeth.

The grass met the flood the same way rain puddles form on land, an indistinct border at first, with blades of grass still peeking out of the mud, like a lawn that had been moistened by a passing shower. Further out the vegetation became more and more covered by fluid until, at the edge of the flood, the ground fell away to opaque, sluggish water in a canal that had once been a street. There, the inundation was so deep he doubted he would have been able to stand on the bottom and keep his head above the surface.

His approach at the edge of the grass created tiny wave-lets in the standing water, which smelled faintly of petrol and sewage. He brushed his teeth and tongue and cheeks thoroughly, then spat the toothpaste out in the brown water. The lump of foam and saliva spread slowly on the murky surface and dissolved into the other chemicals there. He rinsed his mouth with the water that was left in the plastic bottle, before he strolled back to the cot and the others, feeling more ready to meet them.

❨❩

The group was eating breakfast; cereal mixed with rehydrated milk. He disliked the taste of milk, and even more so milk powder, and asked for water to mix the cereal with instead. The meal was eaten in silence, interspersed with only brief conversation about the day's activities and tasks to be done. They sat at the edge of their collapsible cots or on foldable camping stools, not so close to one another as to actually be sitting together, but not so distant that they couldn't hear what the others were saying.

"Have you talked with him?" the dark-haired woman asked Raymond.

"Yes," Raymond replied. "He's local, and is looking for his family."

"Is he unstable?"

"He said he'd spotted some bodies on the way here."

"Where?"

"Rather close by. I'll have him show me on the map as quickly as possible."

"I want you to go there with him."

❨❩

On the large table in the back was a map, the creases wide and fuzzy from repeated folding, its plastic cover scratched and scuffed, and the corners held down by a bottle of water, a small steel box, a stone, and a transparent glass jug.

"Can you tell us where you saw the bodies on the way here?" the dark-haired woman asked him. "We're at this junction." She pointed at a location in the southeastern part of the city.

He took in the map with the city's familiar outline, curvature of streets, vectors of the main roads. "The first one here," he said, indicating at narrow road nearby, mentally backtracking his own movements through the central district.

Raymond leaned over and marked the place with a red ballpoint pen.

"Then another one here, and one or maybe two here." He pointed at a corner further away, but still in the same section of the city, where he had seen the corpses trapped in the little waterfall. More markings. "A convoy of drowned cars here," he finally said and indicated the old road far north on the map, where several parallel scratches sat in the plastic, nearly obscuring the map beneath.

"Thank you," the woman said, giving him a sharp glance as if to assess the veracity of his words, then vanished among the stacks of boxes and crates

Raymond looked at him, brows knit, jaw set. "Can you take me there?"

"In the punt?" he said.

"Yes. It would be a lot of help to us if you showed me where the nearest bodies are."

He nodded. "Certainly."

Raymond's face relaxed. "Thank you."

"Right away?"

"Yes, if you don't mind."

Raymond vanished into the tent and returned with a jacket, a coiled up rope, and a small steel chest with solid clasps on the front and a black handle on the lid.

He picked up his backpack and shrugged into the straps.

"Feel free to leave that here," Raymond said.

He looked at the older man.

Raymond's face had a soft expression. "Come back and eat with us tonight."

"No one will mind?" he said. "I heard someone mention your supplies . . . "

"No," Raymond said. "It'll be no problem at all."

He set the backpack down on the cot and followed Raymond to the punt at the edge of the half-submerged grass.

❨❩

Raymond climbed in first, stepped into the bottom of the narrow craft, then quickly sat down in the pitch from the motion. Brandon waited until the punt had settled, then embarked too, crouched behind the pathologist and picked up the improvised pole that he'd placed carefully on the curving planks. Raymond loosened the knot of neon-yellow synthetic rope that tied the punt to the similarly hued inflatable and tossed the wet length into the rubber vessel. He pushed them away from land and up against the mild, slow current.

The fog moistened their hands and faces and placed a net of jewels on their hair and clothes. After a while the moisture soaked through the most exposed areas on Raymond's thin jacket, turning the shoulders and lapels dark, but the pathologist showed no signs of discomfort. With the added stability of more weight in the punt, he could stand while pushing the boat ahead, which eased the work considerably. He stood behind Raymond and pushed them along the flooded, fog-filled streets. It was cold and quiet. The glass faces of the buildings loomed above them and reflected nothing, not even the mist.

Except for the sound of the water dripping from the pole and the lapping of the flood against the side of the punt and the surrounding structures, the silence was dense and encompassing. Once or twice the dry clatter of something falling or the metal clang of steel pierced the quiet, but nothing tumbled from the glass towers around them, and nothing they could see moved. Yet, every time it happened, Raymond tensed and the ocean of fear that sat inside the man rose up in deep, pounding waves. He wondered what Raymond really was afraid of, what had created that sea in the first place.

He didn't think Raymond would notice it if he steered the punt past the building where his brother Katsuhiro lived instead of directly to the first corpse. When they reached that street he scanned the buildings that stared down at them through broken windows. Katsuhiro's apartment was located in one of the smaller structures, an old storage facility in red brick that had been renovated and divided into offices and apartments. But as they drew closer to the brick building, his heart sank. Almost all the windows that faced the street were smashed, and massive pieces of debris from taller and wider neighbors had fallen on the building, which had collapsed under their weight several places. A torn wall revealed a steel staircase that spiraled up and around but ended in a gap. It reminded him of an ancient brick tower he had driven past once on the southern continent. The tower was considered a historical and archaeological treasure, but since there was no protection of such buildings in time of war, the banks of the nearby stream had continued to fill the bottom levels of the tower with sand and mud. As a result, the centuries-old structure that was covered with intricate decorative patterns and inscriptions had become so lopsided that it toppled and fell just a few months after he visited.

He gazed up at the smashed windows and the crushed floors, which included the southwestern corner where Katsuhiro's home had been, with a deep ache in his chest. He had to believe that his brother and anyone else that might have been with him had managed to get out of the apartment before it was hit by the neighboring building. At street level he spotted the doorway to the parking garage next door that served Katsuhiro's building. Only the upper quarter of the opening was still above water, looking like it was trying to guzzle the flood away. As they slowly passed the entrance, Raymond turned and stared at the dark cave as it receded into the mist.

"If only we could have gone inside that building when there were people there," Raymond said with shaking voice.

He stared at Raymond, knowing how impossible it was to push the door or even the window of a car open once it was surrounded by water. How living bodies trapped inside a vehicle would bang their fists against the nearly unbreakable glass and scream their last breaths into the pockets of air that might collect beneath the ceiling. "Did you manage to get anyone out?" he asked.

Raymond shook his head, tears in his large pale eyes. "No, the garage has been flooded the whole time we've been here."

He swallowed. "We wouldn't have been able to go in there anyway," he finally said.

Raymond shot him a glance across the shoulder, then turned back. "No, not without diving equipment," the pathologist said.

( )

The punt flowed slowly through the brown, smelly water. They arrived at the site where he had seen the corpses trapped beneath the little waterfall by the concrete flower bed. Now a steel chair and an oblong piece of plastic were pulled under by the current, before both objects reappeared a few meters away, where they bobbed in the froth for a short while, before they were sucked back under.

In that current, clothing that was almost bursting and seams that had already ripped were also visible. He staked them a little closer. The small waterfall rushed and bubbled, warbled and sputtered. Caught in its circle of downward motion were two dead bodies, gray and swollen. If he hadn't known they were corpses, he would have thought they were artificial, life-sized beanbag dolls, grotesque caricatures of the human form. Raymond craned his neck and stared down into the undertow, tense, but focused.

"Just a bit closer," Raymond said. A strong resistance to go nearer to the cadavers rose in him, but he ignored it, and brought the vessel closer to the current.

When he had done that, Raymond said: "Are you able to use the pole to push them out of the churning?"

He nodded, but set his jaw. A stench spread from the water, overpowering both the smell of sewage and of gasoline. There, one lump of clothing popped up in the bubbles. He lifted the pole, aimed, and pushed. He hit the body, but it slid past the staff, like a bobbing-apple in a bucket. He lifted the pole again and prodded the corpse from the same side as the rushing water. Something gave, made a wet, soft noise, and the scent of human decomposition enveloped them.

"Careful," Raymond said. "We want them to move, not burst. It'll be best for them and us, believe me."

"Can they actually break?" he said, lifting the staff again and holding his breath.

Raymond glanced back at him, but he thought he saw a smile.

He pushed again, more gently this time, which tangled the pole in the rags that were still on the cadaver, and pulled it away from the zone of confluence. As he retracted the staff, the body came close, almost to the edge of the punt. The cadaver floated just a few meters from them, so full of gases it remained at the surface. He breathed with relief, but that made his nose and throat close by themselves and emit a dry, strangled noise.

"If you're going to faint, please sit down," Raymond said. "I can't jump after you if you fall in."

He crouched down, put his forearm over his nose and mouth and coughed, trying to get more air. The darkness that was closing like an aperture at the edge of his vision receded."There, now," Raymond said. "Let's see what we can do for this poor person." The pathologist leaned over the rim to inspect the corpse, then opened the small steel crate that sat in the bottom of the vessel. From there Raymond removed a square plastic bottle with a round blue cap, a small ceramic bowl, and a bottle of drinking water. The pathologist opened the square container, shook a little of the contents out, a pink powder, into the bowl, and replaced the cap. A little water went into the dry material, then Raymond produced a tablespoon and stirred the mixture into a batter. After that the pathologist took out a horseshoe-shaped mold from the steel case, spooned pink batter into the mold, and put it gently down on the worm-eaten wood of the punt. Raymond returned the bottles to the case, shut it with a snap, and looked at him.

CD

"How are you doing?" Raymond said.

"Fine," he coughed, tears from gagging still in his eyes.

Raymond glanced at the mixture in the mold, then back at him. "First time you've seen a dead body in real life?"

"No," he said. "But not here, not in water." Those he had seen had been so recently dead, so newly emptied of life, they were still very much recognizable as themselves, or they had dried in the sun for so long they were dark and taut like unwrapped mummies, not ballooned up and expanded till they lost all human resemblance.

"Where?"

He told Raymond the name of the location where he had served the longest, the last place, mostly to see how the pathologist would react.

"I understand," Raymond said, eyes flitting over him, searching for something. Anxiety? Brutality? Remorse?

"Some years ago," he said, clearing his throat. "Not that recently."

"The team and I were there too," Raymond said. "It stayed with all of us. We went to many other places afterwards, but none quite that difficult. Or beautiful."

He nodded and coughed. It felt good having told it. And as he had expected, some of Raymond's ocean was from there and similar places, but not all of it.

126

"Well, this is ready now," Raymond said. "Can you take us up against the body?

He pushed the vessel again, slowly, carefully. When the corpse floated right next to them, and it was as if the air itself had putrefied, Raymond fished out two pairs of skin-colored surgical gloves and from the steel box, and pulled them on. Then the pathologist reached over the rim and found the cadaver's head.

The corpse's features were so swollen and rotted he couldn't tell the gender, age, or ethnicity of the body.

Raymond turned, picked up the mold at the bottom of the punt, and pulled the jaws of the corpse apart.

He didn't want to look at the dead mouth but had to, his gaze pulled irresistibly towards the sight of complete ruin. Beneath a row of yellow teeth lay a black tongue as bloated and as swollen as the rest of the body. If his loved ones had died in the flood, was this what they would look like now? That thought made his knees gave way; he gripped the edge of the punt, gagging on saliva from almost throwing up, not getting enough air.

"Better let it out than keep it down," Raymond said and gently closed the cadaver's mouth over the mold. "You'll feel much better afterwards."

But he couldn't. The nourishment he had in him was much too precious to lose to something as stupid his inability to handle a dead body. He clutched the old wood so hard it creaked and let the saliva that welled up in his mouth drip into the water in proxy of the voiding he longed to do. Yet, as he knelt, half-vomiting, on the old wood, the same sensation as the night before fell over him. He was being held by the vessel beneath him, the water it floated on, the street on the bottom, the soil which carried the street, and the sky and the sun above him. It didn't matter how sick he felt, everything was still present.

❨❩

"Done very soon," Raymond said. "Deep breaths, deep breaths, through the mouth, not the nose."

He squeezed his eyes shut and inhaled slowly through his mouth, but the air tasted almost as rotten as it smelled, so he returned to the sensation of being cradled by the landscape and tried to remain there. When he next looked up Raymond had removed the dental cast from the corpse's mouth and placed it in a small plastic bag.

"What do we do with the body?" he said, wiping his lips with the back of his hand.

"Ideally, we would bring it back with us for identification and then give it a proper send-off," Raymond said. "A burial of some sort, preferably not in a mass grave, but that would have been better than nothing. But now we don't have the facilities for such extensive work and there's no one around to do burials or cremations any longer, so we'll tether the corpse here, mark the site on the map, and come back later."

He nodded. Raymond leaned out over the corpse and slowly unfurled the rope he had brought into the brown water, then looped it around the cadaver's ankles where the flesh already bulged from the constriction of the pant legs.

"Have to tie this a little tightly," Raymond huffed, as he pulled the end of the rope together. "Otherwise it'll drift away when the gases leave the body."

"How long will that take?" he said, more to converse than anything else.

"A few more weeks," Raymond said and turned and smiled at him. "Push us a little closer to that traffic sign."

He did, and Raymond slung the other end of the rope around the steel pole that poked out of the surface and made a small but intricate-looking knot. Whatever sign the traffic control implement had once held had broken off, leaving only a lip of curling metal at its top. Raymond then took a piece of plastic with an elastic band and a black marker from the steel cache. The pathologist jotted down a number on the white tag, slipped the band over the foot of the corpse, then left it bobbing in the water.

"There, now we know where that body is," Raymond said, pulling off both pairs of gloves. "Hopefully we won't need to search for it again, whenever the . . . whenever the water recedes."

He glanced at Raymond. There was now a look of utter despair on the pathologist's face. "It will," he said softly. "It will."

20.

The Returned

They continued to the next place he remembered having spotted a corpse. He staked the punt leisurely through the drowned streets, taking them further and further away from the mound and the camp. As they entered a water-filled glass-and-steel gorge that pointed towards the east, the fog thinned. Far in there he saw the ocean lapping, with no boundary between it and the flooded city. The wavelets rose a little as they entered the concrete canyons and were squeezed together, licking the building walls, then sank back into the surface that had birthed them when their energy receded. As he had at the sinkhole by the coast, he could feel the breath from the ocean, the push and pull against the land. He let the punt drift for a moment, shielded his eyes with his hand, even though there was no sun or glare. Out there two seagulls floated on the wind, then dove down to catch morsels from the sea.

"I can see the ocean from here," he said, before he realized that the street he was looking down ended in a wall of mist, as had all the other streets that day. Raymond turned and glanced up at him, but said nothing.

They went on to the next corpse and after a brief search found it floating between the rusty chassis of a family car and the remnants of a van. He maneuvered the punt according to Raymond's directions so the pathologist could prepare and take a dental impression from the body. Afterwards, Raymond fastened a plastic label to the corpse and tied it to the column between the driver and the passenger window of the smaller vehicle.

"Are we heading for the next cadaver?" he said when the dead body had been secured.

Raymond shook his head. "No, that ought to be enough for today. We have a considerable way back. Do you think you can manage?"

He nodded. "You did all the work with the corpses," he said and lowered the pole into the water.

( )

On the way back they passed the maw of the underground garage again. Raymond shuddered and clenched and unclenched his hands, but kept staring at the narrow gap between the ceiling and the water. The pathologist's distress thinned his own self-control at seeing the place that might conceal the bodies of his family.

"There is a diving shop not far from here," he quickly suggested. "We could go there and see if there are any tanks left, and suits."

Raymond turned, rocking the punt, and gave him a surprised look. "You know how to dive?"

He nodded.

"How well?"

"Reasonably well."

"This will be like a cave, completely dark and with many possible entanglements, lots of car wrecks. Have you done any cave diving before?"

"Yes," he said.

Raymond looked nervous and elated at the same time, and inhaled as if he was about to say something, then stopped himself. Finally, it came out as a sigh. "No, I can't ask you to do it. It's too dangerous."

"Only the ground floor is flooded," he said. "The water's not deep, no risk of decompression sickness. It should be fast. Not that much air needed."

"How far to the dive shop?"

"A few hundred meters." Dusk was near, shadows were already growing long from the empty buildings around them.

"We can go there and have a look tomorrow," Raymond decided. "There might not be anything useful left."

He nodded.

☾☽

At the camp, the lamps had been lit against the night, food had been made, and water bottles handed out when Raymond and he returned. He steered the punt almost up on the grass, higher than the rubber rowboat and reached for the neon-colored rope that dangled from it.

"Let me," Raymond said and collected the end, lifted and slipped it in quick sequence, then pulled it together so deftly it looked like the rope had knotted itself. Raymond looked at him, then untied the knot and started the process again. He followed Raymond's solid fingers, but couldn't see how the knot was done. This time the pathologist didn't stop when the knot was formed, but pulled the rope together until there lay a small ladder of white and neon-yellow sailing wire between them.

He smiled.

Raymond grinned, tugged at the end so the entire structure dissolved into a rope again, then pulled it through the ring at the stern of the punt. "We'd better go eat now, the others are waiting."

In the tent Raymond held out a box of wet wipes to him that smelled strongly of disinfectant. "Clean your palms first," the pathologist said. "Then between the fingers, across the back of the hand, and under the nails, then use a fresh wipe to clean your face. If you think you got floodwater in your eyes, rinse them with water from the bottle."

"Thank you," he said, pulled out a tissue and started washing his hands and wrists.

Raymond put the box on the table. "Help yourself to as many as you need. We can't be too careful with the cleaning."

132

"Because the corpses are infectious?" he asked, expecting a yes.

Raymond shook his head. "Unless the deceased died from a very virulent or hardy pathogen, infectious agents will vanish a few days after death. Most viruses and bacteria can't survive for long outside of normal body temperature."

"It's not important to dispose of dead bodies quickly, to avoid contamination?" he said.

"That's correct in areas where there has been an outbreak of disease, which is common after flooding," Raymond said. "But here, where most people were killed by the hurricane, the flood, or hunger or thirst afterwards, the corpses are not infectious. Still, we should practice good hygiene, not the least because the floodwater itself contains a lot of pathogens and chemicals."

"I shall remember that," he said.

They took a stool and sat down among the others. Once again the conversation was quiet, intermittent, and familiar. When everyone seemed to be finished and were holding empty bowls, Raymond introduced them. Their leader was the dark-haired woman, named Leah. Raymond was second in command; they were both forensic pathologists. The woman and the man he had encountered in the rowboat were Gabriele, specialist in emergency psychology, and Jens, expert in disaster medicine. Edouard was a forensic anthropologist and Marten a forensic dentist, both specialized in identifying remains. The team nodded at him and gave him a few curious glances, but asked no questions. Raymond told them he was looking for his brother, that he was local, and that he was going to help them navigate the city.

During the night, when they were all breathing in their cots, bundled inside their blankets, he was wakened by Raymond and Leah talking, but he couldn't make out their words. Whatever the conversation was, if it pertained to someone else besides themselves, or if it was about him, it would come up sooner or later. There was no reason to rush things. The muted conversation blended with the rustling of the vegetation and the water's licks against the bank until sleep caught up with him again.

21.

Dust Dancing in the Air

The next morning was humid and gray, with little motion in the air, but there was a constant chill at the back of their necks and on their hands. Breakfast was cereal with hydrolyzed milk—water for him—and quiet talk. The blond guy he had punched in the boat sat down on a folding stool next to him. He recognized Jens' stubby hair, and the bruise on his face.

"Sorry about the eye," he said.

"No worries," Jens smirked. "You'll get yours."

"And sorry for splashing you," the woman with the long, light brown hair said, sitting down in front of them. She spoke with an accent typical for the countries south on the continent. "But you were so wild, punching and kicking! I had to save Jens." She laughed and the two of them joined in.

They ate the rest of their meal in relaxed silence. When they were done they lined up by the filter system tap behind the tent to rinse their bowls and spoons. Gabriele and Jens vanished into a smaller tent on the other side of the hillock. He crouched by the rubber vessel and the punt to brush his teeth. On the way back to the tent Raymond came over to him.

"Ready to show me that other body, and the diving store?"

He nodded.

☾☽

The fog held a chill, which was not the crispness of late autumn or early spring, or the iciness of winter, but the clamminess of early fall or late spring when the sun is not yet out. It felt as though the summer had already passed, unnoticed and hidden by the mist.

He punted them slowly yet steadily towards their location of the previous day. He disliked using the same route twice in a row, but didn't want the surprise of a blocked road or strong current, and therefore progressed along the same streets as earlier. Raymond slumped in front of him, appearing relaxed, but with every creak or squeak from the broken city around them, each sudden slosh of water on the concrete, or when the punt scraped against something hidden in the water below them, the pathologist jumped. He recognized the hypervigilance and the startling, and tried to feel it too, in order to bring it up and forward, but the moist air seemed to muffle that as well. For a long while there was only the sound of the pole punting them forward through the water.

"It's so quiet I can hear myself breathe," Raymond said.

"I can't recall ever doing that before," he said. "Not here."

Raymond half turned towards him. "Strange, isn't it?"

"I never thought the city would become like this," he said, pushing on the pole.

"It pains me to see it," Raymond said. "No matter where in the world and on which continent it happens. But more so here, where my son grew up, because we were happy here, even without his mother. Were you?"

He thought a little. "Yes," he finally said. "But I didn't know it at the time."

Raymond turned fully towards him and smiled, tears in his eyes. "What happened here has taken place in so many other locations, before as well as after the hurricane. From other causes, to varying degrees of destruction, but the result is always the same. People leave and the site is changed forever, even if parts of it can be rebuilt."

"Other places have been ruined as well?" he said.

"Too many," Raymond said, his sadness blossoming up between them. "The others and I only arrive after it's already happened, but no matter how well organized or justly run or beautiful the places were before, the devastation is always the same."

"I'm sorry to hear that," he said, for want of knowing what else to say.

"It wasn't so bad earlier," Raymond said. "Then there was usually enough money and plenty of will to rebuild and replace. But these days . . ." Raymond swallowed. "It seems very few regions will remain the same, and there seems to be no end to the difficult weather." The pathologist closed his eyes and breathed.

He did the same.

They located the dead body quickly. It was floating in the open water just a little down the street from where he had spotted it the first time. He steered the punt close and Raymond went through the same procedures as the previous day: opened the corpse's mouth to take a cast of the teeth and gums, then fastened an identification tag around the cadaver's ankle. In this street the water held a faint smell of gasoline, perhaps from a ruptured tank in one of the many vehicles that choked the road, or from the underground store of a gas station. The hydrocarbon scent mixed with the stench of putrefaction once Raymond touched the bloated body.

He coughed a few times, but breathed deeply through his mouth as Raymond had told him to and gagged less than he had the previous day. When he glanced at the pathologist, wondering how he could stand the smell and sight, Raymond grinned at him.

"It's the cycle of nature," Raymond said. "It's how things should be, stink or not. If these cadavers didn't decompose or get consumed by other beings, that would be more wrong than them smelling up the place. Everything will end someday, us included."

He had heard that sentiment many times, but resented the notion. For a long time, death had seemed like a punishment, for being careless, ill-prepared, thoughtless, or simply un-lucky. It had taken him a while to see his own views and come to another conclusion. Yet, here, among the ruined buildings and the drowned streets, it did seem like the natural order, of life returning to life, instead of only death.

(()

Finally, Raymond retrieved the finished cast and secured the cadaver's rope to a blackened cherry sapling that stood in a round, glazed pot on a second-story balcony. The small, jutting space was bounded by glass panes set in steel clamps in a slim banister. Two of the wide pieces of glass displayed a web of broken yet still-present material; in another frame the entire pane was missing; but most of them were still there. Raymond took hold of the pot to push the sapling further back onto the balcony, away from the water.

"Don't!" he said just as Raymond shoved.

In total and complete accordance with the laws of phys-ics Raymond's forward motion brought the punt backwards with an equal and opposite reaction. The sudden movement made the clamps that held the pane in the banister directly above them give way, sending a sheet of thick glass towards them, like a solid waterfall. Raymond's hand shot out, seek-ing his wrist. He caught the hand and let it grasp and bear down on him as it had to. For an impossibly long moment, Raymond hung as if suspended in the air, between the falling pane and the water beneath them.

The belt on Raymond's jacket was closer to him than the pathologist's wrist or shoulder was, and he grabbed the worn leather with his free hand and rolled backwards, pulling Raymond with him into the vessel. The punt kicked up two splashes, one as it slid sideways, and another as it crashed into the wall beneath the balcony, while the heavy glass sheet sliced through the air above them. The pane slid into the dirty water, where it hit the bottom with a corner first and shattered into thin, longitudinal shards that collapsed tinkling on the asphalt. Raymond fell with his full weight on him, knocking the air out of his lungs and making it feel like his thighbone had cracked. The punt sloshed up gasoline- and corpse-reeking water, and bounced back from the impact with the wall, but then it floated calmly away from the veranda and the sapling and corpse and glass.

Raymond sat up, pale and drawn. The pathologist glanced at him and then the balcony, and back at him.

He pushed against the wooden bounds of the punt, trying to contain the agony that rose in him, but it rushed up and into his throat before he could stop it. A constricted gasp escaped him and he clenched his jaw so his teeth creaked. Something touched his leg. He tried to scuttle away from it on his elbows.

"Lie still," Raymond said. "Let me check if it's broken."

He breathed and stopped moving, while his elbows and back burned and throbbed.

Raymond felt the muscle with solid fingers, gently and expertly, but it still made him curl up like a grub prodded with a twig, and squeeze his eyes shut.

"It's not broken as such, thank goodness," Raymond said. "But there may be a hairline fracture. You will have to take it easy for a while. We should go back to the camp, we have painkillers and elastic bandages there."

"No," he said, breathing. "If it's not broken, let me rest a little and we can continue." It felt like the muscle was bruising already; it was singing with pain.

Raymond didn't reply, but fished the pole out of the flood canal, shook the water from it, and pushed it against the nearest wall. The pathologist's face looked swollen and his eyes were red. He began staking them up the street in the same direction they had arrived.

After a while he managed to sit up to gingerly massage his shoulders and elbows. Then he looked up at the store signs around them and the position of the afternoon sun, which had nearly burned through the cloud cover.

"We're just around the corner from the dive shop," he said.

"What?" Raymond said. "I was taking us back to the camp."

"Wrong direction," he grinned.

☾☽

The store was where he remembered it, on the first floor of a building with a faux half-timber facade. Three short stone steps led up to its dark wooden door, flanked by diamond-patterned stained-glass windows covered by decorative, wrought-iron grilles. He recalled forgetting those steps and stumbling, almost falling into the store, after having admired their diving masks in all colors of the spectrum and monofins up to a meter long, but not having bought anything because when would he have time to go diving? He had nevertheless signed up for the diving club that was attached to the store, but had not gone to any of the meetings. Now the afternoon sun shone in through the cross street, spreading a palpable heat across the water, the first warmth in days.

Raymond brought the punt up to the door. The dark planks had been set in a herringbone pattern and had a mail slot that gleamed beneath the surface. The door looked like it had been wrenched open, unable to keep the inundation out.

He was relieved when he saw that, because he had worried about how they would get the door open against the weight of the water.

"Let's go in and make ourselves at home," Raymond grinned and pushed the punt through the door. A white wire basket for catching mail from the door slot shone in the water beneath them.

Inside, it took a moment for their eyes to adjust to the darkness. To the left of the door was a desk and a till, still closed in the water. At the back of the small room, below a narrow window with stained, diamond-patterned glass high up on the wall, hung diving suits, masks, fins, buoyancy belts, and even a couple of air tanks. The afternoon sunlight from the open door danced on the turbid water and shimmered across the walls. In one corner a long diving suit floated, startling them both as they first mistook it for a body. Slim wooden chairs, an overturned shelf, and some debris it was too gloomy to make out any details of, protruded from the still surface.

"I guess not many people go diving in a flood," Raymond grinned, prodding some flotsam in a corner with the pole.

He grinned and nodded, now sitting upright in the punt, with the throbbing leg stretched out in front of him.

Raymond pushed them to the diving suits in the back and rifled through them. "This one looks long enough for you," the pathologist said and pulled a red drysuit with black shoulders and neck down from the hanger and handed to him.

He took the suit and began to pull it on to check the fit.

"And here's one for me," Raymond said and pointed at a drysuit of the same make, but in a shorter length and in blue.

The selection of diving masks, mouthpieces, tubing, harnesses and buoyancy belts was so large they had no problems finding something that was untouched by the flood and fit them well.

"I guess we want as short of fins as possible?" Raymond said, gazing up at several pairs on the wall.

He nodded. "See if there are some short ones in a medium."

Raymond unhooked the fins from the wall and handed them all to him. He selected a pair of the shortest fins he could find for the pathologist and himself. Now their eyes had adjusted to the darkness and a flimsy door, nearly bisected by the flood and lying half in and half out of the water, became visible to them on the side wall.

"What's through there?" he said, as if the pathologist would know.

Raymond pulled the zipper of the dry suit up. "Stay in and I'll pull you along."

140

He wanted to protest, but then just nodded.

Raymond stepped carefully out of the punt and onto the floor of the shop and started wading towards the door while guiding the punt with one hand. The water reached to the pathologist's chest.

"Lights," he said, pointing at two yellow underwater torches. Raymond waded over, picked up one of the lamps and felt along its side. The light clicked on, giving a strong, wide beam. "Perfect," Raymond said. The pathologist picked up the other lamp and when it too clicked on, placed it in the punt.

The door on the side wall led to a white windowless space that served as both office and storage. Another door on the far wall probably led outside. On the other walls hung several different diving tanks, single and double. Others were visible in the water.

"Check the doubles first," he said.

"What do I look for?" Raymond asked.

"The gauge at the top and the pressure level," he said. "And a label or letters on the tank itself."

"All right," Raymond said and pushed his way over to the metal canisters. Some of the submerged tanks clanged together in the water. Tiny mayflies with long, thread-like tails flitted in the slanting light from the doorway and the sun outside. The pathologist read the gas mixture and pressure on the tanks out loud to him. In the end they found three tanks with sufficient pressure remaining, singles, but suitable for short dives. Raymond brought them over to the punt one by one, where they lowered the vessel considerably in the water. In the corner behind the door they found a steel pole with a plastic boat hook at the end, and took that with them to use as a better punting pole.

"No phones," he commented after he had surveyed the items that were floating inside the office. He had hoped they maybe had some waterproof sat phones for sale, or had one in the back, but he had seen no such items.

"If you need to make a call, you're welcome to use our laptop in the camp," Raymond said. "It's connected to the satellite network, which is the only thing still working out here. The laptop is still charging, but with the recent sunny weather we're having it will be done soon."

"Don't the others need to phone out too?"

"Of course," Raymond said. "But there should be enough time for everyone."

He wondered what Leah would think of him depleting the laptop's precious power, but he only nodded and said, "Yes, I would like that."

( )

Finally, Raymond pushed the vessel out the front door and climbed back onboard from the stone steps outside the store.

"Thanks for fetching those things," he said, a little ashamed that he had just been sitting there, doing nothing.

"Thank you for not letting me fall overboard at the balcony," Raymond grinned, but then the pathologist's mood fell, all in the same breath. "I . . . I haven't been in boats much, at least not like this. I didn't know it would move like that . . . "

"Don't think about it," he said, glancing up at Raymond.

"How's your leg now, then?"

He stretched the muscle slowly. "Sore, but I'll live."

"Good," Raymond said. The pathologist held his hand out towards the golden disc that still gleamed between the buildings, and measured the number of fingers'-breadths between the setting sun and the horizon. "We have about forty-five minutes left of daylight. Should be enough to see us back."

After he had instructed Raymond how to punt, the pathologist took their newly-acquired steel pole and brought them back to the meadow by kneeling at the bottom of the wood and pushing them slowly yet steadily along. He helped Raymond navigate the flooded streets, and sat as still as possible to avoid rolling the heavily laden craft.

22.

Measurements

They spotted the warm glow from the liquid-fuel lanterns in the tent long before they arrived at the mound itself, the only light among the looming, gutted buildings and the cloud-dimmed sky, and followed it back to their temporary home. He would have preferred the camp to be less visible in the darkness, but did not intend to remark on it. There was no reason to hide, he just didn't like telegraphing their presence so clearly.

Raymond pushed the punt up on the grass until the flat bottom scraped against the waterlogged soil.

He disembarked as gently as he could, but even just a little weight on his right leg shot pain through him, making him wince. Behind him he heard Raymond splash out of the vessel and tie it to the yellow inflatable. He started limping up the slope to the tent and the cot, drysuit in hand, but only managed a few meters before Raymond caught up with him and supported him the rest of the way. When he could finally sit down on the dark blue canvas, his neck and back were moist with perspiration.

"We'd better take a proper look at your leg," Raymond said and vanished into the shadows.

He began to peel the waders off. His body stank from perspiration and the chemical scent of the artificial fabric. He hoped the gentle breeze that flowed through the tent would remove some of the smell.

Jens came and helped pull the last leg of the moist garment off.

"Let's see now," Jens said and crouched down next to him. Bruising bloomed in the skin both in front and at the back of his thigh. Jens pushed and prodded it for a while. "It's not broken, but there's probably a fine hairline fracture beneath the contusions, so it will hurt for a while. I'll bandage it up and you should not walk for the next few days." Jens looked at him, and at Raymond who was now standing next to him.

"All right," Raymond said.

Jens vanished, returned a moment later with a roll of elastic bandage, and began to wrap his thigh from knee to crotch in several layers of cream-colored, antiseptic-scented fabric, which reduced the throbbing considerably. "How does that feel?" Jens finally said, with a grin.

"Much better," he said. "Thank you."

"Oh, there's a mosquito," Jens said and raised one hand over the bandages.

He froze in painful anticipation.

"Just kidding," Jens laughed and patted his ankle instead.

He closed his eyes and groaned, but laughed too.

"Go and get yourself some dinner," Raymond told Jens, who left snickering. Then the pathologist turned towards him. "I'll find you some food and water."

Raymond returned with two bowls of pasta in tomato sauce and two bottles of water.

He sat up on the cot, pulled the worn sleeping bag around him, and ate with Raymond in silence. Behind them, across a low stack of cardboard boxes, the others settled down and started eating too.

❨❩

The next morning it was raining hard, drops crackling on the tarpaulin, yet the wind was still low. Gabriele and Jens and the yellow rubber vessel were gone, but the others stayed in the camp, walking between the large and the small tents

144

behind it. Occasionally, he thought he heard the sinking and falling whirr of a mechanical saw, and the banging of other tools, but couldn't tell with certainty. Maybe he had dreamed it all?

A little later, Raymond came and handed him a bowl of dry cereal, a spoon, and a bottle of water, saying: "How are we feeling today?"

"You really are a doctor," he smiled, unscrewing the cap of the bottle and pouring the water on the cereal.

Raymond laughed and nodded, then turned serious. "Yes, but mostly for dead people."

"Dead people?" he said. "Do they need doctors too?"

"No," Raymond said, "but the living need to find out what happened with the dead and who they were, and that knowledge helps both."

"I understand," he said. "Not a choice one makes without close consideration."

"No," Raymond smiled. "But that goes for all specializations, even the decision to become a general practitioner."

He nodded.

"Better today?"

"Yes," he said, stirring the cereal and water with the spoon.

"Jens is a good physician."

He nodded again.

"We ate nearly an hour ago," Raymond said. "You were asleep, so we let you rest."

"Thanks," he said, chewing. "And thanks for the breakfast."

"Oh, it's nothing."

He ate another spoonful of the thick and filling mixture. "If you bring the tanks over here, I can check the air and clean the tubes and regulators," he said. "Since I'm not doing much anyway."

"What if the air's no good?" Raymond said.

"Let's look at them first," he said. "Even the first ramp of the garage should be above water and is probably not far from the entrance." As he recalled it, the structure had been small compared with the other buildings on the street, at least from the outside. But he couldn't remember if there had been any signs listing subterranean levels.

"You will have to show me how," Raymond said, glancing at him.

"How to clean the diving equipment?"

"No, how to dive."

He met Raymond's eyes. "No," he said finally. "This is not a first-time dive. It's too dangerous."

"If something happens to you in there, I will feel responsible," Raymond said, looking both flustered and shrewd at the same time. "To your brother, your family . . . "

"If I let you come along and something happens to you, I'll be responsible for that," he countered.

"You can't go in there alone, with that leg and everything," Raymond said loudly, brows furrowing together.

"I can once my leg is better," he said, curling a lump of moist cereal into his spoon and lifting it to his mouth.

"No, we have to go as soon as possible," Raymond said thickly. The pathologist's cheeks were red, but the forehead and nose were waxen and gleaming.

"Why?" he said. "What's the hurry?"

Raymond swallowed. "We . . . , we heard noises from inside. Banging. Maybe even yelling. We couldn't reach them. Some of the other emergency teams had scuba gear and rescue divers, but they had already left."

He felt cold. Why hadn't Raymond said that earlier? But there was no time to discuss. He closed his eyes and nodded to communicate his consent.

"We hoped they would make it up to the upper levels so we could help them down from there," Raymond said. "But we never saw anyone on the top floors, even though we paddled past the building several times."

He nodded again, looking at Raymond. "Perhaps it was just noises from the water, or the structure itself?"

Tears stood in the pathologist's eyes. "No," Raymond said. "Those were voices and the signals were three short, three long, and three short."

( )

Raymond composed himself and carried the tanks up from the punt one by one, then the harnesses, tubes, regulators, belts, flippers, and masks, then brought a bucket of clean water from the filter pump. They put the masks in the bucket, rinsed the mouthpieces and regulators, and soaked all of it for a while.

He cleaned the outside of the tanks, checked the letters and numbers engraved on them, and the exact pressure in their gauges again, in the daylight.

"It's been a while since I did this myself," he said.

"Then going through the equipment with me will be a nice refresher," Raymond said. While they waited for the equipment to dry, he described the basic theory of diving and the function of each piece. The pathologist picked up the principles quickly.

"I once wanted to become an anesthesiologist, but changed my mind," Raymond said. "And decades ago I took a basic diving course while on a holiday in the south, so I have at least used a regulator and mouthpiece before."

When the equipment was dry, they tested the regulators and the tubes, divvied up the weights and slid them onto the belts, and fastened the tanks to the harnesses. Then he showed Raymond how to put on the gear.

"We shouldn't dive with old air," he said, "but we don't have anything else. We must check it."

"How do we do that?" Raymond said.

"By smell and taste. Any oily or chemical scent means it's contaminated. There can also be too much carbon monoxide or carbon dioxide, but we have no way of measuring that. Or do you?" Maybe the team had a gas sensor.

"We've got no instrument for that," Raymond said, "but I know the signs of carbon monoxide poisoning. Don't worry."

He pushed the regulator twice, then sniffed the air that hissed out of the mouthpiece. It smelled vaguely of rubber, mixed with the scent of rotting grass and stagnant water from their surroundings. He pushed twice again and breathed the air to taste it, but felt only the faintest smell of metal, which was probably from the tank itself. Raymond tested the other tank.

"Anything?" he said

"Nothing I can smell or taste," Raymond said. They switched tanks and checked them, but the air seemed usable in both containers. The air in the third tank had a distinct fragrance of mud and decomposition; presumably floodwater had leaked into it. He labeled that tank "Unsafe" with a black marker from the table in the tent.

"We can use the air from that tank to fill the drysuits," he said.

Raymond pulled the smallest suit on and he showed the pathologist how to fill the garment with air and empty it through the vents. Then it was time for Raymond to do a test dive in the water right off the hillock. He limped with Raymond the few meters to the edge of the water and helped the pathologist with the breathing apparatus, flippers, weights, and mask.

Raymond gave him a thumbs-up and waddled into the flooding until the pathologist was only visible as a denser shape in the opaqueness, with clusters of bubbles breaking on the surface.

He tried to sniff the air that came up for traces of contamination, but the only scent he could smell was that of the flood.

Raymond was a decent swimmer and learned quickly, yet he felt far from confident or happy bringing the pathologist along on what would essentially be a cave dive. But maybe when Raymond saw the inside of the parking garage for himself, and they pulled out any corpses that might still be there, the pathologist would be more at peace.

That night, after the evening meal, when he lay on the cot in the darkness while waiting for sleep to arrive, he realized that he hadn't thought of the orange case once the entire day.

23.

The Garage

Morning, yet another overcast sky; low clouds of a pervasive drizzle, the drops not heavy enough to pockmark the water, but dense enough to moisten their hair and skin and breathe wetly into the tent. He took the time to shave, brush his teeth, pull his hair into a ponytail at the nape of his neck. Raymond informed his colleagues of their plans over breakfast.

"There is no way I can authorize this," Leah said when Raymond had described what they intended to do. "It's much too dangerous and I won't let you risk the lives of any team members." She looked determined, even a little defiant, yet there was something hollow about her words, as if Leah herself wasn't entirely convinced that they would be obeyed. For a moment her voice broke the quiet of the mound, before it vanished into the silence of the drowned city around them.

Nobody else on the team said anything, only looked at Raymond, waiting for his reply.

"No other team member will be in danger," Raymond said. "We only need the use of both vessels to carry the tanks and lights, and two people to secure the line outside of the underground garage. Those two will safely remain in the dinghy the whole time, with no risk at all."

Leah turned towards him, measuring him up and down with her eyes. "Did you talk Raymond into this?" she said. "And why? How long have you really been in the city? And what exactly are you doing here?"

He shook his head and was about to defend himself, but Raymond was faster.

"I convinced him to do the dive," the pathologist said, voice firm. "That's why I'm going with him. He's an experienced diver. If something goes wrong you have my permission to report it as an unsanctioned activity without your agreement. You will lose no standing in the organization and all the blame will fall on me. Simple as that."

"You bet I will call it unsanctioned," Leah said.

"Well, that's it then," Raymond smiled and stood, seemingly wholly unaffected by Leah's anger and dark promise. "Jens, Gabriele, will you to come with us? You can take the rowboat and bring the longest lines we still have."

"Raymond . . . ," Leah said, searching the pathologist's face with her eyes. "Please don't do this. If we're going to get out of here, we need everyone to be able to haul the vessels past the debris. Please."

Raymond turned toward her with a soft expression on his face. "There may be people in the garage, still alive. We have to help them. We can't just leave them there."

Leah got to her feet and left the circle of folding stools and the tent.

During the rest of the meeting he remained quiet and let Raymond explain where they wanted to go and what they wished to accomplish. He suspected Raymond wanted Jens to be there in case something happened to them during the dive, and Gabriele for the faint but unsettling possibility that there might still be survivors in the parking garage. More people present would be good if anyone needed to be pulled out, even from the relatively shallow depth. The gap between the ceiling and the water at the entrance was more than large enough to swim through on the surface, if necessary.

"We'll go into the first floor initially, stay well away from the cars, and continue up to the second floor, which should be above water," Raymond said, glancing at him for confirmation. He nodded. Jens looked at Gabriele and Gabriele looked at Raymond, but neither of them protested.

150

"What will you do if you find if you only find dead bodies?" Gabrieles asked.

"We'll bring them back here," Raymond said, this time without seeking his approval and neither Gabriele nor Jens questioned the decision.

☾

Raymond and he both changed into their drysuits, aligned and adjusted the straps and tubes, and tested each other's equipment, since there would be little room to do that once they were in the boats. He'd hobbled around a little before breakfast; the leg was still sore, especially if he put all his weight on it, so he was glad he would be swimming instead of hiking. And he looked forward to being in water again, even dirty and dangerous water. If they had to ascend to the upper levels, he would leave that to Raymond. The danger would be much less once they were inside the structure and out of the debris-filled flooding.

They carried the harnesses with the tanks, tubing, and lights down to the two small vessels at the edge of the mound. In the fog the skeletons of the high-rises in the densest part of the city center were faintly visible as jagged shadows to the east. Leah, Marten, and Edouard were nowhere to be seen, but the noises of a saw and a drill coming from the small tents indicated that they were in full activity there and were clearly not going to see them off. Gabriele and Jens boarded the rubber vessel, Raymond and he the punt, with Raymond taking the long steel pole. They transferred the two diving lights to Jens and Gabriele to distribute the weight and let the punt sit higher in the water.

"It's really you that's too heavy," Jens told Raymond and they both laughed.

Gabriele and Jens unmoored the inflatable first, but let Raymond take the lead with the punt. Their progress through the city and fog was slow but unfaltering, since Raymond now seemed to know exactly which streets to pass and which ones to turn down. Finally, they bobbed in silence outside the black yawn that was left of the parking garage's entrance. The sun had climbed higher in the sky, ceased the drizzle, and nearly broke through the cloud cover, which gave the air a reassuring warmth. He helped Raymond don the harness, weight belt, and flippers, making certain all the straps and tubes were connected correctly and sitting comfortably; then Raymond helped him on with his harness, belt, and flippers, and they performed a final check.

Gabriele handed them both a small water-resistant walkie-talkie from a set of four. "These still have some battery power left," Gabriele said. "They're short range but will reach us even from the top of the building, and should be strong enough to go through the walls."

"Thank you," he said. "Good idea."

"Yes, we will be anxious to hear that you are all right and what you find inside," Jens said. They tested the signals, then Jens placed the walkie-talkies in transparent plastic bags and put them into the zippered pockets on the sides of their suits.

They pushed the mouthpieces over their gums, clicked the regulators, and breathed. He helped Raymond out into the murky water first, then lowered himself carefully from the punt. The water was cool, but not too cold. Had it been a question of temperature only, wetsuits would have sufficed, but the drysuits had the additional advantage of protecting them from the dirty water. Jens handed Raymond the end of a rope, which the pathologist looped around the weight belt. He tied the free end to his own belt so it would be easy to get rid of in an emergency. Then Gabriele gave them each one of the yellow lamps, which they lit. Even behind the feature-obscuring mask and mouthpiece, Raymond looked excited and a little nervous.

"Remember to keep your fins away from the floor," he reminded the pathologist. "Bend your knees to get the fins up and kick slowly. We're not in a hurry and it's not far. If we whirl up too much debris, we follow the rope back out. Any

152

kind of problems, use the hand signal right away."

Raymond nodded and gave him the index finger to thumb circle that signaled OK.

He had Raymond dive first to check that the pathologist was breathing well, before he went under himself and swam the few meters to the underwater entrance.

( )

Beneath the surface the opening to the parking garage was a wide doorway bounded on the asphalt outside by narrow concrete cones with reflective tape around the top. The water depth was three meters at the most, but it was as dark as the greatest depths he had been in, and he was very glad they had lights. He kept the bright ray in front of himself and below his body to avoid being blinded, and swam slowly through the doorway, well above the cones and close to the surface. He hoped Raymond was smart and observant enough to enter at the same depth. He had told the pathologist to keep a good distance from any object inside to avoid snagging the diving gear or the rope, but he had no idea how well Raymond would remember that once they were in the dense darkness. Some people became too excited underwater; others were distracted by the new and foreign world. They were going to enter a small space that contained an unknown amount of debris. He hoped he wasn't being too irresponsible by letting Raymond come along. But the pathologist swam well above the cones and towards him at a leisurely and controlled pace. He gave Raymond the OK signal and continued.

Past the doorway, a row of vehicles had been squashed up against the wall, while the parking spaces themselves were clear and had so little debris that the white stripes separating them were still visible in the gloom. The floodwater must have rushed into the garage from the slowly drowning streets at great speed. Further inside crouched the shadows of more vehicles, most of them bunched up together, but a few still parked in orderly rows, just pushed a little sideways from their original positions. Here, thick concrete columns separated the rows of parking spots from the main thoroughfare, which was littered with individual cars.

The cavernous flooded space was dark and completely quiet. Whatever noises Raymond and the others had heard from the parking garage were gone now. Not even the sharp-angled, twisted shells of the vehicles they hovered past gave any boom or clang in passing. Now the only sounds were the slow and rhythmic hissing of the air they exhaled and the occasional creaking of their harnesses and fins. Leaves and twigs floated in the turbid water, like some sort of plankton originating from dry land. He was aiming for a brighter patch ahead; daylight, he assumed, from the level above, when he became aware of a headache and a simmering, oily dizziness that sat at the back of his mind. As he breathed deeper and progressed slowly forward, the headache mounted and the vertigo became a proper reality. A metallic taste appeared at the back of his mouth; not the sharp, coppery tang of blood, but the heavy, dull flavor of lead. Oh crap. His air must be bad after all. He turned to look for the entrance, but saw only the white sailing line that vanished into the silt behind them, and the silhouettes of concrete columns and car wrecks that the beam from the lamp chased up. They were too far in to go back. He had to find the ramp to the second floor. He turned in the direction of the daylight he had seen. The submerged world spun and tipped and his head throbbed steadily harder. He never had headaches, not even after working late at night. It wasn't the weight of the tank or strain on the neck from the horizontal position of swimming. It was the air.

A darkness gaped below him and there was a strange pull in the water. He feared he was blacking out, but it was only a broad, asphalt-covered ramp leading down into the darkness. In the beam from his lamp a reflective arrow flashed at the bottom of the asphalt, pointing further down into the murk, before the illumination was swallowed up by the gloom. A little further ahead, sparkling at the edge of his now tremulous sight, was another arrow pointing up. Raymond came up alongside him and he pointed to the ramp that protruded from the water. The pathologist signaled OK and he pushed off hard towards it.

( )

He more crawled than swam onto the ramp and as soon as he broke the surface he pulled out the mouthpiece, floodwater or no floodwater. He spat and shivered, and greedily pushed the air, surprisingly fresh for a parking garage, down into his lungs. He coughed and huffed while the world tilted so strongly that for a moment he worried he'd slide back down into the water. In the bright light from the steel-grated walls above, he spotted a jeep lodged at the top of the ramp, but on the other side of the broad slant. If the jeep started sliding from their motion, they wouldn't be directly in its path.

Raymond came up behind him and waded onto land. Then the pathologist leaned over him and put him in a stable position, took his pulse, and felt his forehead.

"Breathe," Raymond said, "breathe."

He lay still until the planet's speed around its own axis had decreased and he could feel the asphalt beneath him through the slowly fading headache.

"How do you feel?" Raymond said.

"Better," he said, keeping his eyes closed, just in case.

Raymond took his pulse again, then stepped out of the fins, clicked the harness open, and put the tank gently on the ground, making certain it didn't roll.

"What are you doing?" he muttered, still behind his eyelids.

"I'll go check the upper levels," Raymond said. "Lie still here and you'll feel better in no time."

Raymond was gone up the ramp and past the stuck jeep before he could reply. He heard the hissing from a walkie-talkie vanish with Raymond and was glad that the pathologist was in touch with Jens and Gabriele outside. His heart beat heavily, but steadily. The asphalt smelled of engine oil and gasoline, an uncomfortable and ugly scent, but vague and inconsequential at the moment. A beam of sunlight sieved in through the grating above, casting a spot of blazing illumination further up the ramp, in front of the jeep. Dust swirled in those rays, as it had in the dive shop, resembling tiny glittering stars, or eternally falling worlds.

(( ))

He heard steps on the level above, and then a little later on the ramp directly above him.

"Anybody still here?" he heard Raymond shout.

At least Raymond would get some answers, and he himself would hopefully be able to rule out the possibility that his brother and parents had died in the garage during the flood. If he found no signs of them here, perhaps they were still alive, and had already reached the north.

When Raymond had put him in a stable position, the pathologist had placed his hand under his cheek. He drooled at it like a tired puppy until he was about to fall asleep. Since that didn't seem like a good idea he lifted his head and forced his eyes open. The world remained still and the headache had faded into a thin smoke at the back of his mind, so he sat up and breathed deeply. The hood of his drysuit had been pulled down, cooling his head, and the tank was standing by his feet, the gasoline-iridescent surface of the garage water licking at the edges of the harness. He couldn't remember Raymond having pulled it off him, but the pathologist must have done that. He had forgotten that Raymond was more used to and better prepared for emergency situations than he was.

24.

Chthonic Knowledge

"Nothing," he heard Raymond say. Another radio crackle, then: "No survivors."

A small breeze that carried fresh and nearly scent-free air from beyond the grated walls brushed across his skin. He inhaled it greedily, hoping it would chase away the remains of his discomfort.

Raymond appeared at the top of the ramp, walking relaxedly in the drysuit. Then the pathologist crossed the rays of sunlight, which had almost died down. Maybe the clouds were rolling in again?

"You must be feeling better," the pathologist said, crouched down by him and shone a diving light into his eyes.

He squinted and groaned, turned his face away.

"Good," Raymond said. "Well, as you probably expected, I didn't find anyone, not even on the upper level. There were traces of a campfire and some tin cans, plastic bottles, and clothing. But if there was anyone here after those people were rescued, they left a long time ago." Raymond sighed and sat down next to him on the cool asphalt.

"So what do we do now?" he said.

"I don't know," Raymond said. The pathologist nevertheless looked deeply relieved, as if he had examined himself for a possible serious illness and the tests had turned out negative. "How do we get out?"

"Same way we came in," he said. "I'll use the secondary regulator on your tank. If you call up Jens and Gabriele, they can give us some pulling power once we're closer to the exit. Should be much quicker to get out than in."

"No," Raymond said. "You're a stronger swimmer than I am. You wear the harness and I will use the secondary regulator."

He was about to protest, but then Raymond said: "Besides, one of us must go and check the basement level."

He swallowed. "I was hoping you'd forgotten that," he said.

Raymond gave him a brief smile, soft enough to seem apologetic, but not yielding enough to make it look as if the pathologist had any plans of letting it go. "Most of the noises we heard that time seemed to come from below."

He frowned. "Why didn't you say that before?" Now he had no choice but to go.

Raymond looked at him gently. "Since it was much easier to check the levels above the water than below, it made sense to do that first. Also, if we did find people in the upper levels, we might not need to go any further. Besides, you needed air and rest."

He let go of his annoyance. "All right," he said and slowly stood. He was relieved to notice there was no dizziness or nausea.

"How do you feel?" Raymond said. "If you don't want to go, I can at least swim down to the entrance and see if I can spot anything from there."

He looked at Raymond. "Would you have stopped there?"

"No," the pathologist admitted. "I guess I wouldn't have."

"I'll do it," he said. "I feel fine now."

"Are you absolutely certain?" Raymond's eyes flitted over his face, not only to analyze his facial expression, but probably also to check the color of his skin and the redness of his eyes.

He nodded.

"I'll be frank with you," Raymond said. "Under normal

circumstances I would have taken you to a hospital to breathe pure oxygen for a few hours, then had someone watch you over the night. You should not dive again this soon after a carbon monoxide poisoning, not even to relatively shallow depths like this. But now nothing is normal, and I don't even know what that word means any longer."

He nodded again.

"Swim down," Raymond said. "Take a quick look around, but be fast. If the headache returns, anytime, come back up immediately. I know I can get you out to the others if necessary. Understood?"

"If I stay close to the ceiling it should be done in less than ten minutes," he said.

"Splendid," Raymond said. The pathologist's eyes were moist, shining in the weak half-light from above. "But don't go too near to the ceiling, remember there are sprinkler heads, lamps, and cables there."

He crouched down, feeling no headache or vertigo, and read the pressure in the good tank. There was plenty of air left.

"Is there enough for a short dive and to get us both out again?" Raymond said.

He nodded. "We didn't spend much air getting in."

"How much left?"

"At least twenty minutes," he said. "Although I wouldn't recommend draining it."

"Fifteen minutes then," Raymond said.

He nodded and set the timer attached to the harness at fifteen minutes.

Raymond lifted the other tank over to him.

With the pathologist's help he pulled it on and adjusted and fastened the straps so they were snug, but not constrictive.

"We should bring the other tank back too," Raymond said. "In case we need the regulator, or even find a compressor to fill it."

He nodded and helped Raymond put on and adjust that harness.

"I will wait here till you return," Raymond said. "Then we both swim out. Do be careful. If there was any way I could do this myself, I would, believe me."

"I need to do this too," he said. "Less than fifteen minutes."

"Less than fifteen minutes," Raymond said and patted his shoulder.

( )

The ramp down was immediately below them, a darker patch in the murk. He was reminded of the blue holes he had seen in pictures from the southern continent. They were ancient caves that had collapsed on the ocean floor or been submerged by the sea after their creation. He recalled the black circle in the forest on the way to the city and was glad it wasn't a true sinkhole, just the basement floor of a submerged parking garage.

Raymond told him to stay and breathe the air in the tank for a minute, to check that it was good. He did, feeling no headache or dizziness, only the slight rubber taste from the mouthpiece. When the minute was over, he gave Raymond the OK signal and walked into the flood.

He left the surface and entered the silent darkness, holding the lamp in front and below him, feeling like an astronaut going into unknown space. The ramp led downwards into a deeper gloom, reminding him of a trip to the subterranean train tunnels under the city he had made with Beanie the previous summer. The memory made him curl his lips around the mouthpiece.

Here, the water was even more filled with particles and tiny pieces of debris. Not so strange, since the flood must have rushed sand and mud and gravel from outside and the upper levels down into the basement. He continued slowly but steadily into the level, staying in the upper quarter of the water, well beneath the ceiling, but far enough above the silt on the bottom and the cars to safely use his fins. The right thigh felt good, almost no soreness, or he was so full of adrenaline he couldn't feel it. No matter what, the weightless motion and increased blood circulation would do the leg good.

The reflective arrows that pointed back towards the up-ramp shone in the light from his lamp, easing navigation and allowing him to keep a higher speed. Down here, the cars were even more jumbled and squashed together than in the level above. No vehicle remained in the space it had once been parked in, and few stood upright. Some of them had been hit with great force and had rolled over several times before coming to a halt near a wall or one of the concrete pillars that separated the thoroughfare from the parking spots. He knew that enough water at enough speed was as damaging as stone or steel. He scanned the car windows he could see with the beam of his diving light as he swam past them, and was relieved to see only darkness in them; no Katsuhiro, Michael, or Beanie sagging over the steering wheel or pressing their palms against the glass.

The darkness flowed past him. He followed the arrows in the opposite direction in which they pointed, around the central part of the structure, which contained a stairwell and an elevator, to what he hoped was the back of the basement level. He saw no bodies on the way, no corpses hovering in the water or crumpled on the floor. Except for the concrete and car wrecks, there was only the occasional cloud of engine oil or gasoline in the water, which he avoided when he could. But where he had hoped to find a smooth wall holding back the nethermost water of the garage, he found instead another ramp leading down into even denser gloom and higher pressure. Another basement level. He checked the depth gauge and the watch. There was only air enough to go to that level and back up again. Since there was no time for decompression he couldn't go further down than that level. But if that was the final floor, he had to go there to be certain that his family was not there. He could not leave the garage without doing that. He took a slow breath, feeling no signs of bad air, and dove down into the deepening darkness.

Here, the water was so turbid his light only pierced a few meters into the murk. The layout of the level was similar to the one above, but here the reflective arrows were partly hidden beneath the silt on the floor. Instead, he kept the concrete block of the central part of the structure to his right and noted its position with the compass on the harness. As during breath hold when he glided along the floor of the pool in the honeycomb tower, the diving reflex slowed his heart and lungs. He advanced past the corner of the stairwell towards what he hoped was the final wall. The asphalt was almost clear of cars since most of the vehicles had been pushed up against the walls, even piled up on one other.

( )

Something moved in the light from his lamp, waving like a flag or a hand. In their diving-induced slowed state, his heart and lungs barely reacted, yet the bitter taste of adrenaline appeared on his tongue from the sight. He ceased swimming and swung the lamp up with both hands. In the cloudy beam appeared an explosion of black, elongated bodies, undulating and wafting from the concrete, the narrow shapes fanning upwards from a center that spun like the funnel of a tornado. The cluster was almost as tall as his body and at least twice as wide.

For a moment he didn't comprehend what he was seeing, and just hung there between the floor and the ceiling while he waited for his eyes and mind to finish processing the sight. He took in the writhing, turning bodies. They fluttered in the water like rags in the air. Then it dawned on him what they were. Eels, looking like a single gigantic, entangled organism, feeding on something on the bottom. They were different and yet so similar to his own form, sharing the same basic structure of head, spine and ribs, with his ancestors having diverged from those of the eels far back in the mists of evolutionary time.

He passed the mass of swirling, writhing bodies while he watched them, more fascinated than in horrified. No Drive-Through, yellow letters on the floor announced, and he knew he had reached the bottom of the garage, without seeing the final back wall. He checked the watch, only a few minutes left. Then he lowered the lamp to investigate what the eels were feeding on, and turned. It had to be something large, since there were so many of them. On an impulse he kicked off hard, aiming right for the center of the mass of slim, black shapes. He sped forward and into them, while the cluster of slick forms parted before him. For the second time, the shock-taste of lactic acid burned on his tongue. In their center, on asphalt swept clean by the motion of countless fins, lay a group of human skeletons. They were tangled into one another's arms and ribs, as if they had fused together into a single large body, but that was just an illusion. He had watched enough news footage from sunken migrant ships to recognize the postures. Whoever these people were, they had sought the comfort of each other, holding one another so hard and so tightly that they were inseparable, even in death.

He counted at least four different bodies, perhaps five, their bones picked clean by hungry mouths, with what little meat and gristle that was left on the yellowing surfaces waving slowly in the water, like hair. He scanned them frantically for any signs of clothing or remnants familiar from his loved ones, but saw nothing that he recognized, not even the corpses' postures or sizes. One of them was small, but too small to be Beanie; it belonged to a child. Another was tall and had long blond hair, but was too solid and masculine to be his mother. None of the other skeletons had anything close to his father's straight bluish-black hair. His family had most probably not died in this garage. His search was not over. And, he realized, by finding the eels he had witnessed something that would have been hidden forever had he not taken the chance of investigating the lowest level. Now he had been allowed in on the eels' secret and become a part of their subterranean being, as much as they had become a part of him.

(( ))

But then he couldn't wait any longer, the air was not only for him. He kicked hard to get away from and up and out of the basement levels as quickly as possible, up through the darkness, and was thankful that he didn't have to stop on the way for the nitrogen gas in his blood to leave.

"Four human skeletons, maybe five, on the very last level," he told Raymond when he surfaced on the ramp. The pathologist was sitting on the asphalt, peering into the water, probably looking for telltale bubbles.

"What?" Raymond said, jumped up and came towards him.

He pushed the mask up, spat out the mouthpiece, wiped the floodwater that dribbled into his mouth away, and repeated the message.

"Dear god," Raymond said and looked so sad yet also so relieved that he immediately regretted having wanted to skip the basement, or resenting the pathologist for having to go there in the first place. Raymond's face contracted as if the pathologist was about to weep and something powerful and thrumming rose inside the man. He thought it would dislodge like an old cork from a bottle or a rotten tooth pulled up, but then Raymond clamped down on it with a shudder and the moment was gone.

"How long do you think they have been down there?" Raymond finally said.

"Long enough to have attracted and been eaten by eels," he said.

"Eels?"

"The flooded streets are open to the marsh and the sea."

"How much was left of them?"

"Just their skeletons," he said, meeting Raymond's eyes. "Nearly picked clean."

164

Raymond sat down as if his knees had buckled beneath him. "Could that have been the people we heard banging on the walls?"

"I don't know," he said. "It doesn't seem likely anyone would have survived for long down there."

"Eels, huh?" Raymond said after a short while.

He nodded, the knot of his wet hair bobbing at the back of his head, and sat down too. For a long time neither man said anything.

(( ))

Finally, they became aware of a crackling noise from Raymond's walkie-talkie.

"Raymond, Raymond, are you there?" a voice said over the static and reduced reception.

Raymond sighed and lifted the handset to his mouth. "Still here," Raymond said, "come in."

"Wind's picking up out here," the voice said, so dry and distorted he couldn't tell if it was Jens or Gabriele. "How much more time do you need?"

"Our friend just returned," Raymond said. "We're coming out right away. Over."

"Good. We're ready. Be careful. Over and out."

Raymond looked at him. "Is there any air left?"

He nodded. "Should be fine for both of us. We'll follow the line out, it'll be a lot faster than when we came in."

Raymond wrapped the walkie-talkie back up in the plastic and returned it to the zippered pocket of his dry suit.

He pulled his diving mask back down, put the mouthpiece in, and waded back into the water, with Raymond following. The pathologist took the secondary regulator and when Raymond gave the OK signal, they dove.

The return seemed much shorter, partly, he suspected, because the water was clearer on this level, and a little illumination from the outside still reached in. Raymond hung onto him and kicked only occasionally until they turned the final corner and had the light from the entrance straight ahead. Then they pulled on the white sailing line, were dragged along on it, and exited the doorway considerably more quickly than they went in.

When they broke the surface by the rubber vessel and the punt, both crafts were rocking on the wavelets that were nipping in the street canal, and it was raining heavily. Jens and Gabriele helped them board the rubber vessel, placed the tanks and the lights in the punt, and tied it to the inflatable.

"We need drysuits too," Gabriele said and handed them an oar each. Then they paddled hard to reach the meadow before the night fell.

25.

The Employees

On the way back to the mound, his thigh started to throb and ache. When he stepped out of the rubber vessel and onto the waterlogged grass, pain shot up from the muscle, hard and sudden enough to almost make him stumble. Jens caught his arm and prevented him from falling, and supported him back to the main tent. There, he slumped down on the cot and pulled the drysuit slowly off. The tent flaps had been rolled down and zipped together, but now the wind was so high it rushed in beneath the fabric, bringing with it sprays of rain.

Raymond came over to him with a steel bowl of filtered water to wash his face and hands and any other area of skin that had been exposed to the floodwater. The concave mirror surface of the bowl gleamed with the water it contained, reminding him of a book from his childhood where orbs of magical crystal were used for long-distance viewing, spying on friends and enemies alike. The orbs were so valuable and so coveted that they plunged an entire world into conflict. He leaned forward and submerged his head into the transparent, clean-smelling water, rubbed his face and hands. Afterwards, he shook his hands to get rid of the moisture, wiped the water from his face, and dried himself with the small towel he had draped over the backpack lid.

"Would you like some dinner?" Edouard asked, in an accent typical of the central reaches of the continent. The forensic anthropologist had eyes that were deep green, above a refined-looking hooked nose and narrow lips.

"No, thank you," he said

"You should eat," Edouard said. "Otherwise your leg will heal slower. I'm an expert on bones."

"Maybe later," he said. "I'm too tired now."

"You really should," Edouard said, then shrugged.

He lay down on the cot, pulled the sleeping bag over his body, and listened to the others assemble in the tent, filter water, and prepare their meals.

After a while Raymond came and handed him a bottle of water and a pill. "Here," the pathologist said. "This will help with the pain."

"Cheers," he said and swallowed the small white tablet with some water, then drank a little more, before he lay down again. He soon started to feel drowsy and when the searing in his thigh had quieted enough, he fell asleep.

☾☽

In his dreams he saw a landscape he had seen many times before, but which he had not dreamed of for years.

In a small village in the mountains, situated by a deep, round lake where the pine forest reached almost to the surface of the water, the body of an unknown person was brought to the local church. The winter was so cold and harsh the snow nearly buried the little shrine outside the gate, and the priest could barely keep the candles in the minuscule, slanting-roofed structure burning. To keep the cadaver cold while the priest found out who the deceased was, it was put in the sepulcher beneath the church. But a few days later, when some villagers came to clean the corpse, they discovered that it hadn't rotted or decomposed in any other way. On the contrary, the body's hair and nails had grown and the skin remained smooth and soft. Soon sick and unhappy people from the village started to arrive at the church for a glimpse of the blessed corpse, and rumors of the miracle started to spread in the region.

Not long after, a stranger traveled all the way from the capital in the headland to the village to investigate the marvel on behalf of the central church and the throne. The investigator immediately set about to measure the length of the corpse's hair and nails, listened for faint heartbeats with a small wooden trumpet pressed against its chest, and held a mirror shard near the mouth to look for hidden breath. But there was nothing, no hint of hidden, cryptic life in the body that might have eluded the normal methods of detection. The investigator then crossed the sea of snow that lay between the church and the village and went from door to door to find the corpse's family. But no one was missing any family members, nor had they heard of anyone having vanished from the nearby villages and towns.

Next, the investigator tracked down and interviewed those who had found the corpse and brought it to the church. A young woman said she had discovered the dead body when she crossed the stream at the edge of the lake with her sister. The cadaver appeared among the floes where the current had broken through the ice, and at first the young woman thought it was the beautiful porcelain doll she had seen in a shop during a rare trip to the capital when she was little, and pulled the corpse out of the icy water. One elderly lady said she had found the body in her woodshed, where she thought it was the husband who had left her in her youth that had come back to her, and therefore brought it with her inside. A childless huntsman found the corpse sitting beneath a tree in the forest, identifying the cadaver to be his colleague who had been taken by an avalanche two winters ago. One merchant thought the dead body was the son he had sent away the previous spring to apprentice with a dried-cod seller in a city on the coast. They all came to the crypt to clean and pray for the deceased, and claimed they were the ones who had found the dead body and taken it to the church.

The investigator sent missives to all the nearby villages, but no person was missing and no corpse had been stolen from the graveyards. Finally, she had no other choice but to let each person who claimed to have recovered the corpse care for it as they wished and grant others access to it as they wished as well. But on the last day in the village, the investigator realized who the corpse really was. It was a patient she had once had when she was a young physician traveling the land. She had been fetched to treat a noble heir who had had his feet crushed by his uncle and rival for the estate. She had lost the patient, her first defeat as a practitioner on her own, and only managed to forget about it and continue with a great effort. Now she realized she had lost the patient not due to inexperience or error, as she had always believed, but to political powers she had had no way to understand, let alone fight, at the time. The investigator realized she couldn't change what had happened in the past, but at least now she had a clearer understanding of it, and although she had failed, she knew she had done all she could. Thus convinced, the investigator returned to the capital and filed her report of a true miracle in the village.

(☽

The new day arrived, white and windy, like a stormy morning during holidays at the coast. He imagined he was relaxing in the cabin his family had rented for the summer, while they waited for the wind to die down so they could go for a walk along the beach below the lighthouse. The waves that curled out at sea would be sharp and frothy, even in that steep city canyon which led in from the ocean. And he remembered the last, powerful wave on his long swim back to the beach in the spring when he almost drowned; the swelling, surging force that had lifted him up and up, rushed him forward, and pushed him back on land, and how grateful he had been, even through hypothermia and exhaustion.

A little later he prepared his breakfast with the others, and ate inside away from the gale.

"Raymond tells us you found something interesting yesterday," Edouard said towards the end of the meal, when there were only a few lumps of brown, unsweetened oatmeal left in their bowls.

"Yes," he nodded. "At the lowest level in the parking garage there were four or five skeletons, tangled together so I couldn't see exactly how many they were."

They turned towards him. Raymond's face was bright with expectation, like a father at his child's first recital. From their unsurprised looks Raymond had already told them what they'd found, but now they wanted to hear it from him. He fell into the modus he always did when he had to speak in public, as in his first and only job in the city, or in the countless debriefings he had done before that.

"Beneath the first floor were two basement levels," he said. "Both were flooded to the ceiling and the cars thrown about. I saw no signs of survivors. The skeletons at the bottom level were near the back wall. A school of freshwater eels were foraging on the skeletons. I had too little air to retrieve a skull for identification."

Now Raymond looked so proud he started to feel embarrassed.

"Eels?" Gabriele said. "They were eaten by eels?"

"Yes," he said. "They had apparently been there for a while."

"And you didn't just swim out of there when you saw them?"

"The eels didn't attack, if that's what you mean," he said, smiling.

"Eels," Gabriele said again and shuddered. Jens snickered, and Raymond kept on grinning.

"We sorely lack data on how fast eels eat human flesh," Marten, who he remembered was a forensic dentist, said drily. "Otherwise we could have guessed how long the victims had been there."

Edouard snorted. "We still can. How clean were the skeletons? Most of the flesh left, or just a little?"

"Just a little," he said. "Slivers of gristle, on the arms and legs and ribs. A little hair." He recalled how the hair had billowed in the motion from the long, slick eel bodies as well as his sudden approach. He remembered an acquaintance who worked as a search and rescue diver. The acquaintance once told him that a colleague had developed an intense phobia against hair because she once had to pull from a wreck corpses whose only remaining sign of humanity had been their still-billowing hair.

"What color hair?" Marten said. "Did you see any clothes?"

"Brown hair," he said. "Light brown. Dark blond. Ginger. Just some rags left on the bodies. Can't recall if I saw any footwear."

Edouard glanced at Marten and sighed. "That doesn't tell us much. At least, yes, they have probably been there for a good while, most likely from when the hurricane and flooding hit."

"Any possibility those could have been the survivors we heard?" Gabriele said, looking at Raymond.

"The signals we heard was weeks after the hurricane passed," Raymond said. "Perhaps they did get help after all. I checked all the levels above, including the roof. There had been survivors there, but they were gone, hopefully rescued earlier . . . "

Gabriele nodded quickly.

"There was a central staircase and elevators," he said. "An air pocket may have formed there, but it wouldn't have lasted very long."

Marten nodded. "That's right. But if they were in the elevator, for example, would we have been able to hear them?"

Jens shrugged. "Hard to say. Did you see if the doors to the stairwell or the elevators were open?"

"I followed the central structure because there were fewer cars along it than near the outer walls," he said. "The doors I saw were shut. But there wasn't enough air to check them closely."

Raymond shifted anxiously in the seat, yet continued to smile and nod at him.

172

"It must have been terrible," Leah said, glancing at Raymond. "Finding them like that."

He thought about it. It had been terrible when he thought the skeletons might be his family, but less so after that. "It was tense and rushed," he said. "But the eels were beautiful." He immediately regretted his words. No one would understand that.

But Marten and Edouard nodded, faces calm, even solemn. Only Jens snickered a little and he stopped almost immediately when he realized he was the only one laughing.

"I'm sure they were," Raymond said quietly.

( )

The world was vast and open and seemed to consist of only air and water, waves and sky. The days remained foggy and white; even the dirty floodwater seemed to pale and take on the same hue as it reflected in its waves. The rain stopped after a day or so and he thought the team would resume their work. But instead, several of them remained in the camp, sauntering into and out of the tents, while they fetched objects or crates, prepared the evening meal, pumped water from the filtering barrel into plastic cans and hauled them back to the closed tents.

The first day he spent recuperating after the dive the team seemed busy, constantly on the move. But on the second day, when he mostly sat on the edge of the cot, or took short trips to the latrine site away from the main tent and behind a cluster of bushes, he saw them shuttling between the tents, carrying only one or two objects at a time, returning a little later to pick up another item they easily could have brought with them on the first pass. Moreover, little was done quickly; in fact the more he watched the team members, the more they seemed to be stalling and wasting time, dragging each little task out for as long as possible without it being completely obvious that they were buying time, like employees extending the last chores for the day out so they didn't have to start on something new and could leave on the dot. Was Leah and Raymond's team paid by the hour or had they united in some sort of protest to delay the work?

After more observations it was clear that the only person who was moving about and working at anything close to a normal tempo was Raymond, and that he had not noticed the slowness of the others. Even Leah seemed to be acting only in response to Raymond's requests, or when they were solving a task together, such as lifting a heavy object wrapped in dark fabric from the small tents to the neon-yellow rowboat. He kept his eye on them while making himself as unobtrusive as possible.

26.

An Empty Lifeboat Floating at Sea

On the third day of recuperating in the camp, Jens came over to his cot and said: "Let's go fishing."

He looked at Jens. Was the man serious?

"You can walk again, yes?"

He nodded. "Fishing?" he said.

"Yes," Jens grinned. "Since you are so good at finding eels."

He frowned.

"Relax, it was just a joke," Jens said.

"Do you really have fishing equipment?" he said. Where had they gotten that from? "I didn't know that was standard for identification teams."

"It's not," Jens said. "But come and I'll show you. Dress warmly and put your waders on. I'll wait for you in the rowboat."

He pulled on the waterproof garment, and the jacket over the sweater. It was cool instead of cold, but windy, so he brought the thin leather gloves and the mesh scarf as well, and limped down to the edge of the mound.

In the bottom of the neon-yellow inflatable lay the wrapped, oblong object he had seen Raymond and Leah carry out from the small tent and place in the vessel.

"We're taking this with us," Jens said, patting the black plastic. "If it smells bad, just ignore it."

"Are we burying a corpse?" he asked.

"Yes, we are," Jens said, with a finality that revealed the physician was expecting resistance.

"At sea?"

"No, just somewhere not too close and where we can find it again. We have to mark the site exactly on the map when we come back."

He nodded and remembered the conscientious way Raymond had moored the other corpses they had found further out in the city. "Why are we taking this body away?"

"We're done with it," Jens said, "but we can't keep it in the camp because we have no ice. Do you know how to paddle?"

"Yes," he said and entered the small vessel.

❨❩

Gassy decomposition leaked up from the dark bundle whenever a wave buffeted them too suddenly, or they accidentally made the body shift on the inflatable's yielding surface while they sliced the floodwater with their paddles to make good speed through the street-canyons.

"So what was special about this cadaver?" he said, to distract his mind from the smell.

"Why we had it in the camp, you mean?" Jens said without turning towards him. The emergency medic was sitting in front of him on the opposite side of the vessel.

"Yes," he said over the sound of the oars and the water.

"You have to ask Raymond about that. He wanted to identify the body properly, even though we can't do that now that we're offline. And when the others left they took most of the post-mortem equipment with them."

"Really?" he said, not being entirely certain what Jens meant. He had to make the medic talk more.

"Yah," Jens said in his distinct, mid-continental accent. "Raymond wanted us to do a full post-mortem, in the tiny tent. We don't even have sterile water except for a few bags of intravenous saline, and I wasn't going to let Raymond have that."

"Why not?" he said, still trying to piece together what had happened.

"It's Raymond," Jens said. "He gets these bouts of compulsion, wants to do it one hundred percent correctly, even without the proper equipment. Of course we didn't find out who the person was, only water in their lungs and some broken bones."

"So that's why you can only do . . . dental analysis?" he said.

"Correct. We were still going to try and identify the corpse, but the fingertips and toes were gone. We don't have equipment for DNA analysis, and even if we did, we'd have no power to run the electrophoresis, plus it's near impossible to avoid contamination in the field like this."

"Is that why the other team members left?"

For a short moment their breathing was the only thing audible over the splashing of the paddles. Then Jens finally said: "No, they left with the other groups. They were ordered to. We all were."

"To other disaster areas?"

Jens scoffed. "There are so many of those now, there aren't enough emergency teams to cover half of it. Floods, wildfires, tornadoes, multiple catastrophes on every continent. People like us are shipped out, along with the local military, rescue workers, volunteers, but it's just a drop in the ocean, and has been for the last few years. Much of it isn't even mentioned in the news, because it only gets picked up by regional or national media, and because the international affairs sections are already saturated. But I must say I hadn't expected to do this on the continent where I was born and grew up."

"Did the others go home?" he said, his heart beating faster.

"Yes," Jens said. "Huge forest fires in the east, along with serious drought, so little water to put the conflagrations out with. No continent's sending emergency teams overseas any longer, there's too much to do at home."

He swallowed but said nothing, trying to digest the news. "So why didn't you leave too?" he finally said. "You and the others."

"We were going to," Jens said. "But Raymond refused. He wanted to fix things here, he said, finish things up properly. I don't know why it's so important that we stay here, though. It's not like they could call us deserters. I think it's just Raymond. He can't face another site, another disaster, even if we know they're out there."

"I thought Leah was your leader?"

"She is," Jens said, "but only in name, after what happened on the eastern continent. This is Raymond's show now."

Before he could ask what had happened on the eastern continent, they came to a cluster of cars that they had to navigate carefully past. Then they decided that was as good a place as any other to leave the body.

(   )

They hoisted the paddles out of the water and put down onto the yellow rubber, wetting the bottom of the vessel. Jens threaded a short piece of sailing line through the metal ring at the end of the body bag and tied it with a knot, not as deftly as Raymond had done, but with obvious practice. Then they crouched, took one end of the black plastic each, and heaved the body into the brown flood. The vessel's rubber sides squeaked and the stagnant water splashed, then went still. To his surprise the body was not weighted, but floated, with the air bulging the bag like the sail of a man o' war jellyfish. Jens tied the other end of the rope to a chain link fence that was still standing in the water, perhaps because its meshed and insubstantial form had allowed the flood to stream through it instead of toppling it. That reminded him of two things: his father's oft-repeated advice to be like bamboo and bend instead of break, and a fairy tale from his mother's country about a tin soldier who remained true to his beliefs and staunchly upright even through great adversity. He had not yet found out which country's solution was the best.

178

With the cadaver secured, they sat down and took out the paddles again. Jens was still in the lead and took a wrong turn on the way back to the meadow. Now the ocean was closer, but with it a noticeably stronger motion in the flood-water. They were not far from the street-canyons that led out to the sea.

"We're heading away from the camp," he said on Jens' third wrong turn.

"It's still early," Jens said. "Didn't you say you wanted to go fishing?"

"Don't you have some kind of work to do?" he said. "More corpses to identify?"

Jens laughed. "Leah and Raymond can say whatever the hell they want. We haven't been paid for weeks."

"I thought your organization had big investment accounts," he said.

That's what we all though, Jens huffed.

They paddled on until they reached a street with a view to the sea, not the place he had been with Raymond, but another, similar site. Above them the wind creaked through broken steel beams and clinked in blown-out glass. Here and there draperies waved from the windows like the kerchiefs of fairytale maidens trapped in castle towers, but torn and ripped by the wind and weathered ragged and gray. Through the narrow concrete canyon they could see the ocean, white and frothy and stretching beyond their sight into the mist.

"I nearly drowned this spring," he said, before he thought to stop himself.

Jens turned and looked at him. "On the way here?"

"No," he said. "Before I knew about the flooding."

"Really?" Jens said. "How did you survive?"

"By pure luck," he said.

"We all need a bit of that," Jens said.

They drew in the oars and made certain they were drifting slowly back towards the city and not further out into the ocean. Then Jens gave him a handle of smooth, worn plastic, with a thick fishing line wound around its length, studded with brightly-colored plastic lures. "Mind the hooks," Jens said. "Don't get them into your fingers, or the boat."

They carefully unreeled the fishing lines over the inflatable's side and sank the lures into the water.

"Now we wait," Jens said. "The best part of fishing."

"We shouldn't eat anything we get," he said. "With all the chemicals in the water."

"You just try and catch us an eel," Jens laughed.

☾☽

They bobbed on the wavelets for a long time, in a relaxed, comfortable silence.

"There used to be a factory not far from here," he said after a good while, his voice almost vanishing in the quiet.

"Is it still standing?" Jens said, gazing towards the horizon.

"I don't know," he said. "But we used to be able to smell it and I haven't since I returned."

Jens nodded. "Then at least the production has stopped, most probably because of the hurricane."

He nodded. "Have you been to a place like this before?"

Jens pulled at the line to make the lures move in the water. "I've been to many flooded places, but not as large as this."

"When did you arrive?"

"Sometime after the hurricane. By then those who had been able to evacuate before the hurricane arrived were long gone, and most of the critically injured and sick had been airlifted out right after. The transportation of those who were still left had just started. Things looked very much the same as now, only with worse weather."

They drifted for a while longer. The scent of hydrocarbons wafted up from the licking and dipping surface, making him queasy.

"I'm actually a little glad we didn't leave when the others did," Jens said.

He looked at Jens.

"It did feel too early to leave. Raymond was right about that. It would have felt as if we were running away and just ditched the people that were still here and had no way of evacuating. We did find a few survivors, and helped them find transportation out."

"So there were many people left?"

"Right when we arrived, there was a surprising number of people still here," Jens said. "Some thought they could stay because they had apartments or houses that sat above the water. Others thought the hurricane warning was exaggerated and that it would just be a strong storm that would pass quickly. Yet others had no way of getting out of the city or no place to stay or no funds to pay for lodging elsewhere. But as long as the flooding remained, power and sewage couldn't be restored, and without that it was nearly impossible to make food and have clean water. After a while we found more people who had died from dehydration or starved to death than had drowned or been killed by structures collapsed by the hurricane."

"That's terrible," he said.

"It's not as unusual as you might think," Jens said. "Not even on this continent. Before I met Leah and Raymond, I worked on an ambulance crew in my hometown. We used to find people who had starved to death, and not just old people who lived alone or addicts on the streets, but regular people who ended up not having enough money for food, who had lost their jobs and social benefits. Lots of people not even the food banks and charity volunteers had reached."

He made a sympathetic sound.

"It's always that way," Jens said. "Even natural disasters hit the poor the hardest. We've found the fewest survivors, or even dead people, in the big houses outside of the city center. I guess the owners were rich enough to have other properties they could escape to before the hurricane hit. "

"Did you ever reach the old neighborhoods to the southwest, by the lake?"

"The lake with the artificial sand beach?"

He nodded, wondering if the white wooden building of the boat club was still there, the pines still swaying in the wind.

Jens thought. "We might have reached the outskirts, but it was so far away we only went there a few times. Other teams were much closer."

"Any survivors?"

Jens shook his head. "I don't think so. Maybe a guy with three small kids. Those are the only ones I can remember clearly."

"Lots of dead?"

"Not really," Jens said. "The few houses we checked were empty."

"So what about recently?" he said. "Any survivors now?"

"No," Jens said. "We haven't found anyone alive for weeks, well, except for you."

"No wonder you were so eager to save me," he smirked, turning the new information over in his mind.

"Haha, funny," Jens said, but laughed a little, before growing serious again. "You know what this place reminds me of?"

He shook his head.

"Some years back I worked in search and rescue in the southern ocean. You know, for adventure, a chance to see the seventh continent - the great white desert, and all that. Not much air or ship traffic there, but enough to occasionally need assistance, especially in the spring and summer when it's busiest. Slightly north of the continent, far away from anywhere else, is an island mostly covered in ice looking like a damn fortress, with a crown of piercing cliffs that drop right into the sea. The place is so remote and barren that only birds and seals live there. Well, we received a distress signal from a ship via the search and rescue system on the new navigation satellites, and the positioning was clear, coming from the west side of that island. It took hours just to get out there, and when we arrived, we found an orange life raft, you know, one of those circular ones with a plastic cover, floating on the sea. It was empty, there were signs that it had been used, but there was nobody there. We thought the sailors may have fallen overboard in the strong wind, so we searched the area for a sunken vessel, people in survival suits, or lights from emergency beacons, but saw only ocean and waves. Whoever had launched that raft was simply gone and any ship they had traveled with had sunk without a trace."

He made another sympathetic noise at the back of his throat and imagined the Antarctic island and the empty life raft.

"Perhaps it was not so strange," Jens said. "It's a very remote place with extremely harsh weather. Once a ship has trouble out there, they must either wait a long time for rescue, even with strong satellite signals, or be lucky enough to sit on a reef, or in solid lifeboats. That's bad since a ship can go down in less than thirty minutes, no matter how big it is. And the conditions there are so violent, you need a good measure of luck to survive and even more in order to be found."

He nodded.

"I feel like I did back then," Jens said, pulling at his fishing line once more. "At the end of an empty world. Only this time everyone else is here with me."

"I know what you mean," he said.

Finally Jens said: "I'm feeling seasick now. Let's go back."

They pulled the fishing lines up as gently and as carefully as they had cast them out. Jens' line had caught some plant matter and rotten cardboard, and that was all they got. They paddled the long way back to the meadow slowly and with little talk. When they finally glided up on the drowned grass, their arms and backs were sore and it had grown dark.

In the camp no one asked where they had been all day. Over dinner Jens mentioned that they had gone fishing, but no one commented on it.

"Well, that explains tonight's dinner, then!" Raymond said and laughed, open-mouthed, pieces from the canned salmon and pasta meal still on his tongue and lips.

27.

The Heat Death at the End of the Universe

He reflected on what Jens had told him, that the team were now volunteers, working off Raymond's money, which, perhaps plentiful, had to have some limit. And what would they do, now that the chance of finding any remaining survivors seemed to have run out and the team no longer had the means to identify the dead they did locate? With the rowboat and the punt they'd be able to cross the flooded streets and reach the roads that led north. But perhaps the team knew it would be difficult to find paid work elsewhere, or maybe they had, like him, no home to leave for?

During his service he'd met others who said, during drunken, sometimes weepy circumstances, that they didn't have anything to return to; because their spouse had left them, or their new workplace had restructured, or the spot at the university they'd been accepted to couldn't be reserved. He'd felt differently. There was plenty to go home for: family, friends, even a job if he wanted it. But he wasn't certain that was what he wanted, and therefore, when the contract period was over, he did exactly what he had told himself he wouldn't do: extended it even further. He saw enough people who had done that several times over, and who would keep going until they retreated to instructor work only, were dismissed due to health issues, or died in action. He had been prepared to meet soldiers like that and felt strongly motivated not to travel down that road. He wouldn't come home hurt and return to the unit only a few months later, stitched-up and damaged, but craving more. He had plans for afterwards; the service was just temporary, something he had to do, for himself as well as for others. But as he ought to have known from experience, being away changes you, much of it only noticeable when you come home.

"We knew you'd stay on," his old comrades said as he returned after the holiday and they laughed and hugged each other, in another camp, another country, yet all eerily similar to the previous places they had been, in much the same way as large cities start to look the same once you've seen enough of them. "We knew, because a true killer instinct is so rare," they said. It was supposed to be flattering, but it made him feel that a darkness yawned beneath them, and only the knowledge that going home would be worse than going through with what he'd decided on made him continue.

He tried to go home once more, but that turned out worse than the first time and he knew then that ruination was upon him. It became easier to give in to going back, instead of trying to fight it. But then everything had washed over him and became a part of him and he wanted nothing more than to leave and had managed to convince them to cut him loose, like a shark on a too-thin fishing line. Now he couldn't remember what he told the medical officer, only that it had probably sounded as displaced and uprooted as he had felt, and that had been his ticket out. Nor could he recall exactly what he'd done after he left the camp or where he'd gone, only that months later he had found himself in an isolation ward in a hospital at home, being checked for infectious tropical diseases after having been repatriated by the embassy in the last country he had stayed in. He assumed he had changed so much during his course of freedom that it would be enough to make him stay, and it did. Now some of the sensation from his first time at home, the feeling that he would never be able to return to how things were and how he had been, gnawed at him. But this time it was different; this time it was the city that had changed, not him.

( )

The evening meal was as quiet and calm as always. He looked at the others and tried to discern the reason they stayed behind in the city. Was it because they agreed with Raymond that it was too soon to leave, like Jens, or was it out of an even simpler sense of duty, or something entirely else? Love? Affection? There didn't seem to be much of that between Leah and Raymond, except for a remaining sliver of professional respect. Edouard and Martin were clearly personal friends, as were Gabriele and Jens, with maybe something more between them. The younger team members seemed to respect their two older colleagues well enough, but who knew what had happened in the past and what the team didn't talk about during their quiet gatherings.

His arms and shoulders were sore after the previous day's paddling. The canvas on the cot was drawn tightly across its frame, but being fabric, it could not avoid yielding under his weight, giving no relief to his aches and pains. He turned, still uncomfortable; shifted onto his back; that didn't help either. He could smell his own body; how long was it since he had had a proper shower with soap and warm water? He sniffed his skin again, expecting the reek of perspiration and unwashed hair, but instead there was just a musky scent with a strange, flowery undertone. He hadn't been in smelling range of aftershave or cologne since he went home for Christmas, not even a stick of deodorant since that had disappeared with the large backpack when the cabin was flooded. Was this his natural, unmasked scent, or would the stench gradually increase? He hoped to be gone from the city by then.

In the gray predawn light, he rose and moved quietly to the table behind his cot, the orange plastic case, and the thick wire that coiled out of it to the small solar-cell panel that was rolled out by the closed tent flaps. He hunched instead by the solar panel to find some indication of how the recharging was progressing.

186

"It doesn't work," someone whispered behind him.

He flinched, but remained hunched, made no sudden motion that might wake the others.

"The weather's been bad for so long we haven't been able to use the solar panel," Gabriele continued.

"For the laptop?" he whispered.

Gabriele nodded. "The laptop, the Internet, the rest of the world, or what's left of it now."

"Left of it?" he said, a little louder than he had intended to.

"You haven't been further south?" Gabriele said.

"No," he said.

"Go back to sleep," Gabriele said. "I'll tell you tomorrow."

Gabriele's shadowy form passed a stack of crates and returned to her cot. Most of the team members slept behind a few boxes for the illusion of privacy. He lay down behind his own wall of containers and thought about the heat death of the universe.

Some time, billions of years into the future, the universe would have expanded so much that the stars would no longer be visible from one another. Beings capable of traveling vast distances in space would see individual stars blink like lone lighthouses along a desolate coast. All the energy in the universe would have been recycled from nebulae to newborn stars to supernovae so many times it would be entirely spent and no longer could be used for ordered structures such as planets or stars or galaxies. One by one the lonely, separated stars would blink out and the sky would turn completely dark. For a while photons would be visible in the black vastness, like fireflies on a moonless night or luminescent plankton in the abyssal depths, before they too died down in a sea of everlasting night. Then, all light would be gone from the universe. Was that what every being felt at the moment of their own death?

☾☽

The next morning, Gabriele broke the breakfast silence by saying:

"I'm taking our friend with me to see if we can find more bodies."

Raymond looked up from a bowl of cold, milk-filled gruel. "Be careful," the pathologist said.

"Of course," Gabriele said. "We'll go in the inflatable."

Leah glanced at them above her bowl.

"We'll be back by lunch," Gabriele added quickly.

"All right," Leah said. "But be fast about it and don't forget to mark the map when you return so your trip isn't a complete waste of time, as some of your colleagues' sojourns are."

After he had rinsed his bowl and spoon in water from the filter and placed them beneath his cot, he pulled the waders and the jacket on. Along with the smell of synthetic fabric, the musky-flowery scent he had sensed earlier lifted from the clothing. As he limped down the slope to the inflatable to wait for Gabriele, she came striding after him in her bright red coveralls, holding two bottles of water in her hands.

"How's your leg?" Gabriele said.

"Better," he said.

"I'm sure Raymond weighs a ton," she laughed. "You were lucky not to break the bone clean off."

He smiled.

Gabriele slid across the rubbery side and took out one of the white oars from the bottom of the craft. "Jens showed you how to paddle yesterday?" she asked.

"Yes," he said and boarded the rowboat carefully so as not to stretch his leg suddenly or put too much weight on it. He sat down on the rubber surface, the boots of his waders squeaking against the neon-yellow material.

Gabriele released the knot that held the rowboat to the punt, and tossed the rope into the dirty water.

They paddled down the road, away from the meadow, but in the opposite direction from that in which Jens had taken him the day before, and towards the industrial area in the east. After a while the sun burned through the mist and made the day bright and hot. They heard bird chatter, and a large flock of sparrows took to the air from a roof above them. Water vapor rose from the flooded streets and made the air humid and smelling of rotten plants, old gasoline, and sewage. Further east, the water grew lower and the surface became sticky with half-degraded debris.

"All right, this is far enough," Gabriele said and rested her paddle in the plastic grip on the side of the inflatable. Brown, viscous drops dripped from the scuffed blade into the sluggish floodwater. "Ugh, it stinks."

He rested his oar too and glanced around, but could not see any signs of corpses nearby. He thought he smelled decomposing flesh, but that might be the water itself. The smelly liquid reminded him of a dream he had had in the cabin where a dark lake high in the mountains dried up into mud and all the organisms that lived in its depths were choked and buried in the lifeless substrate. In that dream he had thrown himself onto the ground and clawed into the sludge to save the buried fish, but found nothing but lifeless bodies.

He scanned the nearby car wrecks that lay half-drowned and turned over, and the balconies in the buildings above them. Dirty rainwater had flowed from the verandas so frequently that stains and streaks coursed down them like tears trailing down a face. The tear-tracks suited the ruination of the structures.

"Is there a dead body here?" he finally said. "I can't see any."

Gabriele turned and laughed, one water bottle in her hand. "No, I just wanted to get far enough away that we could talk without being heard." She cracked the cap open with a twist of her hand and held the container up in a toast.

He took the other bottle and returned her greeting, before he opened the cap and drew a small sip of the warm but sweet-tasting water. Then he pulled his jacket off, rolled it up to protect it from the moisture that floated between the bulging ridges at the bottom of the craft, and drank some more.

Gabriele unzipped and pulled down the top of her coveralls, its sleeves flapping down her back. Her black cotton T-shirt had multiple rings of dried moisture beneath the arms and around the neck. "It's hot," Gabriele said, wiping the sides of her nose and upper lip. "Too bad I left my sunscreen at the camp." She winked at him and laughed.

He grinned at her, lifted his bottle and drank again.

(()

"Did you ever reach the neighborhoods in the southwest, by the lake?" he said, thinking now was a good time to ask the disaster psychologist about it.

"Old villas, large gardens?" Gabriele said.

He nodded, and for a moment thought he could smell the wood polish and mowed lawn of the house he grew up in.

"We rescued a father with young children in the area," Gabriele said. "I remember that because he complained that we were late and then Jens talked back at him. Later on we found someone in a hallway, but they had clearly died of natural causes. Is that where your family lives?"

He nodded.

Gabriele smiled, but it was gentle instead of celebratory at the correct guess. "We didn't find many people out there," she said. "We only checked a few houses and they seemed evacuated; closets empty, toiletries gone, no cars in the driveways. Other teams might have rescued some people too."

"Do you know where the survivors were taken?"

"Everywhere there was room for them, any sports hall or school or old hotel, and that still had functional roads so the buses could go there," Gabriele said. "It was so chaotic and crowded that people had to be registered when they arrived at the rescue centers, not when they were found.

"If I were home now," Gabriele said after a while, "I would have gone to the beach with my friends, or to the old waterlily ponds in the botanical garden to read in the shadow of their broad old arches."

"Where is home?" he said.

Gabriele mentioned a city far south on the continent.

"How are things there?" he said.

"Terrible," she said. "A little like here, in fact. It was hit hard by the hurricane and the flood, but there are more canals than here, so maybe the water's drained away by now."

"I'm sorry to hear that," he said.

Gabriele nodded. "The last we heard was that fewer people evacuated there than here. I don't know why, but the warning seems to have been issued much later. There's supposed to be many people left there, even now, but not like here, not like us."

He looked at her, knowing what she meant, but since he didn't want to admit the defeat of his city he remained silent.

"I'm certain a lot of people went to the mountains," Gabriele said. "To the north, in the country, and to the east, away from the sea. But there have been wildfires too, and droughts, the earth so dry it cracked and started to blow away on the winds, turning the old rivers and canals into clay and leaves, so I don't know."

"But you still want to go home?"

"Yes, of course, are you mad?" she said, tears in her eyes. "This isn't my home, it never will be. I am far from home, that's why we're leaving very soon, and you should come with us."

He glanced at her, then swallowed. That was not what he wanted, but he had been expecting it, had been waiting for it since he understood that they were just pretending to work. "Who?" he said.

"Jens, Marten, Edouard, and me, maybe even Leah."

"If all of you leave, then Raymond will have no choice but to follow," he said.

"No, he won't," Gabriele said, shaking her head. "He's too stubborn, too stupid. Born stupid!"

He wanted to laugh, but refrained from it. "If it's so bad in the south," he said instead, "where are you heading then?"

"North, of course," she said. "You told us yourself, there are camps there, water, housing. We can evacuate to there, like intelligent human beings, instead of staying here, like dumb monkeys. Before you came, we thought we were trapped in this city with Raymond."

He stared at her. He had not expected his words and actions to have that effect. He cursed inside. He ought to have told them less, been more stingy with the information, instead of wagging his tongue so much. Now his words had set something in motion he couldn't control.

"Don't look so surprised," Gabriele said. "It's not your fault. It's just how things are now."

"But not always?"

Gabriele shook her head. "No," she said. "We've worked together for many years, many places, many disasters, but finally chaos reached us too. What is it they say? She who lives by the sword shall die by the sword, and she who lives by disaster shall be undone by one. You must know that proverb, since you were a soldier."

"Did Raymond tell you that?" he said, feeling like he'd been slapped in the face. How much had Raymond guessed about him and told his colleagues?

Gabriele shook her head. "No, we saw it on you. We've worked with many different military units in the past. Maybe even yours."

❨❩

He remained quiet for a long time, while he tried to picture the camp and the city with only Raymond and Leah and himself in it.

Gabriele drained the last of her water. "You have to come with us," she said. "Because you know the way out."

"Simply head north," he said. "And stay away from the industrial area east of here."

"But you found a safe and quick way in," she said, squinting at him in the sunlight. "Getting out could take us several days."

"There are probably many ways out of the city."

"You do know we're running out of food, and water too?" Gabriele said. "We're eating well now, but it's not that far away in time."

He didn't know, but he hadn't expected the team's supplies to last forever, particularly not after weeks alone in the field. "If you leave," he said, "there will be more for those who stay behind."

Gabriele scoffed. "I am not saying this only because we need help to find a way out," she said. "I am also telling this for your own sake. You do not wish to remain here with Raymond, no matter how harmless he seems. Take it from someone who's stayed behind with him for years, in other places."

"Then why didn't you leave when the other emergency teams did?"

She looked at him. "You really don't know what happened," she said. It was a statement, not a question. "The team was originally twice as large as it is now."

"Really?" he said, scanning her features for signs of deception.

She accepted his scrutiny by calmly meeting his eyes. "When the order for all the teams to evacuate came, Raymond told us to stay behind with him. But half the team refused, saying it was too dangerous, pointless, that they wanted to go home to find their loved ones, so they gave their notices and left with the others."

"Why didn't you evacuate when you had the chance?"

Gabriele shrugged. "It didn't feel right at the time, it was clear there were countless dead in the city and they needed to be identified, or at least tagged for future work. They have no one else to speak for them. But now we can't access any records, and the chances of identifying anyone have become very, very slim. There are only remnants of people here now," she said, looking at him.

He bowed his head in reluctant agreement. "You're right," he said.

"Then you'll leave with us?"

"No," he said. "But I can mark the route out on the map for you."

Gabriele seemed to take his decision as a personal affront, or perhaps she felt that she had parted with sensitive information to no avail and regretted trusting him with it. Whatever the cause, she quickly decided to return to the camp, saying that she had promised Leah to be back before noon and that the heat was bothering her. They paddled in a strained silence back to the meadow.

28.

In the Crypt at Night

Now that he was aware of it, it was apparent that something was going on. There was a hum of tension between the team members, an avoidance of eye contact, and a silence that could only mean something more. Raymond disappeared, and he didn't know where to, and Leah did the same. He assumed they were on some business together, something they couldn't or didn't want to share with the rest of the team.

"Edouard and I could use some help today," Marten told him after breakfast as they both stood rinsing their bowls. The stream from the tap of the water barrel had been reduced to a thin trickle, the filter beginning to clog after weeks of continuous use.

He marveled at how much Marten, with his short brown hair that grew upwards at a jaunty angle, and calm, gray eyes above a freckled nose, resembled a young man he had served with, a soldier who seemed to never falter no matter how difficult things were or how warm it got. Charlie was calm and courteous, with an effortless optimism he himself had never managed to generate. Charlie was the one who instructed their translators, who was the main contact for the local forces they worked with, who led negotiations to persuade or cajole parties. Charlie worked closely with intelligence and they had probably instructed him many times, yet he managed to retain an air of trustworthiness and honesty.

Somehow, Charlie had managed to persuade some local men in power and their own officers to have an artesian well built in a village near the camp. Charlie helped set up the pumping mechanism himself, long thin tubing that was threaded down into the pipe until it reached the source. The well and its hand pump was opened with as much fanfare as the locals could produce, inviting the whole village and the soldiers to a party that ended late at night without any violent incidents. The cool, clean drops from the pump fell glittering through the sunlight, even more beautiful and valuable than diamonds. On the way back from reconnaissance they sometimes stopped by the well to fill water.

Officially, the well was just a gift from command to the local communities for hosting the unit in their troubled midst, but where the money for the well came from, coalition or contractors or even some aid organization, and whether it was an exchange for prisoners of war, payment for information about some high-value target, a kind of public relations stunt, or simply the realization of a humanitarian ambition on Charlie's behalf, he never found out. The young man talked pleasantly to him, smiling, but offered him as little actual information as possible, just as he imagined him doing in the closed meetings with the local powers. Yet Charlie was more personal and open with just about everyone else in the unit. Had he disliked Charlie, he would have resented him for it, but instead he took an unexpected, platonic liking to the man, and thought of him as a kind of archetypal shadow, only one that cast light instead of darkness. As a consequence, he didn't mind Charlie's distance, which he nevertheless thought ridiculous since they had almost the same training and capabilities, but accepted it benignly, while he tried to eavesdrop on Charlie's stories to the others as much as he could.

He always wondered how Charlie managed to do what he did: sit across the table from and exchange toasts and smiles with people whom only force and necessity kept them from attacking. He never solved the mystery of whether that the humane outlook that everyone pursued their own interests and was at heart well-intentioned towards their own, or caused by something else, something more naive. Because when Charlie and his small retinue followed the local politicians, warlords, bandits, smugglers, or holy men into the houses or huts or tents for social exchange and negotiations, he was stationed outside, at the highest elevation possible, aiming behind high magnification. Thus he never learned how to persuade the enemy to do as he wanted and not as they said they would.

(( ))

Now he couldn't tell if Marten really needed help, or whether it was part of a continued attempt at persuading him to leave with them, perhaps orchestrated by Jens or Gabriele. Nevertheless, he followed a beaming Marten to the nearest of the small tents on the mound. There the forensic dentist pulled the tent flap aside for him so he could duck and enter, welcomed by a smiling Edouard. He felt like a local warlord in a hostile country invited in for talks about ceasefire and ransom.

"I'm sorry that we have been too busy to talk much with you," Marten began.

"It is because we wanted to finish up the rest of our work here before we left," Edouard said. "For the same reason, we were also prevented from accompanying you on your expeditions into the city."

"I'm sure you have seen a lot worse," he said, addressing Edouard. He dared not look at Marten too much, in case he would start to see too many differences from Charlie. He wanted to remain for a bit longer in the illusion that Marten could teach him about Charlie by proxy and thus reveal the secrets of his onetime colleague. Instead he studied Edouard. Now the forensic anthropologist looked taller and more cultured than he had seen him before. He imagined that Edouard, who, judging by his accent, called the center of the continent home, would spend his time in locales that smelled of old books and velvet upholstery and gleaming parquet floors, with the gentle sound of pendants tinkling in lead-crystal chandeliers above. The man seemed to come from an entirely different world than Marten, Gabriele, and Jens, even though they appeared to be the same age. He wondered how Edouard had ended up working for Leah and Raymond.

Behind Edouard stood a long steel table on spindly, foldable legs, a groove going down the middle of the horizontal surface. In the half darkness of the tent he could make out some lumpy shapes in its deeper recesses behind the table.

"Our work here in this city is a little unusual," Edouard explained. "As I'm sure Raymond and Gabriele have told you."

He nodded.

"This is the last one, and we could really need a hand with it," Marten said.

"Please put on two layers of these," Edouard said and held out a box of skin-colored medical gloves. At the bottom of the cardboard only four crumpled and flattened gloves were left. He lifted them out and shook them open before pulling them on gently so as not to pierce or overstretch them.

"Do they fit or does he need another size?" Edouard asked Marten.

Marten leaned forward and pulled at the tip of the gloves to see how much room was left between his fingers and the vinyl. "No, it's fine," Marten said. "This is the right size, and so are his fingers."

"Good," Edouard nodded and crouched to light a steel lantern that stood on the ground next to the forensic anthropologist. A dim, but steady yellow light filled the tent.

"Why don't you open the tent flap fully and roll it all the way up," Marten said, addressing him. "And tie the strings well so they don't fall down while we work."

He turned and collected the taupe fabric in his hands. Behind him, he heard Marten and Edouard lift something wet and heavy up onto the table.

( )

198

As opposed to the corpses Raymond and he had located and tagged in the water, this one had passed through the bloated stage, ruptured along the torso, been hollowed out by the decomposition, and then collapsed in on itself, like a neutron star. The skin looked as dark and hard as if it had been tanned, resembling some of the cadavers, mummified by the sun, he had seen during his service. The stench was slightly less than the bloated bodies he had found together with Raymond, and an almost imperceptible motion of air breathed in through the tent's opening, dispelling some of the odor of death as well as the nausea that rose in him.

He glanced at Edouard and Marten who were busy settling the limbs of the corpse on the table. Lastly, they checked the inside the body bag that they hadn't left anything out, and thankfully zipped the dark plastic up.

"I'll go rinse this," Edouard said and sloshed past him out of the tent. On hearing that sound he had to close his eyes for a moment.

"You'd better put a coat and apron on," Marten said. "There are some in the chest to your left."

Happy to have his attention pulled out of the fog of nausea, he clicked the clasps of the oblong steel box open and took out the uppermost dark blue coat and white plastic apron that lay folded inside it.

"This will be quick," Marten said and rolled out a pocketed cloth full of saws, pliers, tongs, blades, tweezers, files, and what looked like a spatula, out on the edge of the table. "Where are you from, by the way?"

Not even his body's insistent protest against the smell of decayed flesh could dampen the annoyance he felt, as he always did, at that question. "I'm from here," he said. "This city."

"No, I mean, where are your ancestors from," Marten said and smiled at him.

Hadn't that been the first thing Charlie asked him too? Only with an air of easy curiosity instead of prying dismissal, which was what he most often heard in that question, prompting him to indulge Charlie despite his misgivings. Now, as usual when faced with queries about his forebears, he was tempted to give the name of his mother's country, which was on the same continent as the city. But knowing full well what Marten meant, he reluctantly mentioned the name of his father's country on the eastern continent.

"I knew it," Marten laughed. "Though you're too tall to be from there."

"Where are you from, then?" he asked, keeping his voice even.

Marten smiled and named a capital north on the continent.

"How are things there?" he continued, since they were already asking each other slightly invasive questions. Perhaps Marten would be less guarded than Charlie had been.

Marten shrugged and smiled. "Flooded, I think. Maybe worse than here. Depends on how many dikes held in the hurricane or not. They've spent billions on building sea walls and reinforcing the dikes, but only a real storm and king tide could put that to the test."

"Don't you want to go home to see?"

"Not like Gabriele and Jens do," Marten said. "I will return eventually, but for now I feel needed elsewhere."

Wasn't Marten leaving with the others? "Don't you have family there?" he asked.

"When I started this work, it became my family," Marten said. "I'm staying with the group till Leah throws me out."

"God, you're full of shit," Edouard said from the tent opening and laughed.

"So are we all," Marten grinned. "Before all these disasters happened, our intestinal flora was all the rage in medical circles, the new wonder medicine, with the potential to cure everything from cancer to obesity to auto-immune diseases. So don't look down on that, please."

They both laughed loudly, and he couldn't help joining them, a brightness in the smelly murk of the tent.

☾

"Now," Marten said. "Our particular problem is that this person has passed so far into Arcadia, we will have to do something very special to see if we can find out who it is and give them a proper burial. And that's where you," Marten gun-pointed with both hands at him," come in."

"What do I need to do?" he said, relaxed by Marten's speech and their shared laughter.

"This might be a little scary," Marten said. "But if you start to feel queasy, think about what I've just said."

He met Marten's eyes.

Marten looked at Edouard. "Let's start with the right index finger first, that'll be the easiest and might give the best results."

"All right," Edouard said and pushed a notepad closer to him.

He avoided staring directly at the cadaver and instead kept his gaze on the luminous rectangle of the tent's opening.

Marten selected one of the razors on the cloth, then bent over the side of the corpse and did something he couldn't see.

"How does it look?" Edouard said.

"As if we might get something out of this, if we're really really careful and quick," Marten said.

"Hold up your right hand, please," Edouard said and he did.

Marten placed something he at first thought was a piece of rice paper or condom rubber on his right index finger. Edouard took hold of his hand, held it over a plastic inkpad, and rolled his finger calmly from one side to the other on the dark, moist surface. Then Marten pulled his hand over to the paper and rolled his finger slowly across the white surface beneath black letters that said "right index finger".

It was then he saw that what covered the tip of his digit was neither paper nor rubber, but a fingertip from the cadaver, a blackened nail protruding from it like a claw. Suddenly, and without his volition his knees gave way and he had to curl his hands around the edge of the steel table to remain upright.

"Easy, easy," Marten said, the same way he or Charlie would have calmed a village horse.

"I've got it," Edouard said and caught with cupped hands the fingertip that fell from the edge of the table.

"You could have fucking told me!" he yelled when his pulse finally caught up with the rest of his body. This time he didn't feel just sick, but also morally disgusted. Death and everything about it was shameful because it was a defeat. Now it all came back to him.

"And would you have lent science your hand if we had?" Marten said.

"Of course not!" he breathed, glaring at them both.

But then Edouard gave a laugh so deep and sincere he almost began to laugh too.

"Now, now, don't feel too sullied or shocked," Edouard said. "It is only the way we think about death that disgust us, how we label the sights and sounds and smells. Nature doesn't mind, nor does the corpse itself. It might actually be more galling to know we treated them with fear and loathing instead of the same respect that nature lets decay unfold with."

"You still should have asked for permission," he said, now feeling shameful for his initial reaction of disgust. The corpse had been someone's loved one and still was.

"We would have," Marten said. "If there had been any danger of hurting you at all."

He glanced down at the pad that was balancing on the edge of the table. There, a dark blue fingerprint stood out from the white, the ridges and whorls clearly visible, as clear as a signature. "Will you actually be able to find out who the person is . . . from these?" he asked.

"Yes, if their prints are in the database," Marten said.

"And when we're back online," Edouard said. "Whenever that happens."

"What do you do with the names if you identify someone out here?" he asked, voice shaking a little. They must have identified some corpses before the others in the team left.

"We put them on our list of people to be taken back to the coordination center and added to the databases of identified dead there," Marten said. "But since there is no coordination center anymore, we store the paperwork ourselves here in the camp."

"What happens when the dead are identified?"

"Then they are catalogued, and their closest relatives contacted," Edouard said. "So they finally can know what happened to their loved one, and that she or he is dead and simply not missing."

"Doesn't informing the bereaved bring them a lot of pain?"

Marten nodded. "It does, and sometimes they are angry at us for the message. Other times they don't believe it, and think we must have made some kind of mistake."

"This is of course, why it is so important everything is done correctly," Edouard said. "That there really are no errors."

"But when the family accepts it, what happens then?"

"Then they find closure," Marten said. "Maybe not then or very soon after, but slowly and surely, even if it takes a long time. And then they can begin to move on, no longer stuck in the not-knowing."

He almost smiled. It was so much like what he imagined Charlie would have said. On his first return he wondered if Charlie would still be among them, set on the long orbits that would take them further and further away from home. Almost as soon as he was back, he heard that Charlie had been offered a spot in intelligence, but that the negotiator had turned it down and gone home for good to run his family's business selling dishwashers and refrigerators and other kinds of home appliances. The others had laughed at Charlie's choice, saying that the man could really have accomplished something, what a waste of true potential, and he had laughed with them. But inside he had felt relieved. At least one of them had found their way back.

"All right," he said and held out his hands to Marten and Edouard. "Let's do the rest."

29.

The Company, Preparing to March Out

After the last corpse was examined and set adrift on the floodwater inside its own bag, they whiled away the days on the stench-filled banks of the mound, or in the main tent, organizing and reorganizing the equipment that was left. The dental records of the most recently examined corpses appeared by the orange case on the table in the back, the photocopied diagrams filled with handwritten notes were weighed down with a small stone to prevent them from flying away in the sunny breeze. Surgical equipment packed in plastic pouches and new scalpel blades still in silver foil turned up next to the paper records. At the same time crates and boxes changed place in the tent; some were emptied, others refilled, some vanished altogether, in a sleight of hand that was too large and too close for him to see the full extent of.

He thought he detected the process only because he was trained to look for small, yet intentional changes in the environment, and to specifically notice objects and items that were out of place or missing from their original positions. It was a long time since he had first played those games, and it had taken him a few tries to get them right, but once the observational mode had become a habit, it had never left him. He also had a clear feeling that his punt would vanish, so he rolled the drysuit up and kept it and his backpack safely beneath the cot at all times.

The process of surreptitious vanishing reminded him of the story of an ancient war in his father's country. One side had been beaten and banished to the periphery of the nation. But the faction used the time in exile well, strengthened its allies and alliances, rebuilt its forces out of sight of their old opponents, who failed to detect the subtle but definite shift in power that happened outside of the capital and the courts before it was too late and the once-ousted clan rose up again, sparking a new war, which they won, and pushed the other and once-so-powerful clan to the opposite end of the country.

( )

At night he could hear members of the team whisper or move among the cots and crates, but he pretended to be asleep and didn't ask what they were doing or interfere with their activities in any way. He considered it, however. A part of him thought that Raymond and Leah had a right to know. Why should grown people slink around their bosses instead of speaking up directly? Yet another side of him knew Raymond needed the shock, the nasty surprise they had in store for him, in order to be persuaded to come with them. He wanted Raymond to go with them, not remain as the brothers in arms he felt he had left behind, like Kaye, and Michael, and even Katsuhiro and Beanie. He wanted the pathologist to climb into the punt, lower the pole in the water, and travel with them up against the current of the flood, back to the submerged motorway, the broken high-rises, the overturned convoys, the barren towns, the abandoned suburbs, the sinkhole in the mudslide, the tent camps, the emergency housing, and the streets where bags of garbage still lined the pavement and people expected municipal services to return because there still was a community in which to live.

He recalled the empty and unfinished neighborhood he had crossed in the fall, with hundreds of houses that only lacked hedges in the garden or paint on the basement floor, and even more homes that were in the middle of completion, needing tiles on the roof, or a few dry walls. All those houses had room for new inhabitants, new families, and were out of the way of further hurricanes or floods. It was highly possible to resettle people, if only the political will was there. He imagined an end to his journey, away from the water, away from the wandering, and the feeling he had had when he brought the sand from the beach near his grandparents' town to the cabin and poured it into the hearth in the cabin rose up in him in a great warmth that was so strong it seemed almost real.

❆

The next morning at breakfast, the stacks of cardboard boxes and plastic crates had become visibly lower, and, he thought, impossible any longer to fail to notice. But Raymond only looked at him and said so loudly that everyone could hear it:

"You're from this city, what should we see while we're here?"

He almost laughed at the incongruity of the request, but the pathologist remained serious.

"What would you like to see?" he said as evenly as he could, as he would to any other visiting friend, under less moist circumstances. "What are you interested in?" He didn't dare glance at the others to see what they were thinking. Was Raymond trying to sound them out, to see who was still loyal or not, by behaving eccentrically? Or had the pathologist's mind began to unravel?

"It would have to be fairly close since transportation is difficult," Raymond smiled. "And ideally something that would appeal to a lot of different, although well-educated, and hard-working people."

Was there a hint of sarcasm or bitterness in the description? He didn't know Raymond well enough to see through the layers of innocuous-looking gentleness. He chewed on his spoon, the porridge already consumed. "The museum of art history is nearby," he finally said, relieved as the memory of having gone there with Michael a little over a year ago suddenly bloomed in his mind. He hadn't wanted to go, hadn't even known about the place; it had all been Michael's idea. "There are artifacts from all over the world, manmade as well as natural," he said, quoting what Michael had said to try to tempt him into visiting the museum. He trailed off and looked at Raymond.

"That sounds like just what we need. That'll be our task for today, esteemed colleagues!" Raymond grinned. "We must make time for play too, not just work, and some art would feed our souls a little, humans can't subsist on bread alone and so on!"

"That sounds like a wonderful idea, Raymond," Leah said, the only hint of insincerity an almost imperceptible glance of warning at Gabriele, who passed it on to Jens.

"Splendid!" Raymond said. "That's a deal, then, let's get going as soon as we can, now that we have full daylight!" The pathologist gave him a warm look. "And thank you, my friend, for showing an old man respect and making such a thoughtful suggestion."

He nodded at Raymond and rose to clean his spoon and bowl to hide his discomfort at having been pulled into the mind games of the group.

☾

"What the hell are you and Raymond up to?" Leah hissed behind him.

He was standing at the edge of the mound voiding his bladder into the inundation after having brushed his teeth. Aware of his rather vulnerable position and unable to cease his stream, he said as calmly as he could: "Raymond asked for a place to visit. What was I supposed to say?"

"What about 'No, the streets are flooded, we only have two vessels, we're hemmed in by dirty water'! What are you two playing at?"

"Nothing," he said, finally, relievingly done. "Look, I know it's a little odd to go sightseeing now, but the museum is very close. Only the first floors should be flooded, and it'll keep Raymond happy." He wanted to ask her why she couldn't just tell Raymond that she didn't want to go, but that was probably not what she wished to hear, so he didn't say it. Instead he pulled an almost-dry wet wipe out of his pocket and began to clean his hands.

Leah glared at him as if she thought he would intentionally get the inflatable punctured during the trip or interfere with their escape in other ways. "You make sure we all come back in one piece or I will hold you personally responsible, not just Raymond."

He wondered how she was going to do that. Murder them both in their sleep? But best not to give her any ideas. "Of course," he muttered. Then he threw the dry tissue into the dirty slop and hurried away from her up the grass.

( )

"All aboard, all aboard!" Raymond said, waving his hands as if he wanted to pull them into the boats himself.

He hadn't seen all of them take to the vessels before and now he understood why not, and the reason for Leah's anger. With Leah, Jens, Gabriele, Edouard, and Marten squeezed together in the inflatable, there was no room for equipment or supplies, and certainly not one more person. He realized that his hunch was correct. The punt and everything in it would vanish when the group left, whenever it happened. But with the extra vessel, there was room for Raymond and him too, if he could persuade the pathologist to come along. It wasn't all bad.

"Marten, you'd better come over here with us," Raymond said, watching brown floodwater slosh over the low-lying rim of the rowboat.

Marten glanced at Leah, who nodded.

He pushed the punt close so Marten could squeak over the neon-yellow rubber and into the wooden vessel.

"Welcome, Marten," Raymond said and settled into the narrow punt. "Are we ready to go?"

He pushed off from the hillock and steered down the street.

During the half-hour paddle to the museum, only Raymond talked; in the beginning exclaiming inane things like "What a perfect day for a trip!" and "Wonderful weather, how lucky we are today." But when no one else said anything, the pathologist fell quiet too. The rest of the short journey they glared at each other in reproachful, high-density silence, like a dysfunctional family at the dinner table.

Fortunately, the museum of art history was closer than he recalled. Just two streets away, and then the dove-gray building loomed above them in all its classically carved, linteled, and casement-windowed glory. The main entrance consisted of two enormous lime-green oak doors flanked by four pillars of rust-red, black-speckled basalt. The doors were so tall the massive brass handles sat higher on the wood than a grown human could comfortably reach, while the lower panel had a normal-sized door set into it. Thanks to a short flight of stairs made from the same mineral as the columns, the main entrance stood well above the surface of the water. But the small human-sized door was covered with moisture-darkened plywood, and so were all the windows in the front.

"It's the servant's entrance for us, then," Raymond said and grinned in the sunlight.

☾

In the parking lot behind the museum a shipping container had been left close to the back wall. Here, the windows were not covered. Perhaps the staff didn't have time to do it before they had to evacuate, or had run out of plywood and couldn't get ahold of more due to the impending storm. Several of the back windows displayed cracked panes. Most of them were on the upper floors, indicating that the breakage had been caused by the hurricane or subsequent bad weather, rather than by looters or people seeking shelter.

He brought the punt close to the bright blue shipping container, past a maple that still had a thin canopy left. Brown and yellow leaves floated on the dim water, which stank of gasoline. On the opposite side of the parking lot, the front of a white van peeked out of the inundation, gleaming in the sunshine. A warm spring breeze rippled the iridescent surface of the flood and the leaves that floated there. They reminded him of temple gardens, with golden foliage resting on moss so thick and well tended it looked like fur.

He hauled himself from the ribbed container roof and into the deep recess of the nearest glassless window, kicked away the remnants of the frame, and climbed in. The corridor inside was empty, with dry foliage and sand heaped along the walls. Sunlight slanted in through the broken windows, illuminating the dust and heating the air. He leaned out the window and helped Raymond in first, then Leah and the rest of the team.

"Where to?" Raymond beamed and turned towards him with fatherly expectation.

"The classical paintings," he said, to his own surprise. He certainly hadn't planned on playing guide for them, but now that they were here, there was only one thing he'd like to see that Michael and he had missed the last time. He didn't know which floor the classical paintings were on, but recalled that there were maps and directions on every landing, and continued down the corridor towards the stairs. A strong smell of mustiness and mildew hinted that the building and its treasures were well on their way to decay. Something about the moisture-streaked walls and crunch of sand beneath their boots made him miss the weight of a rifle in his hands.

"Are there any mummies here?" Gabriele whispered behind him.

"I don't think so," he said, relieved to be pulled out of his darkening thoughts. "Maybe in the exhibits from the southern continent." He couldn't remember having seen any mummies the previous time.

"Good," Gabriele said. "Because in the museum at home, the mummies have cursed me."

"Oh, really, did you stare and laugh at their rude bits?" Jens said.

"I didn't do anything," Gabriele replied. "But every time I go to that museum, I end up at the glass cage with the mummies in it, squashed by the crowd that's always there, and then I have to look at the mummies for a long time when I don't want to see them. I always plan on going somewhere else in the museum, but then I turn a wrong corner and get pulled by the streams of visitors into the mummy room."

Jens laughed. "So that's how you ended up working with dead people."

"I didn't," Gabriele said. "My job is to treat the survivors of emergencies and disasters. But now I understand why I came here with you! It's the curse of those damn mummies! The last time I ran away from them in the museum, I ended up in a room full of naughty woodblock prints, the only person in the exhibition, because I didn't see the sign above the door."

They laughed with Gabriele and the tension that hung between them lessened.

(( ))

To reach the wing with the classical paintings they passed through the section of artifacts from the eastern continent; past a life-sized statue sitting cross-legged on a giant pewter lotus, display cases with cups made from human skulls, cabinets full of patterned sword guards from his father's country. As they filed past the opening to a room where he remembered a beautiful wooden statue had reclined in red and golden robes while it smiled beatifically at the world, he peeked inside, but the dais that had displayed the figure was empty and only the temple bell that hung above it remained.

Then they entered the exhibits from the ancient civilizations; rows of lion statues with heads of men sporting long beards and conical hats. They passed through the seven-meter-tall and one-meter-wide wood and bronze replica of the gate of earliest known city-state, and into a stone tunnel painted with intricate pictorial script. Beyond this were gigantic obsidian heads with commanding eyes and haughty noses. Still further in was a temple in white marble that had been dismantled piece by piece in its original country, then stolen or perhaps appropriated to the museum and rebuilt there. In the semi-dark room Raymond stumbled on a spotlight meant to illuminate the temple from below and would have fallen if Leah hadn't grabbed his arm.

"Thank you, dear," Raymond nodded, but Leah just kept walking.

In one of the subsequent corridors was an antique mahogany cabinet with row upon row of hummingbirds, stuffed and mounted as if still in flight, sorted from the largest in the back to the smallest in the front, which was barely the size of a bumblebee. The tiny birds were so numerous that they stood wing tip to wing tip on the dusty wood with hardly any space between them. Their metallic green or black or blue feathers gleamed and glittered even in death. He stopped to take in the multitude of little birds, to imprint the sight of their beauty and variegation onto his memory so that it would never fade. But the small beings were too many and too similar to one another for the human eye, and he could barely tell them apart. He then tried to learn their names from the tiny plaques beneath each bird, but the thin, blue-inked cursive had already run and faded from legibility. He wanted to elbow a glass pane like he had done with the tulip window in the house in the suburbs, pull the cabinet door open and remove one shining bird, the smallest and brightest of them. Tuck it into the breast pocket of his jacket to save at least one of them from the humidity and rot, from never being seen and marveled at again as a sign of the energy and evolution that had shaped the bird's entire little body so that it fit its environmental niche so perfectly it could not be removed from the web of life without other parts unraveling.

But then he realized that the birds were long dead and the species they belonged to probably extinct already, and he left them to their decay.

( )

From there they descended the stairs into a deepening gloom and an increasing heat. The smelly humidity that gripped them like a sweaty hand more than hinted of the full submergence of the bottom floors and the merciless moisture that now surrounded the stone walls and rose inside them like water through paper. When they finally reached the gallery of classical paintings, they were so warm and tired of dust and mold and darkness, they slumped down on the benches in the center of the first exhibit, beneath a tall wrought-iron-barred skylight muted by white paint.

The wall in front of them was filled with a single extensive painting, its human figures so large they were almost life-sized. From the dimness in the background two men, one dressed in white and gold and the other in black and red, were striding forward. Behind and around them others were following, glancing around watchfully, yet calmly, carrying muskets, drums, flags, and spears. In the middle of the patrol a little girl and a dog could also be spotted. The two men in the foreground were conversing amicably, even affectionately, no doubt about the current affairs of their city and the long-gone world they lived in. The painting, with its beautiful, staged artifice of scene, layered brushstrokes that created a three-dimensional effect, and colors and highlights that made the luminous parts brighter and the dark parts deeper, seemed like the final victory of art and civilization, thought to last forever.

They watched the painting in silence while they held each other's hands.

30.

The Escape

That night they slept soundly in their cots, worn out by the fight earlier in the day, he assumed. But right before dawn he became aware of shadows moving about in the tent. He opened his eyes, but kept his breath slow and steady and pretended to still be asleep. One of the dark shapes leaned close to him and whispered: "We're leaving now. Last chance to come along."

He propped up on one elbow. "I'll go with you if Raymond does," he said.

Gabriele peered over one of the crate walls, which had become considerably lower the last few days. "We're waking him now."

"Raymond, I'm sorry, but we're leaving," he heard Leah say on the other side of the stacked boxes.

Raymond's reply was full of sleep and he couldn't make out individual words.

"Come with us. Please."

"No!" Raymond said, high-pitched as if weeping. "Why?"

"We need to go," Leah said. "Back to our own homes, our children, parents, relatives, friends. This time we need to save ourselves."

"Are you all leaving?" Raymond said, in the same pitiful voice as before.

"Yes," Leah said.

"Only if you are, Raymond," he said and stood, so that he was visible above the crates.

Raymond, breath rapid and shallow, looked at each of them.

"We have divided the food and water evenly," Leah said. "If you don't come with us, we leave your portions here and bring ours with us in the boats. We don't know how many days it will take us to get out."

Raymond flung his blanket aside and stood. "Very well!" the pathologist said so loudly it was as if the darkness would break. "Just go! Abandon your duties and return home. The faster the better! I will of course revoke your payment immediately!"

"Raymond," Leah said quietly. "The organization is dead. It is nothing but paper and names now. Even De Lotte has gone home to her family."

"I know that," Raymond yelled. "Why do you think I have been paying you myself these last months?"

"I'm sorry, Raymond," Leah said, hands limp along her sides. She lifted a bag from the grass, turned away from them, and started walking. Gabriele and Jens took their remaining belongings and followed her.

It was still dark, but towards the east, the predawn was already blushing the water and the sky. The air was still and cool, yet had the soft moistness that heralds a warm summer day. In the faint light he could see the inflatable and the punt. Edouard and Marten had already boarded one vessel each. Raymond followed them down the slope, with shirttails flying from his unbuttoned shirt, his body shaking with rage.

Gabriele, Jens, and Leah climbed onboard the two vessels that already sat low in the water from the weight. He searched the rowboat and the punt for any signs of the steel crates that contained the list of the dead, but he could only see cardboard boxes of supplies and the team members' waterproof bags. Jens undid the moorings and threw the rope off. It keened through the air for a second before it hit the water. Calmly, Jens lifted the steel pole from the bottom of the punt. From the rubber vessel Gabriele and Leah lowered the white plastic paddles into the water.

"Are you doing this because I made us leave . . . made us leave your nephew? . . . Raymond said, face trembling.

"Be well, my dear," Leah said, but did not look at the two on the meadow. The five on the water got their heavily laden vessels moving, then receded slowly into the dark, like the stars are bound to do at the end of time.

( )

"Thank you, my friend," Raymond said when they were out of sight, looking at him with moist eyes. Then the pathologist retreated up the mound. Most of the equipment on the table in the tent was still there, but the map had vanished. Now only the jug, the box, the stone, and the plastic bottle remained where the map's corners had been, the center empty. Raymond tore open the plastic wrapping of the uppermost bundle of water bottles that were still left and handed him one, along with a packet of crackers.

He fetched his bowl from beneath the cot, sat down on one of the folding stools, and consumed the biscuits with the bottle of water. They ate together as they had done every morning for the last weeks. Then dawn brightened to a wide, cloudless sky. A year ago it would have been a perfect day to go to the beach, or the boat club by the lake, or to a barbecue in someone's green and flowering garden. But now the city was so changed it might never return to the way it had been.

After the meal, when they were both rinsing their bowls in the smelly trickle from the filter barrel, Raymond said: "Let's put on the drysuits and see if we can find some more bodies."

"There might be some over at my parents' neighborhood," he said. "Out by the artificial lake. Jens and Gabriele said they never searched those houses."

"Excellent idea," Raymond smiled. "Do you know the way there without the map?"

"Yes," he said, having plotted the route in his mind a long time ago.

"Good," Raymond said.

They pulled on the warm drysuits that stank of artificial fabric and sweat. His perspiration made the drysuit cling to his body like a second skin, but his thigh had nearly stopped aching. Knowing their destination was far off and would be even harder to reach due to the flood, he packed the last sachets of freeze-dried meals from his backpack in one of the watertight rollbags the team had left behind and tied it to a D-ring on his suit. Raymond did the same with several bottles of water, and slung a coil of white sailing line over one shoulder, no weights or tanks. Together they walked to the edge of the mound while the sun warmed their backs. Raymond put on mask and fins, waded into the brown water from the grass-covered bank, swam a few strokes through the clouds of gnats and flies that hovered above the surface, then turned and waved at him, as if they were going for a swim at the beach.

He slipped his own mask and fins on and went in, grateful for the sharp scent of rubber that rose from the mask to nearly cover the stench of the floodwater. Raymond advanced cautiously down the street, then took a few turns seemingly at random. In most places the water still stood higher than their bodies, and where it didn't, they avoided stepping on the bottom because of the debris that glimmered there, instead swimming past those obstacles. They kept the masks and gloves and hoods on to minimize the exposure to the water and the mosquitoes that buzzed around them.

One summer during his teens he had worked as a lifeguard at the boat club's artificial beach that reeked of wet sand and suntan lotion and echoed with the shrieks of frolicking children and youths. On the tinny radio that stood beneath his tall and laddered chair there had been a competition inviting listeners to phone in and describe the worst summer job they had held. A young man who called in and said he worked as a diver at the municipal water treatment plant and swam in raw sewage every day won the competition. Suddenly his own warm, tedious job of watching the swimmers play at shore of the lake, reuniting lost and screaming toddlers with their parents, while being the target of uppity comments by younger boys, and giggles and surreptitious photography by the girls, didn't seem so bad. However, as repulsive and objectionable as being a sewage diver sounded, he learned a few years later that that was not the dirtiest of aquatic employments, nor was the position of deep sea diver for the offshore industry the most dangerous. Through a friend of a friend he heard that a couple of the people he had trained with for his service had found work as divers at nuclear power plants on the continent. Appalled, but curious about what such a job entailed, and why anyone would want to do it, even for the adrenaline rush or a phenomenal pay, he asked what the nuclear divers did. He was told that they checked and repaired all parts of the power plant that were filled with liquid, including the coolant intake systems, the pipes for spillwater, the wells were spent material was stored, even the brilliant reactor pools themselves. The radioactive water was so hot that the divers had to wear special suits that prevented them from overheating, along with dosimeters at several places on their body. A whole team of assistants stood ready to rinse off all the water and radioactive material from the suits post dive. Despite the safety precautions, that job sounded a lot more dangerous and desperate than diving in sewage. Now he recalled the worst-summer-job competition and the descriptions of a nuclear diver's tasks, and smiled to himself as he eased his way past the sharp, buckled beams of a rusted vehicle chassis that had disintegrated so much it was difficult to see what its original form had once been.

( )

The journey there took three days of carefully navigating the stagnant and dirty floodwater, and three nights of sitting on top of debris, too cold inside the sweat-moistened drysuits to sleep, the stench of sewage and diesel in their noses, while they watched the moon that shone behind the naked canopies of the dead elms that lined the lanes. He tried to remember what the house he had grown up in, and which he had looked after every summer as a student while his parents were traveling, looked like inside, but realized he hadn't been there for over a year, and now all he could envision were the broken rooms of his apartment and the overfilled house he had stayed in on his way to the city. When Raymond and he finally tread water in front of the steep gables and stained-glass windows of his parents' house, the driveway was empty, the garage door open, and the bed in the master bedroom on the second floor piled with winter clothing.

He peered into all the windows on the first floor and those on the second he could reach from the balcony, but the rooms housed only water, drowned or floating furniture, and a few clothes. In the corner of the garden behind the house he spotted through the murky water the traditional stone lantern that he had ordered from his father's country and given to his parents for Christmas. When he saw that he felt a deep sting of regret for not having arrived sooner. The white trellises on the rear south-facing wall peeked out of the flood like bones, still clinging to the house, but the rose bushes that had grown there, which his mother treasured and had always harvested as soon as they blossomed, hung naked and dead. The few leaves that remained on the hedge were brown and dry, the hazel bushes dying in their new and aquatic environment. The rest of the submerged garden sloped gently up toward the meadow behind the property, a soft round field of grass that fluttered in the wind, with the leaden sky like a wound above it. The sight reminded him of a dream he had had last spring, in which he had stepped out of a building that stood on the edge of a cliff in a storm. Roses grew along its walls, glowing red in the tempest dusk, but when he examined the flowers, they cut his hands until they bled. Now he realized that the glass-paneled doors he had exited and the trellises in that dream had been from his parents' house; he just hadn't wanted to realize that after the dream.

Through the windows he saw the antique copper pots were still hanging from their hooks beneath the ventilation hood, but that no sheets of flight information had been hung up on the magnetic plate by the kitchen door, which his parents always did when they went on holiday. His parents were clearly not in the house. That probably meant they had evacuated before the hurricane set in.

"Do you want to go inside to look further?" Raymond asked.

"No," he said. "I can see they're gone, but not on a holiday." Besides, he had no key and was loathe to break the veranda doors and add to the chaos. "If it hadn't been midday, we could have slept here," he said. "At least the second floor looks dry."

Raymond smiled. "No problem. It's better we start on our way back while it's light. Is there anywhere you could call for your parents?"

"Yes," he said. "When the laptop is charged."

"It might be ready when we're back at the camp," Raymond said.

They started on the long and strenuous way back, returning by the same route since they knew those streets were passable. On the last night before they reached the camp, the northern sky flared in shimmering bands of green and white, the rare aurora making the drowned world a little more bearable.

❨☽❩

Raymond opened the orange case with the solid-looking laptop inside it.

"The battery has almost charged enough to switch it on," Raymond said. "Come on, let's see if we can find some more dead bodies in the meantime."

At the site Raymond had picked out, or chosen at random, since they no longer had a map to consult, they looked around for anything that resembled organic decomposition, but found only a rotting, leafless tree, a cardboard box that had been transformed by the wind and the rain into a brown smear on the side of a vehicle, a rich green moss that bearded the water line along the concrete walls that lined the street, and clusters of red mosquito larvae that floated on the warm surface. Raymond clambered up the steps of a wind-gutted building to scan the street, the vehicles, the water, like a captain at sea, but found nothing more. In the distance, they thought they saw the wake of an otter crossing the flood-canal, but when the furry shape climbed up into a window and disappeared inside a ruin, it was only a large rat.

((   ))

"Well, that's the last of the bottles," Raymond said, handing him one of the plastic containers over dinner after yet another pointless swim to a nearby inundated street corner or plaza, which he knew they had searched at least once before.

He smiled, toasted the pathologist and drank, still waiting for the damn laptop to charge. He had hoped the situation would change before the water ran out, or that the visible dwindling of food and drinking water would persuade Raymond to evacuate, convince him that all they would be leaving behind in the city were the dead. But the pathologist simply cleaned some of the empty plastic crates with water from the filter pump, and put them outside the tent. That night was humid, windy, and full of rain, which still happened regularly despite the late spring heat. In the morning enough water had collected to keep them in fluid that day. They cleaned more empty containers and placed them on the slurping grass.

With the inevitable progress into summer, the days grew warmer and the rain less frequent, yet the flood remained. The first morning in which they peered down into the empty containers and saw no water, not even a few drops of dew clinging to the dark blue plastic, Raymond gave him a brittle smile.

"Let's try to find some clean water," he said to quickly drown out the twinge of remorse that for a moment rose in him for not having left with the rest of the team.

"Good idea," the pathologist said and glanced up at him to gauge his reaction. The edges of Raymond's wound were now visible to him, a dim a shore stretching into the night.

From then on they spent their days trying to find drinking water instead of searching for dead and bloated bodies to confirm their own usefulness. They swam to where they thought the water might be the cleanest, away from rusting scrap, the gleaming iridescence of diesel and gasoline, or the frothing of other chemicals, and where there still was some motion in the flood. There they used the filtering device from his backpack to fill several empty plastic bottles. Now the hurt that clung to Raymond like a corpse's fumes seemed to throb in the air, so thick he could almost touch it, and it pained him whenever he moved too close to the pathologist.

(( ))

The days heated mercilessly, and the floodwater they did take the chance of drinking made them sick despite the filters. He seemed to lose his water much quicker than Raymond did, or take the loss less well, and soon he had to remain in the cot to conserve his energy. They had placed the portable beds as far away from one another as they would go in the tent and had stacked the empty crates and cardboard boxes between them for increased privacy. The latrine at the back of the mound overflowed, but they let it, and simply went in the flood when they needed to. While warm but vigorous summer storms raged they could only close the tent and lie still, and when the sun was out they suffered beneath it.

Days later, when the laptop finally blinked on and he barely had the energy to punch in the number Michael had left in the apartment, there was only the static silence of no phone connection.

"I'm so sorry," Raymond said.

Finally, he did what he had hoped he would never have to do, yet what, ever since he had entered the flooded city, he had suspected he someday must. He took out the soda bottle that had accompanied him the entire journey from the cabin. The plastic was so worn the once-transparent material was now milky and opaque, the cork ragged at the edge. Slowly, he extricated himself from the moist fabric of the cot and crawled a short distance away from it. There, he urinated a little into the grass to get rid of the most bacteria-filled fluid, then released the rest into the soda bottle. The process was equally off-putting and relieving, and produced a modest amount of orange liquid. He opened the filter bottle and the empty canteen, and decanted the urine slowly into the filter bottle, taking care not to spill on the cork and sides. Then he pumped the bottle as usual and poured the yellow liquid that flowed out of it into the canteen. That fluid was as close to water as would ever come out of his body, and should be relatively sterile. The liquid was still warm, although the filtering had cooled it a little so it no longer held body temperature. He tilted his head back, held his breath, and drank. It did not smell or taste at all like water. Drinking his own urine felt a little demeaning, and even more penitent, which he quite liked. He held the filter bottle in the air so Raymond could see it above the wall of empty crates between them, but the pathologist declined.

( )

Raymond was still up, clonking empty plastic containers together, feeding him what little of the plastic-smelling, sun-hot water the pathologist managed to catch. Against the dazzling daylight, Raymond was like silhouette seen through a rippling, diaphanous cloth.

His skin flushed and fevered, and all power vanished from his limbs, so he could barely move on the warm canvas. His mouth was so dry the insides of his lips stuck to his gums, with no saliva left to separate them, and his eyes hurt too much to keep open for long. His blood felt as thick and as fetid as the floodwater that surrounded them.

Raymond came and watched him for a while, sadness and pain hanging in the air like the dust he remembered from the war zones in the south.

☾☽

Then the canned dinners and bags of cereal were gone, not just the water, forcing even Raymond retreat to the cot. There, the pathologist remained quiet, not turning and creaking, like he himself did.

"What happened on the eastern continent," he whispered into the tent, hoping that Raymond was awake on the other side of the wall of the now empty boxes and crates between them.

"Didn't Jens or Gabriele tell you?" Raymond asked quietly.

"I want to hear it from you," he said.

31.

On the Eastern Continent

The wall of flying sand churned and swirled towards the small intercity jet, swallowing up even the sun in an embrace so wide it seemed to span the entire plain below. It reminded Leah of the dust storms that rage on Mars in its spring and fall, storms that can engulf the whole planet for months. She braced for turbulence, which was common in the places where she and her team worked. But the air was strangely still, as if the sky itself was holding its breath in anticipation of the approaching storm.

The plain beneath them was even more extensive than the roiling front of sand, a dense patchwork of variegated crops that stretched from the chain of mountains to the north and the west to the mighty river that flowed far to the south. Down there sorghum, winter wheat, vegetables, cotton, and corn grew in unfathomable amounts. Interspersing the fields were cities, towns, and villages, bound together by a web of motorways and roads. The population and its crops had swelled to such numbers they needed multiple dams to keep them with electricity and water, piped in from the southern and rainier parts of the vast country.

On this plain, cold and dry air from the north merged with mild and humid weather from the south, conditions that had been perfect for agriculture for centuries. But then the rain stopped, not just for a year or two, but several in a row, and the mighty river shrunk due to melting glaciers in the distant mountains. Now the water in the dams was almost gone, and the wind chased the rich soil away in constant, thinning gusts. The millions who lived here were hungry and thirsty.

Leah gazed down at the blighted ground below. It reminded her of somewhere else, the last site they went to, or the one before that. The whole year had been a string of places like this, some wetter, some even drier, and some more dangerous than she had expected them to be. She wondered how long they would go on, how long their food and money would last. And what challenges would meet them after the landing here. Whether their help would be useful and bring relief to at least some of the population. Or if, as in the previous place, they would soon have to leave in the heat of gunfire and flames.

The pilot had just enough time to land safely on the runway before the sandstorm swallowed them completely.

( )

The small jet rocked in the storm while the sand sounded like hail on the hull. The others in the team undid their seatbelts, sighed the stale cabin air, snapped the overhead lockers open and lifted their bags and clothes out. Leah handed them the first disposable dust masks of the countless they were going to use on the plain.

They hurried out of the aircraft to the terminal, a new glass and steel wonder born from the country's recent prosperity, now dull and dark in the power outage. The sliding doors were dead. An airport official pushed open a door nearby and waved them inside while the storm blew fine particles around them.

The terminal was warm and dark and full of people, some with suitcases or bags or backpacks, many without, only what they wore and had in their pockets. The people were sitting or crouched or leaned in clusters around the columns in the large room, on the benches, and against the windows. Without the soothing feel of air conditioning the room smelled of fear and sweat and piss, like most of the places the team worked in.

As the team entered the main court in the terminal, the people they passed spotted the plastic bottles of water they had in their hands and the symbol on their bags and surged towards them, shouting for water and food. They handed their bottles out, tried to make sure it went to children, elderly, or the clearly sick, and ran out much too soon.

From the wide central stairs of the terminal a group of men and women in sleek suits and tight neckwear came trotting towards them. The group divided the crowd like water, and stopped in front of the team. Leah greeted the group as courteously as she could, translated by the member of the team who spoke the country's language best. These were an official delegation from the capital here to coordinate the team with the region's own emergency effort.

Leah watched her entire team bob their heads, bare their teeth, and shake hands with the bright courtesy of a diplomatic mission rather than a group of aid workers. Then the delegation took them up the wide central stairs, past the dark but still-open shops in the mall on the floor above, and the equally unlit offices on the mezzanine of the third floor, to the VIP lounge at the top.

The sand clattered on the glass wall that looked out onto the plain and the suspended floor shivered from the motion of their steps. At the center of the concrete-pillared room, twenty battery-powered studio lamps lit a large table like a theater stage or the scene of a crime. White porcelain, silver-covered cutlery, and fake crystal glass set for thirty people glittered and gleamed in the studio lights. On the table were roasted piglets with apples in the mouths, white almond puddings made from the spittle of endangered birds, oysters and crayfish cooled by a dripping ice swan, ribs grilled in dark sauce, barbecued ducks with pancakes, thick bird liver patés, bowls of stews, deep fried vegetables, fish, along with bottles of red, white, and pink wine, as well as liquor made from local crops at least five years in the past.

"We can't eat all of this while people are starving in the terminal downstairs," Gabriele whispered to Leah.

"We have no choice," Leah told her. "If we refuse it'll be an insult to our hosts, and with good reason; this might be some of the final food that's left."

When the speeches and the eating and the drinking was finally over, the team was split into groups of three and brought downstairs to black cars that stood idling outside the terminal.

"Why do we have to go in separate cars?" Leah asked the head of the delegation. "A single taxi van would have had room for all of us."

"Our senior delegates wanted the honor of accompanying you to your hotel, and the cars only have room for three people in the back," was the answer. Thus they sat in the back of the cars, with one man in dark suit and dark glasses in the driver's seat, and one delegate with very white teeth next to him.

During the banquet at the terminal, the storm passed, but the wind was still high. The windscreen wipers on the cars clacked sand and dust instead of rain and water from the glass. In the faint sweep from the headlights the streets were dark and empty, with dust that rushed across the asphalt like snow and collected in mounds and heaps. Vehicles, crashed or abandoned, rose in the lights like ghosts. The motorcade was the only thing that moved, except for the sand.

❨❩

The hotel seemed to be as far away from the airport as it was possible to be and still remain in the city. The foyer and rooms were lit by battery-powered lamps similar to the ones in the airport lounge. Or perhaps these were the same lamps, transported to the hotel in a hurry while their cars drove in circles through the empty streets.

The rooms were anonymously modern: white walls, long curtains, synthetic leather on the headboards of the beds.

Decorative glass sinks, rain showers with no water, long shag carpet in a chic golden color, dividing screens in mahogany and lacquer. Television sets the size of windows, all dead without power.

"May I have your mobiles phones and passports, please," the head of the delegates asked when the team had been given their rooms.

Gabriele gave a start of protest, but Jens stopped her.

"What do you need them for?" Leah asked in an even voice.

"Oh, just for safekeeping and prevention of theft," the head of the delegates explained. "And our phone network is advanced than yours, so we will procure new phones that will work better here."

The others glanced at her, but Leah had no choice but to agree. They dug into bags and pockets and handed the items, more valuable than cash or credit cards, over to the waiting delegates.

Yet, when the officials had left and the team was alone in the darkened rooms, Leah gave them their shared code word for surveillance. The team members nodded silently, understanding that every word and gesture would be recorded, registered, and disseminated via microphones and cameras hidden in their rooms. They should not search for these or try to eliminate them, but instead live like the reality shows on TV where the participants were filmed day and night.

《 》

The next morning the directors of the regional emergency services, the most prominent local politicians and business owners, even the city's mayor, arrived at the hotel, in a motorcade as black and silent as had transported the team. But this time there was no pomp, no banquet, and no lights. The newly-arrived women and men looked tired and pale, with wrinkled trousers and jackets and sweat-stained armpits, as if they had been sleeping in their clothes.

Then came lectures, all performed by one local administrator after the other, who stood perspiring in the bright light from the projector, and were translated by a government-sanctioned language expert who arrived with the locals. The first lectures informed the team, the local politicians, and the central delegation about the geography and history of the region, then on its main agricultural practices, governance, and population distribution. Lastly came something relevant: the region's emergency aid system, its organization and infrastructure, and the recent actions taken against the drought.

Every two hours there were fifteen-minute breaks.

"These chairs have killed my cheeks already," Marten whispered to Edouard, who stifled a laugh.

"Now I would like to invite our guests to present their organization, mandate, and history, as well as practices of aid," the head of the central delegation said.

"Thank you," Leah said and stood, while she mentally summed up what to say in her improvised talk. A little later Raymond and two other of the senior staff did the same. It was no problem. They knew the history and policies of their organization well.

The local administrators and the delegates from the capital sat among them and applauded loudly. Despite the fancy matte wood paneling on the walls, the thick carpets, the modern meeting-room chairs, and the fans that were somehow still going on the ceiling, the room was warm and stale and smelled of cigarette smoke.

At the end of the day, when the orange sky had turned dark, Leah asked, through the team's translator, the head of the central delegates: "When can we start working?"

The delegate only answered with another question. "When will the supplies arrive?"

All hundred tons stood at an airport in one of the neighboring countries, labeled as wood pulp and cardboard.

"The supplies will arrive when we get into the field," Leah replied.

When the lectures were finally over, and they filed out into the foyer with the delegates and the local dignitaries, there was no dinner, no food of any kind, nor anything to drink.

"My colleagues haven't eaten all day," Leah told the leader of the delegates. "Could we at least get some water?"

"We are in the middle of an emergency, madam," the head replied. "There is no food left, in the city or the surrounding towns. You are bringing it with you."

( )

The team climbed the dark stairs and went to their rooms, turned on the faucets for water, but they gave only a slow, brown trickle. When they discovered that, they convened in one room and ate self-heating meals they had hidden in their luggage along with bottles of water, and sat together on the gold-colored long shag carpet.

Then there were no more lectures, no local politicians, no central delegates, not even a word. The team waited two more days in their rooms.

"They're probably searching the rest of our bags at the airport for supplies," Leah said. "We'll wait."

"Does this country really need our aid?" Gabriele asked. "Don't they have huge emergency organizations on their own?"

"They need it," Leah said. "Otherwise they wouldn't have allowed us to enter the country. But not getting the aid now would be worse than agreeing to receive it in the first place. They'll yield. Just wait. Just wait."

While the team members waited, they read books, played cards, drew sketches, wrote diary entries, postcards, and letters.

"It's quiet here," Jens wrote. "Warm and dusty. We are being treated well. The work is going well. Everything is fine." Their communication would be read, perhaps censored,

231

perhaps stopped. But their organization and governments at home knew they were there. That made them almost safe.

"We've been in worse places many times before," Jens wrote.

❨❩

On the third day, a fifty-seat tourist bus pulled up outside the darkened hotel. The team members filed in, sat in the blast from the air conditioning, and took turns using the functional, flushing toilet on board.

They had expected to be taken out into the countryside, to the fallow fields and dust-filled towns to distribute their supplies there. Instead, they were driven back to the airport, which lay halfway between the city center and the smooth concrete back of the dam they could spot in the far distance of the ochre hills.

Now the airport terminal was empty and they were taken to the enormous parking lot in front of the building. There, the tents from the equipment bags they had left at the airport had been set up, the area cordoned by flapping plastic ribbons into a winding snake for queuing, like the line for the security control inside the empty terminal. On the far side the parking lot extended into a graveled plot, beyond which were only dry fields and rows of desiccated corn all the way to the curl of flying sand at the horizon.

The parking lot was full of people, some with bags and backpacks, others holding children or elderly by the hand. Almost everyone wore scarves and masks over their faces to protect against the sand that got everywhere, into the eyes, nose, throat, even between the teeth. Some people had brought stools or folding chairs to sit on. They even saw a few small camping tents flapping in the breeze.

Leah stopped at the edge of the lot to take everything in. A black car came rushing down the ramp from the motorway overpass and stopped right next to her. The head of the central delegation exited, handed her a brand new satellite phone

"You got your aid station," he said. "Now call your organization for the supplies."

( )

While Leah and the team waited for the supplies to be flown in, they split the proximal end of the line in two, one for those seeking food and water, one for those who needed health care as well. They had one of the local aid workers who had arrived to help write posters in black marker on cardboard to direct the waiting people, as well as placards saying that the supplies were on their way but could take some time yet. The crowd made little noise and only a few people pushed to get into the queue for medical attention; the rest waited calmly.

Then the team started the triage, separating the seriously injured or sick from those who were less affected and could wait longer. Fortunately, the heavily wounded and gravely ill were a minority and were seen to relatively quickly. These the local aid workers found transport for to a hospital outside the region which still had water and electricity. Most of the injured were moderately to lightly wounded, and could be dressed, stitched, or splinted with the medical equipment the team had in their bags, with the sick given what few antibiotics and medicines the local aid workers still had.

The people in the line were elderly and infants, middle-aged and teenagers, city people in suits and dresses, suburban families, village farmers, factory workers, domestic tourists, or immigrant workers from neighboring countries. International visitors—excepting some foreign language teachers—rarely came to this hot and dry region, and then only to a city or two in the region that housed especially well-known historical artifacts. But they had fled home and stopped coming when the dust and the lack of water turned from vague rumor to harsh reality. Now only the capital to the northeast still attracted tourists, and their numbers had dropped greatly because of the now exorbitant prices for food and water.

"Please come and welcome the plane at the runway with us," the head of the delegates told Leah. She followed him, the chairwoman of the national aid organization, the rest of the central delegation, and the men in dark clothes and dark glasses. She would have liked to inspect and tally the supplies as they arrived, but she knew which fights to pick and this was not one of them.

Finally the cargo plane with the supplies was about to land, one of the few foreign aircraft to be allowed into the country for weeks. A full row of flags snapped in the wind outside the terminal. There was even a university marching band, their brass and woodwind instruments gleaming in the sun. A crowd of people had gathered and cheered with flags and red balloons to welcome the plane, while another, smaller group of people waved posters and chanted slogans in protest of the foreign intrusion. The press was also out in force, from mature and seasoned journalists with full camera crew and furry microphones, to young and up and coming, filming themselves with their mobile phones on long sticks.

They must have arrived from the capital, Leah thought. Why else were those people in that crowd and not in the lines on the parking lot?

( )

The cargo plane landed with a screech and a puff, then braked for a long while before it finally came to a stop on the hot asphalt. The long loading ramp slid open, revealing pallet upon pallet of crates of emergency rations, medical supplies, and water. The band played snappy marches from the western continent, the TV reporters talked into their microphones while they were filmed by their crews, or filmed themselves, and the large crowd cheered and the small one booed, while forklifts rolled into the plane's interior and brought the life-saving contents out into the sunshine and to the hangar next door.

The delegates and local leaders smiled and applauded and waved, and Leah did the same. She had witnessed similar occasions many times before, the receiving of aid transformed into a media spectacle, often arranged by the aid organization and donating countries, but lately more and more by the recipient of the aid, as a show of goodwill and compliance to the international community, and as a sign of initiative and security for the audience at home. But never before had the ritual been as publicized as this, or as big. When the glaciers in the western mountains started to retreat and the mighty rivers that flowed from them began to shrink, after first having overflowed with the extra meltwater, the nations who depended on this water started to quarrel over what was left. At least two of the involved nations had nuclear weapons. Leah thought she knew what was going on. The country that Leah and her team were in now hadn't been persuaded into negotiations by promises of aid, which had been offered to all the disputing nations. Instead, it was this country that had forced the international community to help them, despite the nation's massive economy and its southern regions still having water and food. This wasn't merely a public relations spectacle; it was a demonstration of power.

Leah expected, when the pallets were forklifted out of the plane, that the crowd in the parking lot or on the runway would start to push and shout, maybe even fight to get to the supplies first. She and her team had seen everything from small tussles to large riots in their work. But here it didn't happen. There were some irregularities in the line, but they were minor and stopped almost immediately once the packs of emergency rations and bottled water began to be handed out. Those who received them clutched the food and water, put it carefully in bags or backpacks, and hurried away out of the queue.

The team ripped the plastic that held the stacks of bottles together, cut open the boxes with sachets of powdered rations, packs of energy bars, and protein-rich gruel, lifted them out of the containers and transferred them to the waiting hands. The line moved quickly, and the team even received a few thanks yous before the waiting people vanished, hurrying home to prepare the food to hungry relatives or friends. The sun was out, it was warm but clear, and more and more people arrived. The team and the local emergency workers handed out food and smiled at each other. This was what they had come to do, this was what truly mattered.

As it always did in the beginning, it seemed as if the supplies had no end, that everyone would get something, that no one would die. Leah nevertheless asked Edouard, who enjoyed logistics the most of the team, to tally the stock from inside the plane, and again in the hangar which the supplies were brought into. Then she asked Jens and Gabriele, who were handing out food and water to the queue, to keep a close count of how many crates they opened and emptied.

"Be thorough," Leah said. "This is very important."

☾☽

That entire day the team performed the joyous work of handing out food and water to those in need. They did that the next day and the next and the next. More and more people appeared at the airport, coming from the city as well as the towns and villages outside. They saw the tails of dust from approaching cars and trucks approach from far across the plain, tall chimneys in the air.

At the end of the week, the delegation permitted the team to send a few members into the field, to travel to a village out on the plain, so far from the city that most of the inhabitants would have problems reaching the parking lot at the airport, even if petrol had been freely available.

The village was more like a suburb, small houses and gardens rising from the flat of the plain between the remnants of crops and blocks of unfinished apartment houses. The village skirted a much larger town, visible as four- and five-story buildings looming in the hazy distance, but the team never reached that place.

Even there, further out on the plain, people knew they were coming, either alerted by the authorities, by word of mouth that spread fast, or perhaps a combination of the two. Thus on their arrival, a line appeared quickly, less orderly than the one at the airport in the city, but also less crowded. Jens and Gabriele handed the food and water out from the back of the truck they arrived in, crates and boxes that had been tallied and accounted for at the airport. Once more, vital supplies changed hands, with no one receiving more than the next.

The mayor and other local dignitaries soon came to greet them, in a strange echo of the delegation of officials that had met the team when they first arrived in the country. Smiles and pats and handshakes, everyone careful not to mention the water crisis in the western mountains. Gabriele and Jens might not be diplomats, but they knew what it was wise to talk about and what it was not. They nevertheless found moments to inquire what help the region had received so far.

"We received help only after a while," the local politicians, teachers, and volunteers said via eager student translators. "When the drought had been really bad for months and the first dam went empty. It was as if they understood the severity of the situation only then, or perhaps that was when the dwindling crops and soaring food prices finally affected the capital."

When the sun went down and the supplies were gone, Jens and Gabriele piled into the back of the truck, closed the gate, and banged on the steel to have the driver start the journey back. The sky was unusually clear, a dry cold wind blowing, breathing long draughts of soil across the plain, making them chew grit and rub their eyes. But higher up, above the horizon obscured by the ubiquitous dust, the sky was clear and dark, and filled with small and bright stars.

◖◗

In this way the team tried to lessen the thirst and hunger they encountered, to buy more time until the country's government could route food and water in from other regions to help the population on the plain, or until their aid organization would realize it was time to send more supplies, if only to continue to curb the crisis in the western mountains. And most importantly, to give the local population, the thirsty and hungry, those who had started to think about leaving and those who had arrived there from other parts of the plain, some hope, give them the knowledge that they had been heard, that the world was aware of their plight. And maybe, maybe, the moist winds would start up again and the rains return, make the dams and reservoirs gleam again and the automated irrigation systems turn the sunlight into rainbows once more. On every overcast day they turned their faces upwards, hoping for a thickening and darkening of the gray, yearning for the distant roll of thunder and the building hiss of rain. But only dust shaded the sky, higher and higher, like a dome of whipping, rushing sand being built from the horizon up while it reached for the zenith, which it would someday eclipse. The only sound that came even close to thunder was the shriek of the sand and the clattering of loose boards in the wind.

Nevertheless, the team ventured out on the plain, to the villages and towns, driving quickly through the silt when it was clear, then crawling back through the flying soil when the wind returned. Every day the stacks and mounds and heaps of food and bottled water, which at first nearly reached the ceiling of the hangar they were stored in, grew shorter and smaller, shrank slowly in all directions, like the water that yet remained at the bottom of the dams, while sand and blow-dried soil collected on the concrete floors, in the hangar as well as the dams.

The youngest in the team had been born recently enough to be fascinated by the vast country and its ancient culture, had never lived in a world in which it wasn't a superpower, and was the only one in the team who spoke its language. Thus, he functioned as the team's own translator, apart from the government-sanctioned ones they had received.

❨☽❩

The only thing the team could do was to make the supplies last longer, for a little while more. They opened all the boxes and the crates and divided the remaining sachets and packets so they could be spread out to as many people as possible and still provide sufficient nutrition.

It was during this work Edouard found what looked like an anomaly in the numbers. He checked and double-checked before he notified Leah.

Several hundred kilos of food, of the most nutritious emergency rations, the most concentrated formula, meant for pulling under- and malnourished children back from the brink of death, but also given in less concentrated form to adults who had been starving for months, were missing. These supplies were the most valuable, but also what they had the least of.

"Check again," Leah asked Edouard. When the numbers turned out to be correct, Leah told Edouard to check the shipment numbers in case they had never arrived. Had the organization sent them too little, or might it at the last moment have rerouted the special food to other places, other emergencies that mattered more and had arisen after the team had arrived at their current location? But that turned out to be wrong. Two different logisticians at the home organization sent copies of the shipping forms, showing that all the missing crates had been sent with the rest of the supplies. The error must be at the team's end, after they had unloaded the plane.

Where had the supplies gone? Leah wondered. To the black market in the city? Or shipped off to the capital to feed a powerful government official's family there? Or to a business tycoon's factory to keep the workers and the production up?

Leah asked the logisticians at the organization to try and trace the packages, then notified her country's embassy in a message the translator encrypted and rerouted via different servers for her, to avoid the missive being caught and read by their hosts. The last person she contacted was a black-marketeer she had had a few run-ins with in the past, a former gunrunner who had switched to smuggling food and water instead, because that was now more profitable than arms.

"Keep an eye out for these supplies. They vanished just a week ago, and should surface soon," Leah told her.

Only two days later the black-marketeer made contact again. Parts of the shipment had been offered, in smaller segments and more easily smuggled volumes, on the international unofficial market. The bidding had already started, the seller some unknown company from the country they were in, probably the last in a long chain of companies neither Leah nor the black-marketeer had the expertise to follow to its source. She sent the information to her closest colleague in the home organization.

"Stay where you are," the organization replied back. "Do nothing to disturb or endanger the negotiations about the western mountains. Confirm."

Leah informed the rest of the team of the situation, exactly how it was; no lies, no reassurances. She preferred that all of her team knew what was going on, in case things turned worse. She trusted all of them. They were all on close terms with compromises, practical as well as political. It was always necessary when working in disaster areas. The bigger the disaster, the bigger the compromises tended to be.

The days passed while the crates of food and water grew fewer and fewer. The team substituted their own high-energy meals with less nutritious ones so they could distribute the better meals instead. Every day there were more and more people coming to their lines. Now the wind seemed to blow more dust than air, whirling up the once so fertile soil in long shrill breaths, as if it were shredding meat from bones.

"Where are the supplies?" the head of the delegation said.

It was a different man than the one who had welcomed them at the airport many weeks ago. Gradually, the members of the delegation had been replaced with new people, new faces. Even the men in the dark suits and dark glasses were not the same as when the team first arrived. Had all the delegates been switched out and why? Was there a power struggle in the capital because of the disaster? Had this reduced the power of the delegates? Or had pressuring the international community into sending the aid and the resources they wanted strengthened those at the very top, caused a reshuffling in the echelons of power? Whatever went on among the elites in the capital Leah and the team could only guess.

"Where is the food and water your organization promised to send?" the new head of the delegates asked through the team's translator.

"All the supplies arrived with us and we have distributed it to the people who live here and needed it," Leah said. The hangar was almost empty.

( )

"Where are the supplies your governments agreed to send in exchange for negotiations?" the head of the delegates asked the next day. "We will check that we were sent all that was promised."

"Everything that was promised has arrived," Leah said. "We have given the supplies to those who needed them. We have asked our organization for more."

"Where is the food and water that was promised us for joining negotiations about the western mountains?" the head of delegates said on the third day. "Our numbers show that we received what was promised, but not everything has been handed out. Where is it now?"

"We have distributed all we had," Leah said. "The way we always do. My team even switched out their own rations so more of the people here could eat better."

The team's translator looked at Leah. How could she be so calm?

"Where are the supplies that were promised us in exchange to stay our hand in the western mountains?" the head of the delegation asked on the fourth day. "Some of the supplies that made it here are missing. We know you took it to sell on the black market. If you don't tell where it went, I have no choice but to arrest you," the head of the delegation shouted and grabbed Leah's arm.

"No, your people did!" the translator yelled, in the language of their hosts. "Your government took the supplies and have auctioned it off to food smugglers! We know that most of it went to the eastern parts of the southern continent. Don't pretend that you don't know!"

While the rest of the team gaped the head of the delegation turned with his entourage and marched back to their black cars.

☾☽

Leah wanted to send the translator to the consulate, but the nearest one was in the capital and there he would be closer to danger, not further from it, even if they had had the means of transporting him there. She considered returning him to his home country with the explanation that he had been let go and was no longer a part of the team. Perhaps that would satisfy their hosts. But she could do nothing until she heard from the organization. That evening she told all of the team to eat their good rations, especially the translator.

They came for him in the long hours between midnight and dawn. No guns or batons drawn, just a murder of men in dark clothes and even darker glasses. No phone call from the reception, no knocking on the doors. They had the key to the translator's room and went right in. But the young man was not there. He was in Leah's room, together with the rest of his colleagues.

The head of the delegates rushed inside, fortified by his cadre. "Detain that foreigner," the delegate said, nodding at the translator. The men took hold of the translator's arm. He pulled himself free, but they only grabbed him harder.

"He has done nothing wrong!" Leah shouted. "He is a part of the aid you accepted. Your government accepted!"

"He is a spy sent to undermine and subvert our government's efforts at creating peace in the western mountains."

"Why on Earth would he do that?" Leah yelled. "The aid we brought is a part of the international agreement. That's why we are here!"

"The western mountains belong to us," the delegate answered. "You are the ones negotiating."

The men in dark suits vanished down the stairs, with the translator held between them. He was shouting. First in the language of their hosts, then in the language shared by the team, finally in his native language that only a few of his colleagues understood and even less of them spoke. But all those who didn't, heard the fear in the translator's timbre and the growing hoarseness of his voice. The men pulled the translator out to the pavement and into a black car similar to the ones that had transported them the first night in the country. The delegate and the remaining men ducked into three more cars. Then they drove off into the dust that whipped the lightless streets.

☽

The team retreated to Leah's room and huddled in the yellow light from the lamps, like early hominids around a fire. They knew what they had to do, what they must in situations like these. They contacted their organization via a phone they had hidden from the delegates and asked for funds, for the release of one of their own.

But there was no reply.

"Just wait," they told each other. "Just wait. It will take a while. It is still night at home. People are sleeping. Just wait."

Even though there were people on watch day and night, exactly for situations like this.

In the morning, which was warm and filled with a thick mist that heated the air like a sauna instead of cooling it with its droplets, the reply finally came: "No funds. No money for illicit expenses. Leave immediately, while we can still get you out. Transportation is on the way."

Leah sank down at the edge of her bed. She could not move, talk, or cry. It was as if she was frozen. She had never been this helpless in her life.

"You have five minutes to collect your things," Raymond told the rest of the team. He knew when to take over. "We must leave for open ground at once."

"No," Leah yelled, her face and heart contracting. "We cannot leave, not without my nephew! Do something, bribe someone!"

"With what?" Raymond asked.

"With money, your money, you have money!" Leah shouted.

"We have no one to ask for help, and even if we did, that would endanger them too," Raymond said. He rushed about the room, grabbing the essentials; their organization IDs, cash, bottles of water. Something was stirring deep inside him, turning like worms in his belly, something vulnerable and full of fear, which he rarely felt in the field. But lately it seemed as if the entire world burned and flooded and gusted and sweated, while the safe and peaceful places slowly vanished, like low-lying islands in a rising sea. He couldn't bear it, the idea of missing the flight, of being detained and taken into the mountains and the giant prison camps there, to become one of a hundred thousand lost and forgotten and nameless. Not even aid organizations like their own were allowed in there; only rare surreptitious footage escaped those camps. He couldn't stay and sacrifice himself to free Leah's sister's son however much he'd like, however much that was his duty, however much that leaving the young man behind would be condemning him to death.

They rushed down the stairs, two steps at a time, to the hotel's back entrance. Leah leaned heavily against Raymond, his hand on hers. They ran out into the paling dawn, the flying sand, and dust. They didn't know where to go, but the satellite navigation signal was clear. They followed it through the empty, quiet streets, until the office high-rises gave way to apartments which yielded to mansions which turned into houses and then finally flattened to fields and meadows, safe for a helicopter to land. There the team activated a distress signal, which blazed through the navigation network like a beacon.

"Next time," Gabriele whispered as they crouched down to hide among rows of desiccated corn, "let's go somewhere less warm and dry."

The mist thinned, yet the morning dimmed. From the horizon in the west, a wall of sand rose slowly, another dust storm. The barely visible shape of a helicopter flying at great altitude managed to just stay abreast of the darkness that unfurled towards them.

32.

Diving to the Bottom of the World

The city had nothing left but water, yet they were slowly dying of thirst. But even now everything gleamed with an inner light and his body on the cot lay inside the softness of his own awareness, as did the sky and the ground. He could no longer distinguish the world from himself as it played out inside him. As thirsty and exhausted as he was, now those sense impressions belonged to the world itself, not to him alone, and therefore they vanished back into the world as quickly as they appeared in his mind, like the fluid of his body in the mounting heat, leaving him empty and content.

( )

"Don't be sad about the birds in the museum," Michael said in his dream. "They are still alive. See?" Michael handed him an object the length of his hand.

He gazed down at the thing in his palm. It looked like a miniature version of one of the antique pistols in the painting in the museum, but the rounded grip and short barrel were constructed of smooth planes of enamel covered in gold filigree. The fine metal patterns described leaves and vines and stylized flowers, accented with cut gems of appropriate color; diamonds, rubies, or agate. The grip and the circumference of the six-sided double-barrel was edged with small white pearls. The hammer, trigger, and trigger guard were made from brass and had leaves and vines carved into them as fine as the filigree on the grip and barrel. The gleaming surfaces and tiny details in the engravings and enamel made him think of the lacquer work and metal carvings of a traditional dagger from his father's country he had dreamed about before the hurricane hit. But whereas that object had seemed, in spite of its beauty and ancient craftsmanship, an ill omen, the miniature antique pistol only elicited wonder in him, despite its martial appearance. Even inside the dream he vaguely remembered seeing a video of such an object online. It was the kind of gift a rich person would have given to delight a child or a fickle lover.

Without thinking or asking Michael about it, he held the gun away from his boyfriend and himself, cocked the hammer, and squeezed the trigger of the tiny gun, as attentive and as careful as he had countless other firearms. He felt the hammer jolt beneath his fingers, and expected the familiar sharp motion and sound from the trigger mechanism. But instead, a clockwork of tiny rotating brass gears that had been as meticulously and ingeniously created as the cuckoo clocks he had seen at the store in the mountains started up inside the gun. A tiny bird with a short beak and feathers in a multitude of colors appeared on top of the barrel. The bird turned and looked at him from side to side and flapped its stubby wings while it chirped and warbled a high-pitched, trilling melody that resembled true birdsong so much it was difficult to admit that it had originated from the clockwork inside the pistol instead of the creature itself. He nevertheless smiled and stroked the bird's many-hued, dyed-feather plumage as if it were the last bird in the world.

When the clockwork came to its end and the tiny brass cogs and wheels inside the pistol had run their course, the two black circles at the end of the barrel revealed themselves as a lid; the bird clicked into a horizontal position, and was pulled into the barrel by a spring almost faster than the eye could see. He looked from the songbird pistol to Michael with tears in his eyes and wanted to tell him how beautiful he thought the artifact was, how grateful he was for receiving it, and how sorry he was for not having found Michael yet. But then he realized that the birdsong came from somewhere else, from outside of the dream.

He opened his eyes, not sure if he had heard correctly. On his chest stood a blackbird, its dark feathers sleek and shining, its beak bright orange, and its eyes as smooth and glistening as obsidian, edged with a thin ring of orange as strong and conspicuous as the color of its beak. He stared at the bird. It made a few more melodious tweets while it took him in with unblinking eyes that seemed to hide the true knowledge of the world. Then the little being pecked at the fabric of his jacket once or twice, flicked its tail a few times, and flew out of the open tent.

(( ))

As the hours slipped away, a simple, causeless joy appeared. Every thought, every sensation, no matter their contents, whether desperate or comfortable, happy or sad, felt like a benediction. Thinking and feeling was a part of simply being, which was deeply blissful in itself, a happiness that seemed integral to existence. It was as if every nerve signal in him was only pleasure, and a calm, quiet softness. He rested inside it and for a long while was nothing but joy.

Then Raymond stood over him, watching him closely, as if the pathologist was searching for something only he could find. He remembered that all of Raymond's patients, at least for the last decade, had been dead. He wanted to tell Raymond about Michael and Kaye and leaving them all behind, but the pathologist just patted his hand and told him to rest. Then he was back in the parking garage, in the drysuit and the diving gear. This time he went into the water back first, like a diver from a rubber vessel. Bubbles seethed around him from his mask and regulator, and draperies of sunlight undulated through the water, as in the coral reefs and coastal shallows of the southern continent. He sank with great speed, much faster than any diving belt would have weighed him down to, and the sun grew more and more distant until it was only a single star far above him, before it too was quenched by the deep. A massive darkness enveloped him, swallowed even his thoughts, then closed like an aperture. The last thing he registered was a vague feeling of wonder whether he would ever wake up again.

But he returned to the view of Raymond weeping above him and the sensation of something finally giving in and going up in the space between them, of dissipating out and into the air and light, no longer stagnant as it had been for a long time, but in motion again, as it had longed and yearned to be.

A helicopter roared above them and an intravenous needle bit into his arm. While the life-giving fluid spread through his vessels and organs, his body was lifted from the ground.

Then there was the smell of fuel and perspiration, and he sat slumped in a four-point harness inside the hum and shake from whirling rotors and a strong engine, the synthetic fabric and curvature of the seat alien after months of wooden floors, cold grass, and slack canvas. Raymond was in the seat opposite him, eyes downcast and cheeks sallow, but still alive. The pathologist looked up, said something he failed to hear over the helicopter's noise; but he could feel the change inside the other man, a shift like in a glacier that has gone past its melting point and is rushing towards the sea.

He smiled at Raymond, then leaned against the window and watched the ground recede. Beneath them the maze of streets and avenues and plazas glittered with water, in lieu of the glass in the towers that now stood dark and broken. A flock of egrets rose from the alluvial plain, scared up by the sound and motion of the aircraft, then settled on the greening trees that bordered the marsh. Even from this height he could feel the surge in the flood beneath them, the breath of the ocean through the city. A little over a year ago he had dreamed of the delta as it was a hundred thousand years ago, thick with trees, undergrowth, and water plants and teeming with fish, birds, insects, and amphibians. But perhaps that dream had been just as much about the future as it had been about the past. Now the freshwater in the marsh had reached a new equilibrium with the saltwater from the sea, one that would allow the delta to re-grow with all its potency and life. He gazed down at the city and its hundreds of pools, ponds, rivulets and streams, and felt deeply fortunate to see it in its new and reborn form.

A PARTIAL LIST OF SNUGGLY BOOKS

LÉON BLOY *The Tarantulas' Parlor and Other Unkind Tales*

S. HENRY BERTHOUD *Misanthropic Tales*

FÉLICIEN CHAMPSAUR *The Latin Orgy*

FÉLICIEN CHAMPSAUR *The Emerald Princess and Other Decadent Fantasies*

BRENDAN CONNELL *Metrophilias*

QUENTIN S. CRISP *Blue on Blue*

LADY DILKE *The Outcast Spirit and Other Stories*

BERIT ELLINGSEN *Vessel and Solsvart*

EDMOND AND JULES DE GONCOURT *Manette Salomon*

RHYS HUGHES *Cloud Farming in Wales*

JUSTIN ISIS *Divorce Procedures for the Hairdressers of a Metallic and Inconstant Goddess*

VICTOR JOLY *The Unknown Collaborator and Other Legendary Tales*

BERNARD LAZARE *The Mirror of Legends*

JEAN LORRAIN *Masks in the Tapestry*

JEAN LORRAIN *Nightmares of an Ether-Drinker*

JEAN LORRAIN *The Soul-Drinker and Other Decadent Fantasies*

CAMILLE MAUCLAIR *The Frail Soul and Other Stories*

CATULLE MENDÈS *Bluebirds*

LUIS DE MIRANDA *Who Killed the Poet?*

OCTAVE MIRBEAU *The Death of Balzac*

DAMIAN MURPHY *Daughters of Apostasy*

KRISTINE ONG MUSLIM *Butterfly Dream*

YARROW PAISLEY *Mendicant City*

URSULA PFLUG *Down From*

DAVID RIX *A Suite in Four Windows*

FREDERICK ROLFE *An Ossuary of the North Lagoon and Other Stories*

JASON ROLFE *An Archive of Human Nonsense*

BRIAN STABLEFORD *Spirits of the Vasty Deep*

TOADHOUSE *Gone Fishing with Samy Rosenstock*